To Linden Ponds
Books-n-Bytes,
Happy Reading!

THE
ROCKETEER'S
DAUGHTER

CLINTON ALDRICH

Once again, to Carol

This is a work of fiction. All characters, organizations, and events portrayed in this novel are either products of the author's imagination or are used fictitiously.

Also by Clinton Aldrich
A Republic's Rise

Though you soar like the eagle and make your nest among the stars, from there I will bring you down, declares the Lord. — Obadiah 1:4

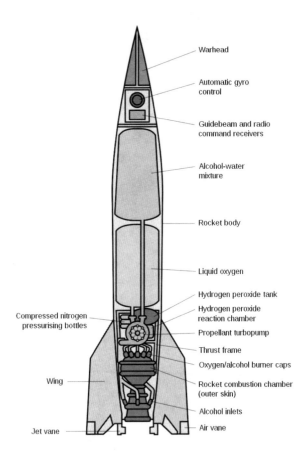

- Warhead
- Automatic gyro control
- Guidebeam and radio command receivers
- Alcohol-water mixture
- Rocket body
- Liquid oxygen
- Hydrogen peroxide tank
- Hydrogen peroxide reaction chamber
- Compressed nitrogen pressurising bottles
- Propellant turbopump
- Thrust frame
- Oxygen/alcohol burner caps
- Wing
- Rocket combustion chamber (outer skin)
- Alcohol inlets
- Jet vane
- Air vane

A4 / V2

PROLOGUE

Cape Kennedy - Florida

July - 1969

Towering 363 feet over Cape Kennedy's wide sandy stretches, the six-million-pound Saturn V rocket stood under a brilliant Florida sun aimed at the heavens like a giant white dagger. Bristling with cables and sensors, it seemed alive – exhaling frosty clouds of liquid oxygen while murmuring like a dormant volcano edging toward eruption.

Over a million people watched from traffic-snarled roadways, crowded campgrounds, beaches, and pleasure boats while closer to the spectacle a former commander-in-chief and First Lady stood among three thousand guests in bleachers. A few miles beyond, in launch control, a palpable tension electrified hundreds of technicians fixated on rows of glowing monitors and closed-circuit television screens.

With less than a minute to launch, men straightened, moods sobered, and eyes focused as a steady masculine voice, piped through headsets and loudspeakers, counted down the final seconds. Then a searing flash of light and guttural earth-shaking growl announced liftoff.

A million throats roared and willed the massive rocket skyward, climbing higher and faster like a flaming javelin, burning through the thinning atmosphere. Suddenly, like a struck match, a fiery blast in the midnight-blue mesosphere triggered first-stage separation.

And then there was a jarring sonic boom.

THE ROCKETEER'S DAUGHTER

CHAPTER 1

Marga Toth jammed the pedals of her bicycle and screeched to a halt at the thunderous sound. Planting her foot, she cupped a hand over her brow and looked over the coastal dunes into the metallic Baltic sky where a fiery-orange cloud rained shards of glowing twisted metal into a slate-colored sea. *Another failure!*

She wiped strands of ash-blond hair from her blue eyes and thought of her father and the men working on this remote sandy stretch in northern Germany on Usedom Island where the Peene River met the Baltic Sea. She imagined their discontent at another unsuccessful launch.

Remounting her bicycle, Marga coasted down a sandy trail lined with gnarled pines, scrub oak, and thorny brambles. Halting on a slope overlooking the sea, she marveled at low-flying cormorants, diving osprey, and scampering plovers watched over by squawking seagulls hovering in the wind.

Inhaling the salty air, she smiled. Her love of nature and open spaces had made for an easy transition to the pastoral coastal setting three years earlier, days after her thirteenth birthday. Along with its natural beauty and remoteness, the Peenemünde Army Research Center offered refuge from Germany's war-ravaged cities. Here, aside from the roaring howl of rocket engines, life was normal.

Marga lived with her parents in a modest but comfortable house, attended school, took violin lessons, and belonged to the local chapter of the League of German Girls.

She pedaled past machine shops, warehouses, cranes, and storage yards sprouting from the wild landscape and skirted a rail line with a clattering tram that shuttled workers through the base. As guard dogs barked from behind camouflage nets concealing anti-aircraft batteries, searchlights, and smoke generators, Marga was reminded that Peenemünde was at war in the summer of 1942.

It was dusk when she arrived home to a two-story white-washed brick cottage with tidy black shutters and a steep slate roof, one of many similar dwellings in the orderly neighborhood housing Peenemünde's engineers and technicians. Propping her bike against a white picket fence enclosing a small garden, she noticed tendrils of smoke twisting from the chimney.

"I was getting worried," her mother said as Marga entered the kitchen through the screen door. Tall with an imperious air, Erna Toth wore her straw-colored hair in a bun. She stood at the counter stirring a bowl of cake batter with a wooden spoon.

"I'm sorry, Mama. I stopped to speak with friends."

"Which friends?"

"Anna Spitzer and her brother, Jonah. They'd gone crabbing and had a basketful."

"Well, save your idle chats for daylight hours."

Reaching for a glass in the cupboard, Marga huffed. "Mama, you worry too much."

Erna cast her daughter a stern eye. "Heed my words and"—she pointed her wooden spoon—"I'll have no backtalk. Now, wash up. We're eating in the kitchen tonight."

Marga became aware of men's voices coming from the living room.

"Your father is busy. Dr. von Braun and some of the others are here. Go in, pay your respects, and hurry back."

Marga quickly smoothed her skirt and hair and pushed open the swinging door leading into the living room.

"Wash your hands first!" Erna blurted out, but Marga was already in the next room where she found half a dozen men, enveloped in a cloudy tobacco haze, huddling over a set of blueprints.

"It's the only logical explanation," Dr. von Braun said as he stabbed a red pencil on the blueprint. "Excess heat buildup is burning through the nozzle throat…Here!" He drew a circle.

"So, we apply a cooling element for thermal insulation," her father said, tapping the blueprint with a finger.

A chorus of voices agreed.

"While we're at it," said Jurgen Miers, a design engineer, "let's integrate heat resistant graphite vanes…Jet exhaust is wreaking havoc on the current aluminum ones."

"Good point," von Braun said. He began scribbling in the margins.

Harold met his daughter's eye and smiled. "*Liebchen.*" He kissed her cheek.

Von Braun looked over his shoulder. "Ah, there she is! Peenemünde's own Shirley Temple! Come and give your uncle a hug!" They embraced. "And what mischief have you been up to?"

Marga twisted a shy smile. "I…I saw the rocket test today… over the sea…I'm sorry."

Von Braun's steely blue eyes shimmered as he playfully pinched her chin. "Fret not, Marga dear. Even in failure, we gain valuable knowledge."

Marga suddenly became self-conscious under the collective gaze of the engineers around the table and remembered her manners. She politely greeted them but saved her last acknowledgement for Ulrich Mainz, a twenty-one-year-old engineer and mathematics prodigy recently assigned to von Braun's rocket design team. Ullie, as his colleagues called him, was the youngest and, in Marga's estimation, handsomest of her father's cohorts. She harbored a secret crush for the young engineer with light brown hair, soft caramel eyes, and chiseled dimples.

He rewarded her with a smile.

Marga's pulse quickened, and she cleared her throat. "I just wanted to say hello." She smiled, curtsied, and turned toward the door to the kitchen. Glancing back, her eyes met Ullie's. His smile lingered.

"Tell your mother her strudel was scrumptious!" von Braun called as Marga pushed open the door.

"I heard that, Wernher!" Erna stuck her head into the living room. "See what I make when one of those infernal things you blast into the heavens *doesn't* explode!"

A collective laugh erupted from the men around the blueprint and they returned to their work.

"Why does Doctor von Braun insist I call him uncle," Marga asked her mother, who was at the sink washing a coffee pot. Marga sat down at the kitchen table and began spooning a bowl of barley soup.

"He's known you a long time, dear. Even, before our days at Kummersdorf."

Marga fondly recalled their small brick cottage on a tree-lined street at the artillery base 25 miles south of Berlin where Germany's early rocket research took place under the watchful eye of her father, Dr. von Braun, and the engineers now working at Peenemünde.

"Is Papa in trouble?"

Erna looked over her shoulder. "What makes you say that?"

"Well, today…the missile…"

"It wasn't the first failure and won't be the last, dear." Erna ran the water. "Rocketry is complicated. They're practically inventing the science."

"Do you think they'll ever succeed?"

Her mother faced her as she reached for a dishrag. "Don't concern yourself with such thoughts. Worry about school…and your chores. And don't trouble your father with silly questions. He has enough on his mind."

Marga took a bite of a dinner roll and announced, "Portia asked me to go to the beach tomorrow."

"What's wrong with the lake?"

"Nothing, but she's going to the beach."

"You know the sea makes me nervous."

Poking her spoon through her soup, Marga wrinkled her brow. "I promise not to go into the water."

"Who else is going?"

"I don't know…Felix maybe. He always tags along."

"He's a good boy…I like his mother." Erna peeked over her shoulder. "Though, he is a boy."

"Mama, you always…"

"I always nothing, Margarethe Toth! I know things you don't. I was once your age—thought I knew everything!" Erna balanced a hand on the sink. "He is sixteen. And boys that age—any age, for that matter—get ideas."

"Not Felix."

"Not Felix," Erna sarcastically muttered returning her attention to the sink. "You may go, but no swimming. And wear your sun hat and a shirt over your bathing suit. I don't want you to burn your shoulders or have Felix getting any ideas. And home by four."

"Mama!"

"Home by four!"

CHAPTER 2

Marga and Portia wore black one-piece bathing suits as they sat on beach towels along a flat, sandy stretch beneath an azure sky rippled with thin, stringy clouds. Lying on her back, Marga also wore an unbuttoned collared shirt but kept her straw hat at her side while Portia, propped on elbows, stretched her long legs under the sun. Alongside them, wearing checkered swim trunks, Felix balanced on his knees wrapping a strand of kelp around a finger.

"Gee, Marga, are you going to wear that shirt all day?" Portia asked. "We are at the beach, after all."

Marga screened the sun from her eyes. "Mama insisted."

"How will she know?" Felix asked, swatting at sand fleas.

"The way yours will." Marga sat up and reached into a small canvas bag and retrieved a bunch of grapes. "When you burn your arms and shoulders." She began divvying up the grapes among them.

"I heard Frau Grimke is giving us a poetry quiz Monday," Portia said after popping a grape into her mouth.

Felix made a face and shook his head. "I hate poetry."

"You should put on your hat," Portia said, turning to Marga. "Your face is turning pink."

Marga grabbed the hat and propped it on her head.

"I don't understand why it's even important," Felix added, letting sand pour through his fingers. "Poetry…who cares!"

"Mama has a book of sonnets," said Marga. "She keeps it in her bureau – locked."

"Maybe they're dirty sonnets," Felix quipped with a sly smile.

Marga gave him a scowl. "Felix, you're so…"

"Immature," Portia remarked.

"It was a gift Papa gave her when they were courting," Marga explained. "She just happens to treasure it is all."

Sitting back smirking, Felix turned to Marga. "Well, you've got nothing to worry about. School comes so easily for you."

"That's not true," Marga declared lifting the brim of her hat. "I have to study too."

"But you…you simply see it—or however you do it—and it's there, like a picture in your head." Felix lobbed a grape in the air and caught it in his mouth. "The rest of us have to study for hours. It'll take me all night to memorize just one of those dumb poems."

"I'm not a parrot, Felix! I still must *learn* the material."

"Well, your brain is like a…sponge. It's scary."

"Just because you don't understand something, doesn't make it scary," Marga huffed. "Papa says I have a gifted mind."

Portia nodded. "It's true. You have a great memory."

Felix chuckled. "Elephants have great memories." He narrowed his eyes inquisitively. "Maybe you're part elephant!" He waved an arm mimicking an elephant's trunk.

"You're so annoying," Portia teased, flicking a pinch of sand at him before turning to Marga. "I know! Recite a poem for us!"

"Oh, no, let's not," Felix grumbled. He chucked a grape into the dunes where a seagull promptly swooped upon it.

"Please?" Portia insisted, poking Marga with a sandy toe.

Marga shrugged. "I…I can't think of one…"

"*Freiligrath!*" Portia blurted with a clap of her hands.

"Are you kidding?" Felix uttered.

"Well, plug your ears then," Portia scolded. "I think a poem would be nice. Please, Marga…proceed."

"*Freiligrath*, huh?" Marga shifted her gaze to the sea.

"In that case, I'm going swimming," Felix announced.

"Good!" Portia replied, wrapping her lanky arms around her knees.

"Okay, how about this one," said Marga. "*O lieb, so lang du lieben kannst*. By Ferdinand Freiligrath." She cleared her throat. "O love, as long as love, you can. O love, as long as love you may. The time will come, the time will come. When you will stand at the grave and mourn…The sure that your heart…"

A thunderous, distant roar interrupted the moment, and like an approaching giant's footsteps, shook the ground. Startled, Marga glanced over the dunes toward an area two miles up the coast where Marga's father and Dr. von Braun and their colleagues conducted rocket testing and development. A billowing, ashen cloud was spiraling skyward, casting a shadow over the Baltic.

* * *

Among ten engineers watching through a thick glass partition, Harold anxiously studied the searing orange flames shooting from the vibrating conical exhaust nozzle of a test-fired engine. Beside him, Wernher watched with a telephone receiver pressed to his ear and a stopwatch in his hand.

"Toth!" Wernher bellowed over the thunderous roar that shook their reinforced bunker. "Forty-seconds!" He held up the stopwatch and beamed. "The film cooling barrier appears to have done the trick! No burn-through! Good work!"

Smiling, Harold glanced at the engineers around him. They'd solved a nagging problem–the build-up of excess heat burning through thermal protective liners causing in-flight explosions. Arms folded, Ullie Mainz gave Harold a congratulatory nod. Harold reciprocated and allowed himself to bask in the engineering victory, if only for a brief while.

* * *

Returning from the water, a hand cupped over his brow, Felix studied the distant cloud.

"How's the water?" Portia asked squinting against the sun.

"Cold. We won't be swimming much longer this season." He slicked back his hair. "It was strange, the water began shaking around me."

"It sounded like a good test," said Marga rising on her knees.

"You mean it didn't blow up," Felix snickered.

"Do you think they'll ever get one of those to fly?" Portia asked brushing sand from her ankles.

"Count on it," said Felix. "And when they do, England will regret having started the war."

"What do you mean?" Portia asked.

"I'll show you," he said retrieving a discarded beer bottle from the dunes. "I heard father talk about it one night." He drew a large circle in the sand with his foot. "Say this is France or Holland." He stepped a few paces to the side and drew another circle. "And this is England." He dug a divot in the center with his toe. "That's London." He returned to the first circle and placed the bottle in the center. "Now, this is our rocket with a warhead."

"Warhead?" Portia asked.

Felix smirked. "A big bomb, dummy. Now, the missile is launched like this." He stood and raised the bottle over his head, tracing an arcing trajectory through the air toward the divot in the second circle. Making a whooshing sound, he mimicked an explosion as he ground the bottle into the sand. "Boom, right into London."

"But how much damage can one rocket do?" Portia asked. "I mean, don't bombers carry tons of bombs…each?"

"And yet, the Union Jack still flies over the Houses of Parliament," Marga remarked.

Clearing his throat, Felix frowned at her reference to Germany's failed air campaign during the Battle of Britain. "It won't be just one rocket," he said, bouncing the bottle in his hand. "Five, ten, maybe more, fired at once. They're cheaper than bombers, not to mention safer too, since we won't risk the lives of aircrews."

"Well, I don't see it happening any time soon," Marga said. "Just yesterday another one blew up."

Felix waved a dismissive hand. "They'll figure it out. Smaller, simpler rockets have been mastered. The A-4 is bigger and more complicated. The real hurdle is guidance."

"How *does* the rocket know where to go?" Portia asked.

Felix scratched his head. "Father sort of explained it to me once. He said there's a radio compartment with gyroscopes." He tapped the neck of the bottle. "And they steer the missile. You know, up…left…right…"

"You mean its horizontal and vertical axis," Marga said.

Felix gave her a peeved look. "Yeah, that. Anyway, these gyroscopes send commands to servomotors." He traced a finger down the side of the bottle. "To here, at the base where they control the movements of rudders and vanes…"

"Vanes?" Portia interrupted.

Annoyed, Felix pursed his lips. "They're like small wings positioned inside the exhaust port where the flames shoot out." He tilted the bottle exposing the bottom. "As these vanes move, they deflect the flames, thus steering the rocket."

Portia continued to appear puzzled.

Marga poked her. "It's like watering your garden with a hose. Picture the water as flames shooting from a rocket. When you place your thumb over the nozzle, you deflect the water's flow to the right or left. On a rocket, vanes act as your thumb, and this alternating pressure does the steering."

Portia shrugged. "It seems like a lot of work."

"Oh, it's absolute genius," Marga said with a proud smile. "Papa says one day rockets will take us to the moon."

"The moon?" Portia snorted.

"That's just double-speak," Felix countered. "To hide what the rockets are really for."

"You mean, flying bombs," Marga said.

"Think of it," he said. "Flying to the moon sounds harmless, if not silly. But using missiles to attack your enemies… well, if they found out what was going on here, they'd try to stop it."

"Oh, enough rocket talk," Portia huffed, clapping sand from her hands. "Marga, dear, you never finished the poem."

"Oh, no, not again!" said Felix, clutching the top of his head and wincing.

Portia frowned. "You didn't let her finish."

"Actually, we were interrupted by the engine test," Marga said.

"Yeah, the engine test," Felix quipped, bouncing a grape off Portia's knee. "Although, I'd settle for a rocket engine anytime over Freely-gath or any other poet for that matter."

"It's, *Freiligrath, dummkopf*," Portia said. Her expression brightened. "I know!" She stood, brushing sand off herself. "Let's go for a swim, Marga. You can finish the poem there!"

Felix jumped to his feet. "I'll hold my breath underwater then!"

"Fine!" Portia answered.

"And I'll wear your hat when I do!" Felix crowed, snatching it off Portia's head and bolting for the water.

"Hey! It's my mother's!"

Playfully shrieking, the girls ran after him and tumbled laughing into the surf.

CHAPTER 3

I t was late at night, and low skimming clouds occluded a three-quarter moon in the Baltic sky. Wearing an overcoat, his face shadowed by a fedora, Ullie made his way through the park, harboring an uneasy feeling he was being watched. A branch suddenly snapped. He held his breath, looked around, and made a fist around a set of keys inside his coat pocket. Another snap, then footsteps and a figure emerged from a thicket.

"You're punctual as usual," said Ullie.

"Do you have it?" a man asked stepping forward.

Ullie held out a small hardbound book, when a flashlight's searing beam invaded the moment.

"Run!" Ullie cried, stuffing the book into his pocket.

"Halt!" a constable shouted, wildly sweeping his flashlight through the darkness before blowing a whistle.

Sprinting in opposite directions, the men darted around trees and bushes, their footsteps fading into the night, and they were gone.

CHAPTER 4

In a cool, dark room two stories beneath the Treasury building in central London's Whitehall section, Major Harrison Brightwell stood beside an illuminated projection screen holding a wooden pointer. Tobacco smoke swirled in the projector's beam like playful ghosts.

Addressing the darkened silhouettes of four men and two women seated around a conference table, he continued the briefing. "Our latest intelligence indicates the Germans are on the verge of getting one of these to actually fly." Brightwell placed the pointer on a grainy image of a rocket perched on an elevated platform.

Brightwell, now in his mid-forties, had spent his entire career in intelligence and harbored few regrets other than his failure to dissuade Prime Minister Neville Chamberlain from believing Adolf Hitler's promise of peace in Europe in exchange for Germany's annexation of the Sudetenland. Flying home from Münich, a smiling Chamberlain had waved the signed guarantee given him by the Führer. "He gave us his word, Harrison…We have peace in our time, old man."

Pointing to the rocket, Randolph Hayes, assistant director of Britain's Imagery Intelligence Branch, asked, "What exactly is that?"

"The Germans call it the *Aggregat-4*," Brightwell replied. "We call it the A-4. It stands 14 meters high, weighs 13 metric tons, generates 25 metric tons of thrust, and can climb to an altitude of 80 kilometers with a range of 270 kilometers."

U.S. Army Air Corps Lieutenant Colonel Tom Porter cleared his throat and spoke next in his Texas drawl. "So, that I can explain it to my brass, Major..." He began writing on a notepad. "You're saying this missile is 46 feet tall, produces 56,000 pounds of thrust, reaches over 50 miles high, and has a range of ...let's see, kilometers to miles...that would be...?"

"In this case, sir," said one of the two female stenographers in the room, "approximately 165 miles."

"To do what?" asked Alistair Hewett, deputy liaison to the British prime minister.

Gripping the pointer behind his back, Brightwell cleared his throat. "Deliver a one-ton explosive warhead, sir."

For a few seconds the room was silent except for the projector's rattling fan and the scratch of shorthand from the two stenographers.

"Who in bloody hell's name created such a thing?" Hayes thundered.

The projector made a clacking sound as the slide changed to a photo of a handsome, charismatic-looking man with movie-star looks.

"This man did, sir. Dr. Wernher von Braun...thirty years old...a mathematics genius. Descends from Prussian nobility and is currently a major in the SS. He answers to a chain of command but, make no mistake, he's the brains behind this operation."

A new slide appeared, a black-and-white high-altitude photograph of Peenemünde's rocket development complex with grease pencil markings identifying key locations.

"In this heavily wooded 2.5-by-4-kilometer spit of sand flanked by the Peene River and Baltic Sea lies the Peenemünde Army Research Center." Brightwell moved the pointer over the image. "As you can see, it's well defended by radar-guided anti-aircraft batteries, troop barracks, and an adjacent *Luftwaffe* base."

Brightwell moved the pointer to the bottom of the screen. "This village, a kilometer to the south, is Karlshagen an old settlement—there long before the Nazis built their base." He dragged the pointer north along the coastline. "These carefully laid out buildings are residential quarters. And here"—he slid the pointer upward— "are production plants, storage yards, warehouses, hangars, machine shops." Next, Brightwell focused their attention on a cluster of buildings. "And here are their engineering and design shops to include a modern wind tunnel. And, farther up the coast, behind this large, elliptical sand berm, is Test Stand Seven—their primary missile testing site. As you can see, it's state of the art, with a launch stand, flame pit, gantries, observation bunkers, mobile cranes, and labyrinth of water lines, storage tanks, and pumps beneath a reinforced concrete apron."

"What's that large building outside the berm?" someone asked. "The one with the railroad track leading to the launch stand?"

Brightwell's pointer found the structure. "It's an assembly building where missiles are put together and readied prior to launch. The rails are used to transport the rockets into place."

"And those curious circles…west of the launch site?" Hewett asked.

"They're liquid oxygen storage tanks, sir."

"Liquid oxygen?" said Hewett. "For breathing?"

"Propulsion, sir. This rocket uses a mixture of liquid oxygen, ethanol, and water."

"What's that large, fenced-in area to the west?" Porter asked,

Brightwell faced the screen. "A *Luftwaffe* test facility, sir. To our understanding, their air force is working on some kind of pilot-less rocket plane."

"Pilotless rocket planes…missiles?" Hewett thundered. "What the devil's going on, Brightwell?" The table creaked under his pressing hands. "When and how did this all come about, man?"

"Sir, Germany has had a robust rocket program for years." Brightwell cleared his throat. "Ironically, we had a hand in it."

"*Us?* How?" Hewett demanded.

"As part of the armament restrictions placed upon them by the Treaty of Versailles. You recall, sir, the treaty abolished Germany's air force and placed strict limits on artillery development."

"So…?" said Hewett.

Brightwell sighed. "Sir, nothing addressed rockets."

"I beg your pardon?" Hayes stammered.

"Gentlemen, the treaty put strict limits on their naval and military rearmament. But nothing addressed missile research and development. They've been working on the damned things for years."

A long silence ensued.

"Good God, man!" Hewett blurted out, thrusting his pipe at the screen. "What about us? Can we do that?"

Brightwell pursed his lips. "No…no, sir. Not yet, at least."

"*Yet?*" Hewett snapped.

"Truth be told, sir, we're years behind them… many years."

Hayes shifted uncomfortably in his chair. "Can we at least shoot the bloody things down?"

Brightwell stood silent, surveying the shadowy figures before him.

"Yes or no, Brightwell?" Hewett asked sharply. "Can we shoot them down? The prime minister will want to know."

Brightwell tapped the pointer against his leg. "Reports have its speed at three to four times the velocity of sound, sir. Not only won't we be able to shoot them down…we'll never see them coming."

There came another long pause before Hewett cleared his throat. "And how reliable is this intelligence? Who exactly is providing it?"

"I can only say, sir, we have elements on the ground."

"Elements?" Hewett challenged. "What sort of elements?"

Brightwell straightened and cleared his throat. "Critically situated elements, sir."

CHAPTER 5

"Marga, hurry up or you'll be late!"

"I'm ready, Mama!" Marga said as she burst through the kitchen's swinging door.

"How many times have I told you? Be careful when charging through that door!"

She straightened her daughter's collar and handed her two paper sacks.

"Two lunches, Mama?"

"One is for your father…He never came home last night."

"Was it he who telephoned so late?"

"He worked all night. Go to his office. But don't linger or you'll be late for school!"

"I promise I won't," Marga said, hoisting a canvas knapsack over her shoulder and reaching for the violin case on the counter.

"And straight home after your music lesson, understood?"

"Yes, Mama!" Marga blew her mother a kiss and headed out the door.

＊ ＊ ＊

Marga pedaled her bicycle past bustling tool-and-die shops, warehouses, and a sheet-metal plant. Despite few automobiles, she still contended with trucks, forklifts, tractors, and a slow-moving train of flatbed cars rolling through the industrial complex. Reaching a group of buildings, she parked her bicycle outside one labeled TECHNICAL DESIGN and trotted inside carrying her father's lunch.

Walking past offices with prattling typewriters and ringing telephones, she entered a long and narrow room with low-slung ceilings, luminous light fixtures and large, bright windows. To get to her father, she had to amble past a dozen drafting tables where rocket designers labored over large technical drawings and work desks where engineers, using slide rulers and pencils, scribbled calculations, spoke on telephones, or studied blueprints.

She knew some of the people working at their desks and smiled at them as she passed. Most either did not look up or met her smile with a nod. All seemed fully absorbed in their work.

When she reached her father's desk, she found him standing with his back to her while conferring with two engineers. Waiting patiently, she eyed a chalkboard with complex diagrams. She couldn't understand the mathematics or intricate equations, but she vividly retained the information as if her brain had taken a picture.

"Hello, Marga."

She turned. "Dr. Mainz"—her cheeks grew warm—"it's so nice to see you…again."

Grinning, he looked at the chalkboard and asked lightheartedly, "Have you decided to join our ranks?"

Blushing, Marga held up a paper sack. "Oh, no. I brought Papa his lunch."

"The way you studied those figures…I thought perhaps, as they say, the apple doesn't fall far from the tree."

She looked at the chalkboard. "Oh, Herr Doctor, I wouldn't know the first thing about any of it."

He stood beside her. "It's not too difficult, actually. For instance, take the diagram…the one in the middle. The top number represents mass, in this case, a rocket. The number on the left is velocity, and the number at the bottom is the coefficient of—" He suddenly laughed. "Listen to me going on."

"Oh no!" she replied. "I find it fascinating! I can repeat it back to you, if you'd like!"

Ullie scratched his nose. "What do you mean?"

Still smiling, Marga shrugged. "I see things and remember them. I get it from Papa, I think."

He chuckled. "Okay, let's test this memory of yours, shall we?"

Welcoming his attention, she nodded.

"Turn your back and tell me the equation to the right of that diagram I began to explain."

When she turned around, she noticed a bald janitor in blue coveralls emptying a wastebasket in the corner. He seemed to be watching her with interest. She smiled at him, but he quickly looked away.

Marga furrowed her brow and closed her eyes. "Let's see…The trajectory angle of 47 degrees is in direct proportion to the square route of V minus…"

"*Mein schatz!*" her father had finally noticed her when he'd turned around to place a stack of folders on his desk. He gave her a peck on the cheek and looked at Ullie. "Are you corrupting my daughter with impure engineering thoughts?" he asked with a chuckle.

"Oh, no, Papa! Dr. Mainz was kindly showing me what you do here." She held out the paper sack. "And, Mama sent me with your lunch."

"Ah, Harold," a silver-haired man in a lab coat announced. "You're lucky to have such a pretty girl bring you your lunch."

Her father smiled. "Huber, you recall my daughter, Marga."

"Yes, of course. I remember you from picnics at Kummersdorf."

Marga curtsied. "A pleasure to see you again, Doctor Vollen."

Her father glanced at a wall clock. "You'd best be going, *Liebchen*. You'll be late for school." He kissed her forehead.

"Will you be home for supper, Papa?"

He tweaked her chin. "I'll try."

"Please do!" She hugged him and then turned toward where Ullie had been standing, but he was gone.

Once outside, as she hurried to her bicycle, someone called her name. She turned. It was Ullie walking towards her. A flurry of butterflies tickled her stomach. "Doctor Mainz," she said.

"Oh, please, call me Ullie."

"Okay…Ullie."

"I see you have your violin case with you."

"I have lessons after school, in Karlshagen."

"Yes, your father once mentioned you take lessons. Said you play beautifully."

She blushed. "He would say that."

Ullie looked around and cleared his throat. "Marga, could I ask a favor?"

She straightened. "Of course!"

"Could I trouble you to deliver this?" He held out a book. "It's for a friend in the village, Tomas Fromme, at number 6 Mittelstrasse. It's a white cottage with brown shutters. If he's not home, his wife knows to expect it." He handed her a thin hardbound volume. She saw the title was *Daybreak* and the author was Friedrich Nietzsche. "I've been so busy lately. I haven't had time to get it to him."

"I understand," she said. "Papa never came home last night… Things *must* be busy."

He smiled. "Thank you, you're doing me a great favor."

She placed the book in the basket on the handlebar of her bicycle. "Good-bye, Dr. …" She smiled. "I mean, Ullie. I'll make sure your book gets delivered."

Pedaling away, Marga glanced over her shoulder to see Ullie smiling and waving at her. In response, she trilled her bicycle bell.

* * *

"Do you think it wise to bring the girl into this?" Janko asked Ullie when they met up in the boiler room.

Ullie sighed. "Relax, she's simply doing me a favor, nothing more."

Janko pursed his lips. He was unconvinced.

"It's fine," said Ullie. "She'll drop off the book, and Tomas will handle it from there. It's a temporary solution." He glanced at his watch. "I have to get back."

Janko Novak's bald head sat like a boulder atop broad, rugged shoulders. His nose disfigured, a vertical scar from forehead to chin gave the impression his head was fused together. A decade earlier, as a mechanic at the Polish embassy in London, he'd gone to work for Britain's MI6–foreign intelligence. A German, Russian, and Polish speaker, he wore a red triangle on his coveralls identifying him as a prisoner-of-war and special detainee volunteering to work for the Germans; a ploy on his part to embed himself into the enemy's ranks and continue the fight from within. Having been a trusted hospital orderly and translator, he ascended to his current position in Peenemünde as janitor—someone with access to buildings, file rooms, and the men working there.

"We just don't need anyone asking questions."

Ullie clapped Janko's muscular shoulder. "Relax, she's a nice girl doing me a simple favor."

"There's an old saying," Janko replied. "Three may keep a secret if two of them are dead."

Ullie straightened his tie. "The American, Benjamin Franklin, I believe." He cleared his throat. "Leave the thinking to me, Janko. I'll let you know if, and when, any legs need to be broken."

CHAPTER 6

A breath of golden leaves floated from poplars and birch trees as Marga approached the two-story white-washed home with brown shutters matching the address Ullie had given her. Dead geraniums filled a window box, and scattered leaves covered a short brick walkway leading to the front door.

She looked at the book in her hand, took a breath, and marched forward. After ringing the buzzer, she waited. No one came to the door. She rang the buzzer again. A minute passed and still there was no answer. She looked at the book, then at the number on the door. She debated whether to leave it but decided against it.

Turning to the street, the door latch rattled. Marga turned back. The door creaked open and a woman, hastily cinching a robe, stuck her head out from behind the door.

"May I help you?"

Marga stepped forward. "I was asked to deliver this book."

"Who sent you?" The woman looked up and down the street.

"Dr. Mainz."

"Oh, yes, of course." She held out her hand. "I'll take it." A man suddenly appeared behind her. He was shirtless and wore suspenders to support his gray uniform trousers.

"From Ullie," said the woman handing him the book.

He took it, thumbed the pages, and nodded to Marga. "Thank you." He turned away into the house.

The woman raked her rumpled hair and smiled. "I'm sorry, I don't know your name."

"Marga…Marga Toth. I live on the base."

The woman smiled. "Thank you, Marga. Maybe we'll meet again. Good-bye."

CHAPTER 7

"I look like a Dutch boy," Marga said as she stared into the mirror at her bobbed hair, cut that afternoon by her mother in preparation for attending the annual Winter Relief Charity dance. She tried parting and splaying its amber strands with little success. "I look like a child."

"You are a child," said her mother, standing next to her. She was busy applying lipstick. "Someday, when you're older, you can choose to wear your hair as you please, but for now…"

"And this dress!" Marga contemplated the powder-blue dress with short white puffed sleeves and Peter Pan collar her mother had insisted she wear.

"What about it?"

"It's…*plain!*"

"Your aunt Elsa in Düsseldorf sent it to you as an early Christmas gift. It's beautiful, and you're lucky to have it. There's a war on. Everything is in short supply." Erna adjusted Marga's collar. "Some people have only one pair of clothes and shoes let alone a party dress."

As she studied her reflection, Marga fanned the hem of the dress. "I look like…like… Alice in Wonderland!"

"You do, darling," said Erna, running a hand over her daughter's head. "With a Dutch-boy haircut, no less." She kissed her, and stepping for the door announced, "Finish up, we're leaving shortly."

Marga sat looking at her reflection in the mirror. Between her haircut and dress, she looked awkward and immature. She thought of Ullie. *Would he be there? Would he even notice her and if he did, would he think she looked like Alice in Wonderland with a Dutch Boy haircut?*

"Marga!" Her mother called from the hallway. "We're going!"

Standing and looking in the mirror, she sighed and reached for her clutch bag and a set of gloves before answering, "Coming, Mama!"

* * *

Upon arriving at the assembly hall, Marga watched her father deposit an envelope she knew contained money, into a red can watched-over by a member of Peenemünde's Hitler Youth chapter. The teenage boy nodded and thanked Harold. Inside, Marga surveyed the festive environment. It had been decorated with glowing Chinese lanterns and colorful paper streamers. A small orchestra was playing a traditional Bavarian folk song. There was a large dance floor with many couples dancing. Others sat at tables surrounding it—the men in suits and ties; the women in dresses, their hair in stylish Marcel waves, ring curls, or long bobs. Those wearing makeup did so sparingly, keeping with National Socialist norms. A decorative silhouette of a rocket hung over a bar where men in lederhosen served draft beer alongside tables filled with platters of potato salad, boiled cabbage, coleslaw, and roasted schnitzel.

A group of friends immediately surrounded her parents, and Marga slipped away. Clutching her sequined purse, she wandered through the crowded hall until she spotted Ullie across the dance floor standing by a punch bowl chatting with two engineers she recognized from her father's shop. Glancing at her parents, who were still engrossed with their friends, Marga ventured forward, stepping around dancing couples and drawing closer to Ullie. But then a blond woman in a much more sophisticated-looking dress than hers sidled up to him and thread her arm under his. He smiled and handed her a glass of punch. The woman looked radiant as she mouthed, "Thank you."

Marga halted, then began to change course when her eyes met Ullie's. She tensed, wanting to pivot and hide in the crowd, but he smiled and motioned her over.

"I've been meaning to thank you for delivering that book," he said over an accordion's trill.

"It was nothing," Marga replied, feeling her cheeks grow warm.

"You know these gentlemen," Ullie motioned to the two engineers.

Marga politely nodded to them.

"And let me introduce you to my date, Gerda Hewel."

"So, this is your little errand girl," Gerda commented. She balanced her punch glass inches from her lips. "She's adorable."

Adorable?

"She's Harold Toth's daughter," said Ullie.

"Oh, yes, darling. You introduced us at the office."

Darling?

Marga cleared her throat. "It's nice to meet you, Fräulein Hewel."

"You're still in school?" Gerda asked.

Marga straightened. "I attend the Gymnasium in Karlshagen."

Gerda slipped a cigarette between her lips and smiled. "Your dress..." She tugged at one of Marga's puffed sleeves. "So... cute. I'm sure your mother worked very hard on it."

Marga looked down at herself. *Alice in Wonderland.*

She suddenly felt an arm placed around her waist from behind. "There you are, *Liebchen*," her father said. "Are you enjoying yourself?"

"Yes, Papa." She leaned into his embrace.

"Well, run along and see if any of your friends are about."

Marga turned to Gerda. "It was nice meeting you, Fräulein Hewel." She nodded at the two engineers. Then, smiling at Ullie, she said, "Nice to see you again."

"Likewise," he said. "And thanks again."

* * *

Polka music coursed through the steamy, cheerful hall as Marga sat at a table nursing a glass of carbonated Fanta, a Coca Cola substitute fashioned from beet sugar and apple pulp. Twisting her glass mindlessly, she watched the couples as they danced, some with practiced footwork and others reluctantly shuffling in circles. She smiled at Portia dancing with her father, her friend staring at her feet as she awkwardly kept pace.

"Sit up, dear!" her mother suddenly remarked, slightly out of breath, as she and Harold quick-stepped past the table.

Frowning, Marga straightened up until they drifted away, then resumed her relaxed posture. Glancing at a wall clock behind the orchestra, she worked at suppressing a yawn when a hand appeared in the corner of her eye. Looking up, it was Wernher von Braun flashing a broad smile.

"Care to dance with your Uncle Wernher?"

Flashing a shy smile, Marga met her mother's gaze across the dance floor. Erna motioned for her to stand.

Nodding, Marga complied. "Of course, Herr Doctor. I'm honored."

Slipping his warm hand into hers, he led her onto the dance floor. He guided her through a waltz at a slow, graceful pace.

"Are you enjoying yourself?" he asked.

"I am," she answered glancing at his feet to emulate his steps. "It's all so nice."

"The rocket on the wall." He motioned to the cutout. "We had it made in the sheet-metal shop. Even had it painted in the black-and-white checkered pattern we use on our test models."

"It's lovely," she said as they spun through the center of the dance floor. "Tell me, why the checkered pattern?"

He glanced over his shoulder at the cutout. "Simple. It allows us to determine if the missile rotates during launch."

Marga wrinkled her brow. "Not a good thing, I suppose."

He smiled as he shook his head. "No, my dear, it's not." He steered them between two slower-moving couples. "Your Papa tells me you're doing well in school."

She nodded. "I have a good teacher."

"That's good to hear, though I lament our education system isn't what it used to be."

Looking around to see if someone might be listening, Marga lowered her voice. "Despite wearing her National Socialist Women's League pin every day, Frau Grimke, to her credit, manages to steer our lessons from political ideology to history, poetry, and mathematics. She once said, 'A well-rounded mind comes from a well-rounded education.'"

Von Braun chuckled. "She remembers how things used to be. Not to mention, you and most of your classmates are children of scientists and engineers—learned men who value education. Besides, we are rather isolated here, away from doddering bureaucrats whose business is to check on such things." He sighed. "It'd be a shame to waste so many young talented minds. For instance, your father tells me you have somewhat of a gift."

"You mean my memory?"

He nodded. "An eidetic memory—sometimes called a photographic memory—it's a rare asset, Marga. Use it to your advantage."

"But what do I do with it?"

"You should be asking, what do you *want* to do with it?"

"Could I build rockets? Like you and Papa?"

"With a proper education…"

"But I'm a girl."

"Well, if Hanna Reitsch can test-fly airplanes and Leni Riefenstahl can create epic films…Why can't *you* design rockets?"

"Do you really think so? Though, the way things are going…"

"Marga," he said. "Things aren't always going to be like this."

She met his gaze. "You mean the war?"

"This war will end, and then…"

The waltz abruptly ended, and the quick tempo of a spritely folk tune drew an approving sigh from the dance floor.

"I don't think I can keep pace to this," Marga said, studying the swift dance steps around them.

"The *Zwiefacher*," he chuckled. "My parents loved it. Come, we'll sit and finish our talk."

Sitting, Marga took a drink from her tepid soda. "Can I ask you something, Herr Doctor?"

"Of course."

"Is it true that rockets could one day reach the moon?"

A pensive look crossed his face. "I believe that with enough engineering and mathematics, just about anything is possible."

"Will it happen in our lifetime?"

"Yes, actually. I believe it will." He laughed suddenly. "My goodness, a girl your age comes to a dance and spends her time speaking of rockets and going to the moon. I should think you'd be more interested in boys or who's wearing what or dancing with whom."

She sighed. "Mother says I'm too serious-minded."

"You have a good mind, Marga. Capable of remarkable things, if you apply yourself."

She looked thoughtfully into her glass. "Can I ask another question?"

Wiping aside a lock of damp hair, he nodded.

"Will these rockets end the war?"

"That's interesting. You said 'end the war.' Most would ask, 'Will they win the war?'"

She shook her head. "I'm sorry. I shouldn't talk about things I don't understand."

He placed his hand over hers. "I think you understand perfectly, dear."

"Oh, my!" Erna uttered, sinking into a chair alongside von Braun fanning herself with a hand. "It's been ages since I've danced so much."

"Punch, darling?" Harold asked, leaning over his wife.

"Yes, please," she huffed.

"Wernher?"

He shook his head and chuckled, "No, thank you. I should be getting back to my table. They'll think I've disappeared!" He turned to Marga and pinched her cheek. "Thank you for the dance. You're a natural." He turned to Erna and Harold. "Your daughter was a most charming dance partner. You should be proud of her. She's smart, charming and… She'll do great things someday."

* * *

As couples and families drifted homeward, Marga and Portia stood outside the dance hall where a full moon cast a cool brilliance around them.

"I can't wait until I attend one of these with a date," said Portia. "I had two glasses of punch. The real punch. Can you smell it on my breath?" She exhaled close to Marga's face.

"What are you doing?"

"Didn't you have any?"

"No, Mama would kill me if I went to the punch bowl."

Portia hiccupped. "It's why you have someone else get it for you."

"Gee, I didn't think to do that. Besides, Mama would know if I'd been drinking."

"How?"

"How?" Marga laughed, waving a hand before her face. "Sometimes I wonder about you."

"I saw you talking with Ullie and his date."

Marga gazed longingly at the moon. "He looked so handsome."

Portia playfully tugged Marga's hair. "His date thought so too."

Marga crossed her arms. "I really don't care anymore!"

"Don't you ever wonder what it would be like?"

Marga sighed. "Are you going to start wondering about your first kiss again?"

"You never think about it?"

"Not like you?"

Portia grinned. "Not even a kiss from…Ullie?"

"Well…maybe it's crossed my mind, but…Oh, stop it, you're incorrigible!"

"I can't wait to be kissed," Portia exclaimed, spinning around.

"Ask Felix to do it and get it over with," Marga snickered.

"Oh, please. It'd be like kissing my brother. No, I'd like my first real kiss to be passionate and memorable."

"I think I'd like to be in love for my first kiss. If it were to be Ullie…"

"Don't hold your breath," said Portia. "He looked pretty cozy with his date."

"He did...But..."

"But...but...but! Face it, Marga. It's never going to happen."

Marga frowned. "How do you know? Circumstances change. Mama always says—"

"There you are!" Her mother suddenly appeared out of the darkness, tucking her purse beneath her arm. "Have you been waiting long?"

"No, Mama," said Marga, straightening up.

"Good evening, Frau Toth." Portia hiccupped again.

"Did your parents leave early?" Erna asked Portia.

"Yes. Mama was tired so Papa took her home."

"Well, you're welcome to walk with us. It's not safe for young women to be out alone at night."

Marga rolled her eyes.

"Thank you, Frau Toth, I'd like that."

"Are we ready?" Marga's father said as he joined them.

"We are," her mother replied. The four of them headed off, her parents leading the way with Marga and Portia holding hands and softly humming a childhood song.

CHAPTER 8

Wearing Ullie's shirt from the previous night's dance, Gerda glanced over her shoulder toward the bathroom where he was showering. Standing at the desk in his small one-room apartment, she began sifting through his papers and letters.

"Let's see who's my competition," she muttered, perusing a letter sorter crammed with postcards and envelopes. A card from Salzburg told of a day touring the old city and of a Mozart recital. "Annabelle, huh?" Another, displaying Hamburg's medieval skyline was signed, *Onkel Kurt*. Next, she rummaged through a few drawers but found nothing interesting.

The address book was full of information. *Stephie lives in Dahlem, Ireen in Erfurt, and Angela in Geesthacht. Good to know.*

Retrieving a leather briefcase from beneath the desk, she randomly pulled out a file causing technical drawings to spill out. Cursing, she hastily gathered them up and while doing so noticed the words State Secret stamped atop each page. She returned them to the briefcase and replaced it under the desk.

Turning to a bookshelf, she ran a hand over several volumes and took note of their titles. *How to Raise Mushrooms... A Brief History of Saxony...The Life of Baron Ernst von Holbach.* She came to a small volume titled, *Silesian Poems* lying face down. Curious, she picked it up. Something rattled inside. She opened it and found a false compartment containing a thumb-sized, Minox camera.

The sound of the shower suddenly stopped. Fumbling with the camera, Gerda jammed it inside the book and hastily replaced it on the shelf.

"See anything you like?" Ullie asked. He stepped from the bathroom drying himself with a towel.

She pulled down the first book and asked, "Are you raising a lot of mushrooms these days?" She smiled. "Building rockets doesn't keep you busy enough?"

He took the book from her and returned it to the shelf. "Cheap buys...five for five marks." He kissed her. "Get dressed. I'll take you to breakfast."

"We did work up an appetite." She caressed his cheek. "Give me a few minutes."

She took her clothes into the bathroom and closed the door. The faint residue of her perfume hung in the air.

* * *

He waited until the shower started before inspecting the bookshelf. He reached for the volume of Silesian poems. He'd left it face down. It now faced up. He chided himself for his carelessness in leaving the book in the open for anyone to peruse. He opened it. The camera had been handled, for he always left it with its tiny Minox label facing upwards. It now sat inverted. The shower stopped and he replaced the book on the shelf.

Minutes later the bathroom door opened and Gerda emerged dressed and smiling.

"You aren't dressed," she remarked fastening an earring.

He studied her.

She reached for a hairbrush. "What is it?"

He shook his head. "Nothing. Give me a minute." He slipped on boxer shorts and asked, "So, what do you like to read?"

She turned smiling. "A good spy novel is fun."

"Is it?" He reached for a pair of slacks.

"The hero always seems to be dashing, handsome, and a good lover."

He slipped on a shirt and glanced at the book with the hidden camera. "Sounds like quite the life."

Helping fasten his buttons, she flashed a mischievous grin. "It does, doesn't it?" She raised herself up on her toes and kissed him. "Let's go," she whispered. "Before I change my mind about breakfast and pretend, you're a dashing spy."

CHAPTER 9

Werner felt Harold grab onto his arm to steady himself on the high scaffolding above their precious rocket poised on its launch stand. They inspected its radio compartment's assembly of wires and gyroscopes—critical in guiding the missile following its launch. Sweeping a flashlight's beam through the interior, a tiny sparkle shimmered under the light. Harold retrieved what turned out to be a metal shaving and handed it to Wernher who frowned. Like Harold, he was aware that under the harsh stresses of flight, such debris could catastrophically damage the missile. It had happened before.

"All the compartments are vacuumed twice in the assembly hangar," Wernher grumbled. "Perhaps we should insist on three times." He pocketed the metal shard and looked toward the ground where tanker trucks slowly withdrew from the missile now brimming with liquid oxygen and ethanol. Harold extinguished his flashlight and gave him a nod. Wernher turned to two technicians in coveralls watching from the adjacent gantry. "Klaus! Jurgen! Close her up!" He pointed skyward. "We're going!"

* * *

At the base of the rocket, Ullie and a group of technicians inspected rudders and stabilizing fins. Ducking beneath the exhaust port, he eyed four graphite vanes and gave each a quick tug before reemerging. He cupped a hand to his mouth and shouted to a technician atop a ladder. "All set, Leo?"

Emerging from the engine compartment with a socket wrench, Leo hollered down, "I adjusted the fastener on the oxygen distributor!" He flashed an A-OK sign. "We're ready to seal her up!"

"Come down then!" Ullie uttered, fingering three hexagonal nuts in his lab-coat pocket. He then stopped a technician carrying the engine hatch toward the rocket. "I'll do it, Ernst!"

"But, sir…" Ernst replied, glancing up at the open compartment.

"I want to give it my own final look," said Ullie, taking the hatch from his hands. "I assured Dr. von Braun I'd personally double-check the burner cups."

As Leo stepped off the ladder, Ullie climbed up and peered inside the engine compartment to inspect the hydrogen peroxide tank. Running a finger along the aluminum feed lines, he casually tucked the three hexagonal nuts into a nest of wires and, for good measure, loosened a rubber coupler on a fuel hose before sealing the hatch.

"All set, Leo!"

"*Jawohl, Mein Herr!*" Leo enthusiastically replied. "Today, we reach the stars!"

* * *

Wernher and his team watched from a concrete bunker outfitted with closed-circuit television monitors, glowing instrument panels, and a periscope.

"Thirty seconds," a voice announced through headphones and loudspeakers.

Wernher pressed an eye to a periscope.

"Twenty seconds…"

A controller abruptly declared, "Initiate hold!"

Wernher turned to the technicians monitoring the rocket's vital signs at an instrument console.

"We have an irregular ammeter reading," said a controller, flipping a toggle switch.

"It might be a voltage regulator," said another.

"Well, get it fixed!" Wernher snapped as he peered back through the periscope, his arms draped over its handles like a submarine commander. Eyeing the black-and-white-checkered A-4, he studied its sleek riveted lines and sharp-angled fins. Sunlight suddenly broke through the clouds and glimmered off its conical nose. He took it as a good omen and wondered if today was the day when Man would soar higher and farther than ever before?

"We're go for launch, Herr Doctor!" a controller announced through Wernher's headset. The countdown resumed. When it got to zero, flames and a thunderous growl shot from the rocket. Umbilical cables fell away, and the A-4 climbed, one…two meters.

Suddenly, its fiery tail extinguished. The missile balked and hung in the air like a stage-struck actor forgetting his lines. Staring in disbelief, Wernher and his team watched as their creation toppled sideways and smashed onto the concrete apron, triggering a blinding flash and a ground-shaking explosion. Lights flickered and monitors went blank. Pressing an eye into the periscope, Wernher stood motionless, mocked by a dark, swirling cloud enveloping the launch stand. Another failure.

* * *

Amid wailing sirens and blaring horns, Ullie halted his stopwatch. Three-point-seven seconds.

"Damn it!" Harold exclaimed. "A turbo pump or steam generator must have failed! Something caused that engine to shut down!" He turned to Ullie. "You ran the cold calibration test, right?"

"I did. Everything checked out. No leaks or ruptures. Jurgen ran it with me."

Looking out the smoke-covered window, Harold declared, "When they put out the fire, I want to be the first out there!" He faced Ullie. "I want you with me!"

Ullie met his eye and nodded. "I was hoping you'd say that."

* * *

Mimicking the stunned looks of disappointment around him, Ullie pocketed his stopwatch and peered out a reinforced window at billowing smoke and lapping flames. For an instant, guilt rankled his senses, but it quickly passed, and he wondered if his act of sabotage had played a role in today's failure or if numerous other potential malfunctions had plagued the launch.

CHAPTER 10

Marga pedaled toward Peenemünde's heavily guarded front gate where machine gun toting sentries checked everyone entering and leaving the base. She had her violin case slung over one shoulder and her canvas bag over the other and carried a book and paper sack in the basket on the front of her bike. As she approached the gate, a hand snatched her handlebars.

"Hey!" she blurted out as she planted her feet on the ground to keep from falling. She turned to the uniformed figure clutching her bike and noticed a set of youthful eyes peering out from under a steel helmet.

"You're subject to search, Fräulein," the young man said.

Marga huffed, "I don't understand? The guards all know me. I take music lessons in the village."

"Things have changed!" He tugged his collar tab emblazoned with SS runes. "We're now in charge of security, and anyone coming or going is subject to search. No exceptions. Now, your case. I must look inside."

"You want to look at my violin?"

"Please." He held out his hand.

Sighing, she slipped the case off her shoulder, unsnapped its latches, and opened the lid. "See, nothing but a violin."

He took it out, turned it over, and shook it.

"Hey, be careful with that!"

He shot her a stern look and returned the violin to its case, then reached into the handlebar basket for the paper sack.

"It's an apple and a muffin," she said.

He peeked inside and put it back before retrieving the book. "*Tales of the Caribbean,* eh?" He smirked as he thumbed through a few of its pages. He placed it back in the basket and pointed to her canvas bag. "I must look inside."

"I'm going to be late for my music lesson," she protested.

He waggled his fingers in the direction of the canvas bag.

Rolling her eyes, Marga slipped it off and handed it over.

He peered inside, then began rummaging through her sheet music, pencil box, and...

"Give me those!" Marga snatched from his hand a box of feminine napkins.

"Are those...?"

"Shut up!" Her cheeks flushed as she stuffed the box into her bag. "Can I go now?"

Straightening, he cleared his throat and waved her through.

After replacing her bag and violin case on her shoulders, Marga began to pedal away. The young guard called out after her, "What's your name, Fräulein?"

She glanced over her shoulder at him but kept going.

CHAPTER 11

Tomas Fromme pressed a handkerchief to his nose. The stench of sewer lines that had ruptured in the wake of a bomb strike to an apartment building on Invalidenstrasse was overwhelming. Looking up into what remained of the structure, he was taken aback by the absurd sight of Berliners going about their daily lives. A plump, bald man sitting in his armchair smoked a pipe and read a newspaper while his apron-clad wife worked in the kitchen, even as a bucket brigade outside sifted through the rubble of their building.

Turning a corner, Tomas peeked over his shoulder before continuing for half a block to Ludwig's three-story brick walk-up.

"Tomas," Ludwig said as he admitted him to the small apartment with a threadbare couch, two mismatching chairs and a coffee table with a white lace doily. The room's cheeriest feature was a wind-up gramophone on a corner table with a framed print of Toulouse-Lautrec's *Jane Avril Dancing*, hanging on the wall above it.

Tomas put down his valise and tossed aside his service cap.

"You must be exhausted." Ludwig put an arm around his shoulder and led him to the sofa. "I know I am, having spent another night in the cellar, courtesy of Herr Göring's air sirens." He huffed. "Call me Meyer, indeed. I mean look at this place," he said pointing to cracks in the ceiling and walls as evidence of Berlin's frequent air raids. He turned and handed Tomas a bottle of wine. "Be a dear and open that."

"Riesling," Tomas commented as he took out a penknife from his pocket and removed the cork. "Things can't be all that bad."

"Don't kid yourself." Ludwig reached for two glasses. "If you want anything in this town, it's the black market or you go without."

"Isn't it dangerous?"

"Everything is dangerous these days, love. Not to mention, we scrape by on corn-silk tobacco, chicory coffee, and ersatz schnitzel, which is all I have in the icebox."

"I'll settle for the Riesling," Tomas said, pouring the wine.

"How is Sylvie?"

"She keeps talking about having a baby."

"Do it."

"I have enough worries with just us two." He shook his head. "A baby would complicate things."

Ludwig stepped to the gramophone. "Never leave for tomorrow that which you can do today. Besides, think of the fun you'll have trying – or so I hear." A speaker suddenly crackled with Marlene Dietrich's husky, sultry voice crooning "Hot Voodoo."

Tomas chuckled. "You haven't changed at all since we were kids. You're still as obstinate as ever, you silly queer. They could put you in jail for listening to her."

Ludwig returned to the sofa and took his glass. "They could put me in jail for a lot of things. Besides, I like Marlene. I see her as a kindred spirit. Did you know that back in her theater days, she'd perform in several plays at once? She'd act a scene in one theater, scoot out the back door, hop the train to her next engagement where she'd say her lines, and then move to her next gig."

"Sounds exhausting."

"Sirens like her usually are, love. Trust me."

They sampled their Riesling, and Tomas cleared his throat. "Ludwig, I admire your spirit but…You are careful, aren't you?"

Sniffing his wine's bouquet, Ludwig flashed a curious glance. "Careful? You mean with…?"

"Men, the black market…" Tomas nodded toward the gramophone, "Music..."

"Darling, it's why I'm so perfect for this work. I've lived my life in the shadows. I know the art of illusion. It's ironic, isn't it, that someone like me risks his life to save a society that would just as soon keep me silent in a corner."

"Why do it then?"

"And miss all the fun?" Ludwig tossed his head of silky sand-colored hair and downed his wine. "Not a chance, love. I'm in until we evict Uncle Adolf from the Reich Chancellery… the bastard!"

Tomas reached inside his valise. "In that case, you'll need this." He placed *Tales of the Caribbean* on the coffee table.

Ludwig picked up the volume and inspected the binding. "Oh, but to be on a warm beach in the Caribbean." He smiled. "Maybe someday." He poured more wine. "For now, I have to settle for the public pool near the Zoological Garden…At least until it gets blown to bits."

"Just promise me you won't take unnecessary chances. It could compromise our entire operation."

"I've been taking chances every day of my twenty-five years on this earth, darling!" Ludwig raised his glass. "Now, tell me all about the tall, handsome men on the Baltic and what I'm missing."

CHAPTER 12

Wrapped in a peacoat, denim pants, and hat, Ludwig walked through Berlin's early-morning fog until he reached a squat brick building in the shadow of a bomb-damaged warehouse and came face to face with a green-eyed black cat studying him through a dirty window.

"Its name is Himmler," said Arno Huff, the thirtyish postal clerk with somber eyes, who answered the door. "I don't know where he came from, but he's decided this is home."

"Why Himmler?"

Arno grinned. "It makes me look like a good Nazi. What neighbor would denounce someone with a cat named Himmler?" He petted the purring ball of fur. "Not to mention, he eviscerates rats with a striking efficiency."

Ludwig handed Arno the copy of *Tales of the Caribbean*. "Here it is."

Arno ran a finger over the binding. "Come inside and have a cup of coffee…the good stuff."

Ludwig shook his head. "I have to go." He touched Arno's cheek. "Be careful, love. Someday this will all be over." He nodded toward the book. "And, we'll create our own Caribbean tales."

Arno smiled. "If only."

Ludwig kissed Arno's cheek and walked away, vanishing into the mist.

CHAPTER 13

"Tighten your belt," Flight Sergeant Carlisle Mead announced through an intercom to his backseat passenger—a covert operative from Britain's Special Operations Executive—as he advanced the throttle of his Westland Lysander sending the specially designed airplane for clandestine operations roaring across a remote French meadow. As they climbed into a moonlit night, flames belched from the engine and the craft nosed downwards.

"Bollocks!" Mead blurted, pulling back the yoke and throttling the engine with little effect. The Lysander plummeted into the forest. Thrown from the aircraft and barely conscious, he watched his rear-seat passenger, silhouetted by glowing flames, crawl from the burning wreckage, dragging a leather satchel to the base of a nearby tree before collapsing.

CHAPTER 14

With a clattering mechanical growl, the Foch-Achgelis 223 banked over a Russian village. Looking up, Colonel Wilhelm Ernst squinted at the sight of the forty-foot-long aircraft with a conventional body of an airplane and dual 39-foot three-bladed rotors mounted on outriggers in place of wings. Descending like a gangly metallic insect, it hovered ten feet off the ground before gently setting down outside the village.

The colonel adjusted his cap and peered curiously as a woman jumped from a side cargo door. Lean and fit, she wore her flaxen hair in a French braid beneath a field cap with a death's head insignia over the bill. He figured she had to be important to be dressed in tan jodhpur trousers, a black Panzer jacket, and knee-length riding boots. A holstered six-shot pearl-handled revolver strapped to her hip mimicked that of a western gunslinger. She tugged at snug leather gloves as she approached the colonel and four German officers standing watch over three Russian soldiers.

"Fräulein Geisler, I presume?" said the colonel.

"Call me Freida," she said, eyeing the three Russians. "Are these the prisoners?"

Looking her up and down, the colonel cleared his throat. "I was under the impression Sicherheitsdienst was sending a...how shall I say..."

Freida opened and closed her leather-bound hands as if preparing to strangle someone. "Herr Colonel, you were expecting a hairy-knuckled ruffian? One of Röhm's leftover Brownshirts, perhaps?"

The colonel smirked. "Anything you're capable of, Fräulein, my own men are more than adept at."

"Yet it would seem that you and your so-called men have failed to obtain the information demanded from brigade headquarters."

The colonel stiffened. "I've shot a dozen men and hung a score of partisan women. These are brutish people, Fräulein—used to hard lives. Anything we threaten them with is but an extension of their pitiful existence."

Freida drew a twin-edged dagger from her boot and stepped before one of the Russians – a general officer. He looked into her eyes with an air of indifference as he tugged on his cigarette and blew aside the smoke. She moved to the next man – a political commissar. Assigned to Russian army field units, they were responsible for ensuring proper adherence to Soviet political ideology. Usually shot on site when captured, he avoided her scrutinizing gaze. Freida placed her dagger under his chin and raised his head to look into his dark eyes. Flicking the blade so that it pricked his flesh and drew a speck of blood, she moved onto the next prisoner, a young lieutenant.

"He's the German speaker?" she asked the colonel.

He nodded.

"How old are you?" she asked the Russian.

His lips quivering, he answered. *"Zwan…Zwanzig, Fräulein."*

She smirked. "Twenty? What a shame…to die so young." She pressed the tip of her dagger to his cheek. "If you tell me what I want to know, you'll live."

Straightening up, he looked sternly toward the horizon and announced, "I'm prepared to die for Mother Russia!"

Grinning, Freida leaned close and whispered, "I'll give you your chance."

She turned toward the aircraft and called over her shoulder, "Herr Colonel, tie their hands and put them aboard!"

"Where are you taking them?" he demanded. "They're *my* prisoners!"

"Not to worry! I'll drop them off shortly!"

The colonel turned to one of his captains. "Accompany the Fräulein!"

The officer looked at him and then toward the strange flying machine.

The colonel noticed the captain's hesitance. *"Now,* Captain!"

* * *

As the spindly aircraft's engine revved and its rotors turned, a crew chief helped board the three prisoners and sit them on the metal floor where they were joined by the captain, who sat facing them. Leaning into the cockpit, Freida gave the pilot a thumbs-up and the *fa* 223 rose to a hover and gently climbed skyward.

At five hundred feet, Freida stepped to the open cargo door and looked down at the ground. Reaching for a pair of headsets, she slipped one on the Russian general and the other on the young

German-speaking lieutenant. Wearing her own headset, she keyed her microphone. "Ask the general where he buried our Enigma machine," she said, referring to the highly classified wooden shoe-box-sized unit used by *Wehrmacht* field units to encipher and decode messages.

The lieutenant turned to the general and asked.

Pursing his lips, the general shrugged.

Freida turned to the crew chief, snapped her fingers, and pointed to the Russian commissar. The crew chief dutifully raised him to his feet, and she motioned toward the open cargo door.

His face terror-struck, the commissar dove for the deck and wrapped his arms around the crew chief's legs. Freida turned to the German captain who remained frozen—seemingly from shock—until her hard stare willed him to action.

"Tell the general I'll throw him out!" Freida hollered over the whining engine.

The lieutenant translated, stammering the words.

The general shrugged.

"Toss him!" Freida barked.

The commissar shrieked as he went out the door.

Her eyes on fire, Freida turned to the general. He remained unmoved.

Freida turned to the captain and crew chief. They pulled the general to his feet.

He tensed. A long, wet stain spread down his trouser leg. "*Nyet! Nyet!*" he blurted.

"Either he talks or he goes!" Freida yelled into her mike.

The lieutenant quickly translated her words.

The general raised his bound hands pleading.

Her jaw set, Freida exclaimed, "Pitch him!"

The crew chief and captain manhandled the general toward the door's edge where the wind fluttered his hair and the tips of his boots hung over the side.

"Last chance!" Freida shouted.

The lieutenant barked her final warning.

His eyes wide and face ashen, the general turned to the lieutenant and spoke frantically.

Freida yanked the general back from the door's edge and pushed him to the floor. *"Where is it?"*

"He says it's hidden in the village well," said the lieutenant. "In the center square."

Freida shouted at the lieutenant. "If he's lying…!"

The general babbled in Russian.

The lieutenant translated. "He promises it's there!"

Freida tapped the pilot's shoulder, and he handed her a radio transmitter. She used it to relay the information to the ground.

Turning to the general, she said, "Now, we wait."

They circled one thousand feet above the Russian steppe for an hour before a radio call from the ground announced, "Item retrieved."

The lieutenant conveyed the message to the pale and anxious general, who sat back relieved.

Straightening her Panzer jacket, Freida turned to the door and curled a thin, grim smile. Turning to the captain and crew chief, she nodded at the general and keyed her internal mike. "Toss him."

The captain and crew chief raised the general to his feet.

The general protested.

The lieutenant said to Frieda, "He said he gave you what you wanted!"

She remained unmoved.

His eyes dark and menacing, the general barked in Russian at the lieutenant.

"What'd he say?" she shouted, her hands balled into fists.

"He said…Tell her I'll be waiting for her in hell!"

The general spit in her face.

Her eyes burning, Freida wiped the spittle from her cheek then snatched the general's tunic, spun him around, and heaved him out the door.

CHAPTER 15

Deep within a maze of corridors inside a nondescript gray building in the heart of Berlin, SS-Oberführer Gerhard Pringer stood with hands behind his back watching Freida Geisler examine a collection of fire-singed items spread over a table. He admired her coiffed golden hair and slender feminine lines beneath a tailored black pin-striped suit and pencil skirt.

"So, Herr Oberführer, whose garage did you empty?" she asked.

He replied, "Those items were recovered from the crash site of an RAF Lysander in France."

"Maquis?" she remarked, referencing the French resistance group.

"I'm sure they were involved," he said stepping alongside her. "You'll notice two copies of *Defense de la France,* a scurrilous French resistance newspaper."

She picked up one of the partially burned editions before setting it down among a first-aid kit, flotation device, maps, charts, and a slim volume titled *Tales of the Caribbean.*

"So, what am I looking at?" she asked.

"Your next assignment."

She turned with a curious gleam in her eye.

Pringer extinguished the lights and activated a slide projector. The wall over the table lit up, revealing an image of the Lysander wreckage. He advanced through images of the recovered items. *Thunk, thunk, thunk* the projector sounded as slides were advanced until stopping on an image of *Tales of the Caribbean*.

"It meant little to us at first," he said. "It's just a book. But then, two things caught our attention. First, books are for leisure, not something clandestine operatives have time for. Secondly," he advanced the slide to show an image of the book's German text. "Are we to believe British agents read obscure books in German?" *Thunk.* "And, we have *this* curious item." He adjusted the focus. "Tucked in a corner of the back page…a partial stamp."

Freida narrowed her eyes as she deciphered the red lettering. "Peene…li…bry."

"Peenemünde Free Library," announced Pringer. "The stamp must have lacked sufficient ink."

"And this means what?"

The slide changed to reveal an image of the book's spine with a carefully drawn narrow slit along its seam. Next was another image of the binding, this time peeled back to show a strip of microfilm. The slides that followed were blueprints of electrical circuitry and other technical drawings.

Her face aglow from the projector's light, Freida stated the obvious. "Herr Oberführer, there are spies at Peenemünde."

Pringer lifted his head to look her in the eye. "Yes, Freida, there are. And you're going to find them."

CHAPTER 16

Perfume, cigarettes, and perspiration scented the air as Ullie joined a flood of workers stepping off the tram that had taken them all to Peenemünde. Approaching the Technical Design building, Ullie slowed his gait at the sight of uniformed SS guards at the entrance checking identifications and bags. Waiting his turn, Ullie watched as the man in front of him had his briefcase searched and papers reviewed. They patted him down and removed his fedora. The hat was thoroughly checked, with a finger slid under the hatband for good measure before it was returned and the man sent on his way.

Ullie was motioned forward.

"Briefcase," one of the guards ordered, holding out his hand. Ullie hesitated. "Briefcase!" the SS man snapped.

Taking it by its handle, the guard stared at Ullie. "Your palms are wet, Mein Herr. Any particular reason?"

"I have nothing to hide," Ullie replied motioning to the briefcase.

"Arms up," the other guard demanded. He began to pat him down. Finding a fountain pen in Ullie's breast pocket, he pulled it out and unscrewed it. Meanwhile, the official rummaging through his briefcase retrieved a cardboard tube of Bromo-Seltzer tablets. He opened the container and poured the contents into his hand. Apparently satisfied, the guards replaced Ullie's items where they had found them.

"Go!" said the SS man, snapping shut the briefcase.

Ullie entered the building and went straight to the men's room, where he barged into a stall, leaned over the bowl, and vomited. Composing himself, he wiped his mouth and flushed the toilet. He then closed the lid and placed the briefcase atop it. He lifted his tie, snaked out a tightly folded document inserted within its narrow fabric and unfolded it. After flattening the creases in the paper, he slipped the document inside the briefcase.

Ullie exited the stall and checked his appearance in a mirror when the men's room door opened, and two men entered.

"Did they get you too, Mainz?" one of them asked.

"Why do you think he's in here?" said the other, clapping Ullie's shoulder. "He crapped himself!"

The two men laughed.

Ullie gave a weak smile and grabbed his briefcase. "If only suspicion and harassment could launch a rocket, we'd be on the moon by now."

Reaching his desk, Ullie was startled by Harold's voice. "So, what do you think?"

Ullie feigned ignorance as he stuffed his briefcase under his desk. "About what?"

"Our little greeting this morning? Nothing like trust in the workplace."

"I'm surprised it's taken this long."

Harold slipped on a lab coat. "Why do you suppose they're starting now?"

"It's the SS. It's what they do. Trust no one, suspect everyone."

"It's not like we aren't under enough pressure." Harold shook his head as he stuck pens and colored pencils into a pocket protector. He glanced at a wall clock. "Join me in the wind tunnel when you get settled. I might have a fix for that lateral fin oscillation issue."

"I'll be right down," said Ullie.

He waited until Harold left, then opened his briefcase and retrieved the folder with the document smuggled in his tie. Proceeding to the file room, he opened a metal cabinet and returned the document of technical drawings to its proper folder. Someone entered the room behind him. Ullie turned. It was Janko. The janitor stood in the doorway pushing a large trash barrel on wheels.

"They know," said Janko.

Ullie gave a cautious look over the janitor's shoulder into the office where the engineers went about their work. "It's just routine security checks. Nothing to worry about."

"Is that why you're so pale?"

Ullie stepped forward. "Don't get distracted."

"I hope this doesn't involve the girl."

Ullie cleared his throat. "You leave her to me. Understood?"

Janko drew a wry smile. "You do your job, and I'll do mine."

"Just do as I say."

"I do as I see my duty…Herr Doctor. Now, excuse me, I have work to do."

CHAPTER 17

A thunderous roar echoed over the Baltic and Peenemünde's white sandy shores as an A-4 rocket soared skyward while engineers inside a concrete bunker monitored glowing gauges and flickering monitors. In the background, a flight controller's measured voice crackled through a speaker counting off the seconds since launch. "Ten…fifteen…twenty…All systems responding!"

From an observation balcony, Harold clutched a stopwatch while Wernher peered through binoculars. At his side, an auburn-haired secretary scribbled his observations into a notepad.

"Swinemünde reports positive tracking, fifty kilometers down range!" the flight controller's voice echoed through the speaker, referring to the tracking station on Usedom's eastern tip on the Baltic.

"Kolberg reporting, one hundred kilometers down range!" came the next position report seconds later.

Wernher and Harold exchanged glances. They dared not smile.

"Abeam Koslin, one-hundred-fifty kilometers!" the speaker broadcast, reporting the missile's position relative to the Polish town 7 miles inland from the sea.

Harold glanced at his stopwatch. Anticipation electrified his senses.

"Fifty-five…fifty-six…fifty-seven…Apogee and engine shut-off," the flight controller's voice announced through the speaker.

Harold halted his stopwatch. He met Wernher's eye. They'd done it. Years of painstaking research, punctuated by repeated failure and disappointment, finally overcome.

"Wernher." Harold held out his hand.

Wernher pushed it aside and embraced him. "We did it, old friend!"

"The world will never be the same."

"Not ever again!" Wernher declared. He turned to his smiling secretary and kissed her on the cheek. "This is your victory too!"

"Impact reported!" an engineer clutching a telephone called to Wernher. "In the sea…between Leba and Rixhoff."

* * *

Pocketing his stopwatch in the flight-control bunker, Ullie leaned against a wall and peered through a window at the vacated launch stand from where the A-4 had ascended minutes earlier. He weighed the incredible and grim milestone just achieved and realized the world had changed forever. The age of the bomb-laden piloted aircraft had just been rendered obsolete. Henceforth, a weapon could be launched beyond the atmosphere at a distant target without its author ever seeing his objective or his victims knowing of its approach.

CHAPTER 18

Beer mugs overflowed and Jägermeister and schnapps poured liberally at the officers' club as a piano played *"Jägerlied"* to accompany a chorus of cheerful singing voices. The laughter and raucous banter echoed throughout the room as the men celebrated the world's first successful ballistic missile launch. Seated at the bar, his eyes pink and glassy, Harold stoked his pipe. Alongside him, Hermann Goetz took a long pull from a beer stein and placed an arm over Harold's shoulder.

"Did you ever imagine, Harold, back in our university days that any of this would ever happen?" Goetz snorted. "Do you recall, Dr. Fuchs…his rocket club—*our first launch!*"

Harold slapped the bar chuckling as tobacco smoke shot from his nose.

"How it veered sideways," Goetz continued, "burning a trail across that meadow…between that cow's legs!" They laughed. "Now, look at us!" Goetz pressed his moist forehead against Harold's. "This, changes everything. Space, the moon itself is now within reach!" He clutched Harold's shoulder. "Think of it, man, the moon!"

"Let's drink to it!" Harold quipped, raising his mug. "To the moon!"

"To the moon!" Goetz hoisted his stein.

"What's this talk of the moon?" Wernher interrupted as he clamped a hand on each of his colleagues' shoulders.

"I was just telling Harold," said Goetz. "Today we took a big step toward it."

Through a hesitant grin, Wernher looked around before softly saying, "We're a long way from the moon, Hermann. A *very* long way."

"Perhaps, but it's simply a matter of physics, mathematics and"—Goetz burped—"thrust dynamics! We just need to..."

"We just need to focus on our task," Wernher said, gently squeezing Goetz's shoulder. "That being the development of ballistic missiles." He spoke as if addressing everyone within earshot. In fact, many had turned to listen. "Today's accomplishment is the first step in the right direction, but there's still much to do—in particular, guidance and flight control. That, I'm afraid, will take some doing." He hoisted his mug and smiled. "Therefore, I can optimistically announce, we all have job security in the near future!"

A cheer sounded. Mugs and bottles were raised. The piano keys trilled a quick cadence of *"Horst Wessel Lied,"* the Nazi Party anthem, which men proudly stood to sing.

"Ironic," Harold remarked over the clamor. "Without them—the Nazis—we wouldn't be here."

Taking a drink, Wernher answered, "It's but a means to an end, Harold. Someday our work will be for the betterment of humanity."

"Humanity..." Harold shook his head. "Let's drink to it then. To humanity!"

* * *

Across the room, Freida Geisler's smoky eyes watched over the brim of her champagne glass. So, the rumors were true. The Nazi high command's suspicions of Peenemünde's scientists were justified. They were interested in—distracted by—space travel more than the rocket program's objective, which was destroying Germany's enemies.

She waited until most of the scientists had filtered out. With their arms around each other, they sang college hymns and silly tunes. She ordered a sherry at the bar and turned to the man on a stool beside her.

"Have you a light by chance?" she asked, her cigarette balanced between plump, ruby lips.

Hermann Goetz slid his bloodshot eyes towards her.

She smiled.

He felt his pockets and produced a lighter. Striking a flame, he angled it to her cigarette.

"Thank you," she said, taking a puff just as her sherry appeared. Goetz raised a hand indicating he'd pay for it. "Thanks again." She took a sip and sat on the stool beside him. "I'm Freida."

"Hermann…Hermann Goetz." His thinning straw-colored hair was damp and disheveled, and moisture dappled his forehead and rosy cheeks.

"That's my father's name," she lied, smiling. "I don't suppose you operate a streetcar?" She took a puff.

"No." He shook his head, cupping his nearly empty beer mug with both hands as if praying to it. "I'm an engineer."

"A rocket engineer?"

He nodded, slurping the last of his beer.

She signaled the barkeeper for another.

"I should call it a night," he said through a burp.

"Oh, have one more." She inched closer to him. "I want to hear more about what you do."

An overflowing mug was set before him. She raised her glass in a toast. "To new friends."

He raised his mug. "To new friends."

"So, what exactly do you do?" she asked.

He suppressed another burp. "My wife always says, Hermann, don't be a bore. Rocket talk is dull."

"Is she here?" Freida looked around curiously.

He shook his head. "Düsseldorf. She refused to move here—the end of the world she calls it."

"That's a shame," she brushed his hand. "You must get lonely."

"It's for the best. I work long hours…She'd be bored silly."

"You aren't working tonight."

He grinned. "Ah, tonight…We celebrated. You probably heard."

"Heard what?"

"We made our first successful rocket launch today."

"Fascinating." She sipped her sherry. "And where did this rocket go?"

"Eighty kilometers into the stratosphere, before falling into the Baltic," he announced giddily.

"Excuse me, Fräulein," a uniformed officer interrupted. Younger and handsomer than Goetz, he held a beer mug and smiled confidently. "Perhaps you'd care to sit with me and my friends." He nodded toward a corner table where two other uniformed officers sat smiling.

Goetz fell silent and turned to his beer. Freida eyed the officer and then his friends. One blew her a kiss. Projecting a faint smile as if she might accept the offer, Freida motioned the officer closer. Grinning, he leaned in when she viciously jammed her three-inch heel into his knee. Wincing, the officer reeled, grabbing his leg. Freida snatched his collar, put her lips to his ear and hissed, "*Piss off!*"

Shoving him away, she watched him limp back to his waiting friends, who looked stunned. Smoothing her shiny coiffed hair, Freida turned back to Goetz and smiled as if nothing had happened. "Now, Hermann, you were saying?"

* * *

From the kitchen, Janko watched. He found the episode troubling—this beautiful young woman preferring the older man's company. There was more to her actions than a casual interest in a middle-aged rocket scientist. No, a woman like her, had a motive and Janko suspected the worst.

CHAPTER 19

Marga walked her bicycle along a wooded shortcut to the base when a man surprised her by emerging from a stand of trees.

"Good afternoon, Fräulein."

"Oh!" She was startled. "You scared me!" The man wore an SS uniform and looked vaguely familiar.

"I'm sorry…I didn't mean to."

"What are you doing here?"

"Waiting for you."

"Me? Why?"

"I want to talk to you."

"I have to get home," she said, pressing on. She now recognized him as the guard who had searched her days earlier at the front gate.

He trotted after her. "Can I walk with you?"

"I can't stop you, though mother has cautioned me about speaking with strangers."

"I'm not a stranger. You know me."

She gave him a miffed look. "Only because you stopped and searched me."

"I was doing my job."

"That wouldn't convince my mother."

"Perhaps she'd feel different about an SS man."

Marga scrunched her brow. "You're little more than a boy."

"I'm nineteen!"

"Is that supposed to impress me?"

"How about knowing that I like you?"

She narrowed her eyes warily. "I don't even know your name."

"Walter...Walter Mitz...SS-Oberschütze."

"Is that a high rank?"

He cleared his throat. "No, but it's not the lowest either."

"Well, Walter Mitz, nice chatting with you, but I must get home." She pedaled away and turned onto the asphalt roadway leading to Peenemünde's main gate. Glancing over her shoulder, she saw that he appeared crestfallen. Guilt rankled her for she wasn't accustomed to being rude. She stopped and sighed and called out to him. "Okay, Walter, I'm Marga...You can walk me to the gate."

Grinning, he ran to catch up to her.

Pushing her bike, Marga asked, "How can you like me when you don't know anything about me?"

"I know you like to read."

She stopped. "What's your point?"

"That we aren't strangers."

Frowning, Marga pressed on.

"Marga...wait!"

She turned, hinting a scowl. "What?"

"The gate sentries...They were questioned the other day... about books leaving the base." He clutched her handlebars. *"Tales of the Caribbean* came up."

Marga's heart skipped.

He grinned. "Don't' worry...I didn't say anything."

"It wouldn't matter," she said defiantly. "I didn't do anything wrong. It's just a book."

"I believe you."

She wrinkled her brow. "Why are you telling me this?"

"I told you...I like you."

"Thank you, but I'm not worried."

"No, you don't seem to be."

She gave him a hard stare then turned for the gate. "I'll see you around, Walter."

As she approached the gate, Marga's heart was pounding. Would the guards notice her hands shaking?

"Papers, Fräulein," a gate sentry said to her extending his hand.

She handed him her identification with trembling hands.

"Are you nervous?" he asked.

"No...just winded from riding my bike."

He reviewed her credentials and handed them back.

"Very well, you may pass."

Marga took her papers and walked her bike fifty feet from the gate and stopped to put them away. Turning back, she saw Walter speaking with the guard she'd just encountered. They looked in her direction.

Marga turned, mounted her bike and pedaled away thinking, Ullie, where are you?

CHAPTER 20

A breeze ruffled Marga's skirt and played with her hair as she balanced her bicycle with an eye on the Technical Design building. She was hoping Ullie kept to his routine and took a mid-afternoon walk. Biting her lip, she looked around. He was late. *Perhaps he isn't coming – detained with an engineering problem or meeting.* She sighed. She couldn't loiter or someone would notice.

To her delight, Ullie exited the front door and he stopped to speak with a colleague before turning onto a footpath leading behind a neighboring hangar. Setting off, she coasted behind him and called his name.

He turned. "Marga…?"

"Something's happened," she said stopping alongside him. "The gate sentries were questioned about books leaving the base. They were asked about *Tales of the Caribbean* specifically."

Looking around, he smoothed his tie and, with a disarming smile, said, "Come, let's walk." They proceeded at a leisurely pace behind the hangar, the faint sounds of the lapping sea nearby. "First of all, you did nothing wrong," he assured her. "This is a highly classified base, and security is constantly assessed."

"But why ask about the book? What if I'm questioned?"

"Can I trust you?"

"Yes, of course."

He cleared his throat. "Truth is, Marga, I was randomly selected to participate in a program evaluating our security measures."

"You mean, the sentries at the gate?"

He nodded. "They're constantly being tested for contraband entering and leaving the facility. Books, personal items, anything that can be used to smuggle something."

She looked puzzled. "What can be smuggled inside a book?"

"That's not the point, Marga. It's about, do the sentries pay enough attention to detail to remember specific items which, if it were later learned were used in a nefarious manner, could be tracked down and anyone involved with them questioned."

"I think I understand. But why did you have me do it?"

He smiled. "A little trickery."

"Trickery?"

He chuckled. "The sentries are young, often bored and distracted. It's easy for them to stay focused on someone like me. However, introduce a young and fetching girl like yourself…" He arched his brow. "They may tend to overlook things and spend more time focusing on you."

Blushing, Marga laughed. "Oh, Ullie…Really? I don't believe you!"

"It's true but," he clutched her bike's handlebars. "You aren't to repeat a word of this to anyone."

She shook her head. "Of course not!"

"I'm sorry if I caused you any embarrassment."

"You didn't. It all makes perfect sense now."

He gave her his best smile. "Our secret, right?"

She nodded. "Our secret…Ullie."

CHAPTER 21

The evening was cool and visited by a pale moon. Freida's heels clicked along the sidewalk as she approached the four-story apartment building whose chimneys expelled cozy trails of smoke. She looked up at the illuminated second-floor window with drawn shades and then at the large brown envelope in her hand. She entered the building, climbed the stairs to the second floor, and knocked on Hermann Goetz's door.

Goetz answered and, not wearing his glasses, narrowed his eyes at his unexpected caller. "Yes?"

"Dr. Goetz," Freida said pleasantly.

He wrinkled his brow. "Fräulein…"

"Freida. Remember?"

He cleared his throat. "Yes, of course. What…What can I do for you?"

"I'd like to pick up our conversation from the other night."

He rubbed his nose thoughtfully. "I have to admit, I'm a bit fuzzy on the entire evening. I apologize if I said anything untoward."

"Nonsense, Hermann," she said stepping around him and into his small apartment. It smelled of stale tobacco and ersatz coffee. "I found our conversation most stimulating." She eyed the bed and peeked inside the small bathroom, then moved to a seating area with a small couch, two chairs, and a coffee table. There was a radio on the bureau. She turned it on. A jingle in English for furniture polish tittered through the speaker.

"Please…!" he protested shutting it off.

"Hermann, I'm surprised. There are harsh penalties for listening to foreign broadcasts."

Frazzled, he put on his glasses and exclaimed, "I must have twisted the dial inadvertently… I have no idea. You aren't going to…?"

"Oh, Hermann, please," she said amused. She removed her coat and knitted beret. "Is there a place to hang this?" She held out her coat with one hand. Her other held the large brown envelope that would help her persuade Goetz of what he had to do.

As Goetz placed her coat on a door hook, she noticed him eyeing the envelope nervously.

"Come, Hermann," she motioned to the couch. "Let's sit and talk."

She opened the envelope and spread out several photographs before him on the coffee table.

Goetz reached for the photos. "My wife…? Children…? Our home?!" He glared at her. "What is this?"

"Hermann, you and I are going to reach an understanding."

"I…I don't follow!"

"My name is Freida Geisler. I work for state security… Sicherheitsdienst. SS intelligence branch."

"S-D?"

She nodded.

"What…what would you—they—want with me? I haven't done anything!"

"Oh, Hermann," she laughed. "If you were in trouble, I'd have you hanging by your thumbs by now." She patted his hand. "Hear me out."

Goetz stood and pointed to the door. "I want you to leave – now!"

"Sit down!" she snapped.

His face turned beet red. He stared at her for a long moment before relenting.

"As I was saying," she said, "we're to have an understanding. One in which you'll report to me anyone undermining Peenemünde's ongoing research."

"Undermining research?"

"I'm a spy hunter, Hermann. There are spies here, and you're going to help me find them."

"Impossible!"

Freida held up the photos. "Fail me, Hermann, and…well, you wouldn't want anything to happen to them…would you?" She raised a finger. "However, in return, your children will attend the best schools in Düsseldorf, and your daughter will be excused from summer labor duties, while your wife will have a maid—a Polish girl—to keep house." Freida looked down and adjusted her lapel. "Now, Hermann, do we have an understanding?"

He remained silent.

Freida stood and stepped to the door. "I forgot to mention… It would be a shame for Inge, your children's schnauzer, to be taken away since her family would no longer be there to care for her."

Goetz studied the faces in the photos.

Freida buttoned her coat. "I need an answer, Hermann."

With a defeated look, Goetz nodded.

"Good," she said. "I'll be in touch."

CHAPTER 22

Having dined on pan-seared veal and roasted potatoes, Ullie and Dr. Fredrich Stroudt, a propulsion engineer on von Braun's team, finished their apple tarts in the Adlon Hotel's dining room. Ullie couldn't help but admire the décor of potted palms, crown molding, brass light fixtures, and crystal chandeliers, which evoked a pre-war elegance at odds with the hotel's brick encased lobby and basement bomb shelter.

The two men reclined in cabriolet chairs and ordered brandy that soon had the desired effect on Ullie's octogenarian travel companion already fatigued from their day's journey to Berlin.

"I'm afraid," said Stroudt suppressing a yawn, "that I'm fading." His colleague dabbed a napkin over his lips. "It's been a long day."

Ullie glanced at his watch. "I can't say that I'm far behind you, Herr Doctor."

"Come then," said Stroudt, leading the way into the lobby. They shook hands. "Good night, Dr. Mainz. I shall see you in the morning."

Ullie waited until the Peenemünde engineer disappeared behind elevator doors, then claimed his overcoat and hat from the coat-check girl. Outdoors the season's first snowflakes danced in the wind as he stood under the Adlon's front awning facing an almost empty Pariser Platz and adjacent Brandenburg Gate.

"May I summon you a car?" a uniformed porter asked.

"I'm walking, thank you." Ullie centered his trilby and strolled into the night.

Fifteen minutes later, he knocked on the lacquered front door of Ursula's fashionable Unter den Linden address. It was his first visit and the third time he'd met her. Their two previous encounters had been at an acquaintance's Berlin home over cocktails and once in Berlin's central train station where he passed her a photo album with hidden microfilm of missile documents. She answered the door wearing a low-cut pearl-white chiffon evening dress with rouleau shoulder straps and a glimmering silver necklace encrusted with green emeralds. Her platinum hair was stylishly bobbed. Tall and elegant, she looked much younger than her forty-plus years.

"Ullie, darling!" she said pecking his cheek. "Come in." She took his hat and coat.

"Ursula, I see Berlin continues to agree with you."

She raised a thin eyebrow and looked him over. "I see Peenemünde is keeping you fit. What's her name?"

"*His* name is Doctor von Braun, and he keeps me plenty busy."

"Come and tell me all about it," she said, taking his arm and ushering him into the spacious living room. He admired a Picasso above the fireplace and the white, chamois furniture, porcelain oriental lamps, and taffeta curtains complementing the room.

"Offer you a drink?" she asked.

"What are Berlin's current penchants?"

"How about Dewar's?"

"In these times?"

Unscrewing the cap, she smiled and poured. "You take it neat, as I recall."

Accepting his drink, he held it to the light. "Black market prices must be draconian."

"I manage," she said with an assured smile.

They sat on opposite sides of an oval glass coffee table. Reaching for a cigarette, Ursula gracefully crossed her legs in a practiced manner designed to draw a man's attention. Sipping his drink, Ullie admired her lean, winsome lines. He had heard she'd modeled during the Weimar years, her smoky eyes and remarkable face gracing billboards for Muratti cigarettes and Henkell sparkling wines.

"I was pleased to find your invitation waiting for me," he said. "I wasn't sure we should meet."

"I thought it important…Besides, well, let's just say, anyone watching knows I'm accustomed to handsome gentlemen callers."

"I'm flattered."

She took a pensive drag. "I'll get to the point. I'm told the Führer expects Peenemünde's rockets to change the course of the war. He was recently briefed at his East Prussian field headquarters by von Braun and other officials. He was shown footage of rocket launches and provided generous estimates of their potential."

"How generous?"

"Enough so that he's authorized significant resources to their development."

"How could they have told him that? I mean, their payloads are limited and their accuracy abysmal."

She smiled. "No one wants to tell the emperor he has no clothes."

"You mean admit Peenemünde's rockets won't save the Third Reich."

"Hitler is convinced they will. Therefore, the more he pours into the project, the more he bleeds Germany's war machine and buys time until a second front can be opened in the West. That being said, he's also of the mind that if the Allies prevail, all vestiges of the Third Reich are to be destroyed to include Peenemünde and all its work. He specifically tasked Himmler and his SS to devise contingency plans."

"I'm sure von Braun will have a plan to counter such a thing. After all, it's his life's work."

"If he survives, Ullie."

He shook his head. "Ursula, there's too much documentation – not to mention what I've managed to get out."

"You've done a wonderful job, Ullie, but it represents only a fraction."

He frowned. "I can fit only so many pictures into a book binding."

"No one is blaming you." She drew a puff. "However, in light of this possibility, you're to gather the A-4's most vital and indispensable records—the data that, if destroyed, would set back the field of rocketry many years."

Ullie listened attentively and took a drink.

"There's another consideration," she said. "Our friends, the Russians, have gotten the upper hand in the East. It'll be a bloody road but, in the end, they'll prevail. And when they do, they'll advance through Germany like locusts—devouring everything in their path, to include Germany's spoils."

"Like ballistic missile research."

She nodded. "It's little better in their hands than the Nazis. The West fears what Stalin could do with it."

"You mean he might look beyond the Rhine," he said.

"The Russians once chased Napoleon back to Paris. It may prove too tempting."

"I can probably condense the information to a few hundred pages," he told her. "Then what?"

"You're taking it out."

"To England?"

She took a drag nodding.

"On who's authority?" He tried not to appear peeved.

"Mine. You work for me, remember?"

He shook his head. "No, Ursula. I'll do what you ask, but I'm not leaving."

"Ullie, listen to me. Spy rings are like musical chairs. Eventually, the music stops."

"And someone gets left without a chair."

Her tone softened. "Let me do this for you."

He thumbed his chest. "I'm the only intelligence asset you have on the Baltic. Without me…" He shook his head. "No, I'm staying—musical chairs or not."

"London is demanding that information and who better than you to deliver it?"

"Let them come for it then."

She sighed and downed her drink. Then she held out her glass and rattled its ice cubes. "Be a darling?"

He took the glass and turned to the bar when, stepping past the fireplace, his foot caught a brass lever triggering the hissing sound of gas.

"Just set it back into place," she said.

He reset the lever and the hissing stopped. The faint odor of propane lingered.

"You should have that fixed."

"What makes you think it's not?"

He found her tone odd but refreshed their drinks and sat back down. "What about you? Aren't *you* concerned about being left without a chair?"

Her eyes grew distant. "I remember a time when Germany was a tolerant, cultured society. Sure, we lived in a monarchy, but it wasn't repressive. One could practice their faith, read their author of choice, and express themselves artistically." She took a long drag and sighed a breath of smoke. "When they started burning books and limiting speech, I knew I had to do something." Her voice suddenly loud and defiant, she added, "If it costs me my life, it'll have been a life well spent."

"Well, I don't intend on leaving you behind to fight the battle alone."

"I miss that…The cockiness and incorruptibility of youth…It's what will win this war in the end. You'll see."

A clock chimed in the foyer, and he glanced at his watch. "It's getting late. I should let you get to bed."

She stood and tamped out her cigarette. A sweet, feminine musk scented the air as her dress settled over her lissome body. Extending a slim, ivory hand, she smiled seductively and said, "Be a darling then, and tuck me in."

CHAPTER 23

The shades in Ullie's apartment glowed under the morning sun as Gerda's naked figure tiptoed across the room and slipped under the bed covers. She smiled and listened as he whistled in the bathroom while shaving.

Following his recent trip to Berlin, she'd sensed competition for his affection. The scent of another woman's perfume had greeted her upon opening his suitcase. And she'd fished out a note from his address book thanking him for "an evening's pleasure" in a delicate script.

Ullie emerged from the bathroom toweling his face. He grinned. "I think we should conserve water on Sundays, do our bit for the war effort, and shower together. What do you think?" He stepped to the foot of the bed.

She rose on an elbow and smiled. "I can think of something better. We can shower together... every morning."

He chuckled. "I think the fellows in the dormitory would grow suspicious of stockings hanging out of the windows."

"Scandalous!" she tittered, sitting up and allowing the bedsheet to fall away. "Ullie... Do you love me?"

He arched his brow and cleared his throat. "Gerda..."

Giggling, she lay back and raised a leg, making small circles with her foot while playfully singing, "I know what you do...I know what you do..."

He eyed her curiously as he wrapped the towel around his neck.

Sitting up, she cast a mischievous smile and slowly opened her fist.

Ullie froze.

Balancing the micro-Minox camera in her palm, Gerda raised it to her eye and, pretending to snap a picture, said, "Smile, dear!"

Ullie dropped his towel and tried to snatch the device from her.

Laughing, Gerda pressed it to her bare chest.

"Gerda!"

"I had a feeling you were using that little girl on her bike to deliver more than books."

His eyes smoldering, he snapped, "Leave her out of this!"

"She has a crush on you...poor thing." She sighed. "What if I were to run your errands from now on?"

Ullie crossed his arms and frowned.

"It's what any wife would do for her husband." She worked her way to the foot of the bed with the camera tightly clutched in her fist. "I love you, Ullie and I'd never hurt the one I love. Besides, soon we'll be..."

His eyes narrowed. "We'll soon be what?"

Letting the anticipation build, she gently rubbed her navel.

"Gerda, are you saying...?"

Beaming, she announced, "I'm pregnant, darling."

"Gerda!" He snatched her wrist. "How do I know...?"

"It's yours?" She laughed. "It's been only you, Ullie." She traced a finger over his chest. "Do we really want to argue this before a magistrate?"

"Gerda…"

"Shhh…" She brushed her lips over his. "Say you love me. I know you can. And you will mean it."

"Give me the camera," he said.

"First, I need to know how you feel, dear. I can wire my mother the wonderful news. She can get a travel pass. A simple ceremony will do."

His jaw set, he stared into her dancing eyes.

She drew close. "Should I send the wire?"

He remained unmoved.

"Darling?"

He sighed and finally nodded.

"Oh, Ullie," she pouted. "A girl dreams of a proper proposal."

Meeting her eager gaze, he took her hand and cleared his throat. "Gerda Hewel…Will you marry me?"

Her cheeks warm and smiling, she opened her fist to finally relinquish the camera. "Of course, darling. We're partners now."

CHAPTER 24

"Have chapters seven and eight read by tomorrow," Frau Ilsa Grimke announced to her classroom of pupils. She turned and nodded to a thin, yellow-haired boy in the front row who dutifully rose and called the room to attention. Chairs scraped over the floor as Grimke stepped to a gramophone and flipped a switch. A record began spinning and "*Horst Wessel Lied*" crackled through its speaker prompting the class to extend their arms in a National Socialist salute and sing.

Side-by-side, their arms raised, Marga and Portia absently voiced the words honoring a Brownshirt thug killed in a street fight with communists. The music concluded, Frau Grimke replaced the record arm on its cradle and faced the members of the class standing at attention. Eyeing her charges, she waited a long moment before uttering, "Dismissed!"

The students gathered their books and eagerly headed for the door.

Marga turned to Portia. "I'm going home first and then we can—"

"Marga?" Frau Grimke called to her.

Clutching her books, Marga looked up.

"I'd like a word."

Portia nudged her. "Teacher's pet."

Frau Grimke did seem to like Marga, but Marga didn't especially care for the frumpy, middle-aged teacher and her bureaucratic air. Alone together now in the classroom, Grimke's stubby heels echoed off the gypsum walls festooned with swastika pennants and portraits of Ludendorff, Hindenburg, and Hitler as she walked around her desk and sat in one of the student's chairs. She motioned for Marga to sit down in a chair beside her. "Marga, you are a bright and gifted student, and with such a gift comes responsibility."

"What kind of responsibility, Frau Grimke?"

"We are National Socialists, and we owe our talents to the state."

Marga wrinkled her brow. "But what could I possibly do for the state?"

"I'm recommending that you sit for an exam."

"An exam? What kind of …?

Grimke held out a sealed envelope. "Give this to your parents. It explains everything."

* * *

"What are your thoughts?" Erna asked Harold as she hung her clothes inside an armoire in their bedroom.

He sat on the edge of the bed, buttoning his pajama top. "I'm wondering what Marga thinks."

"It's not up to her," Erna said tersely, closing the armoire and facing him. "This is an honor—obligation even."

"But it's her choice if she chooses to take the exam."

"Nonsense. It's ours." She leaned over a bureau and brushed her hair in the mirror.

Harold looked up at his wife. "If she does well, she could be sent to Berlin to do…cryptology…radio work…who knows what."

"In a little more than a year, she'll be eighteen and mandated to serve in the Reich Labor Service." Erna slipped off her robe and climbed into bed. "Would you prefer she work in a munitions plant or some farm in the East?"

"Perhaps she won't pass," Harold remarked getting under the covers.

Erna snorted a laugh. "Our Marga? Don't be silly, dear. She'll pass." She turned off the light. "We know how bright she is…It's time others knew as well."

CHAPTER 25

A rendition of "*Ach wie ist's Möglich dann*" came to a sudden halt as Frau Rainer dropped her arms and shook her head in frustration. Lowering her violin, Marga momentarily glanced at Portia, clutching her oboe, then at their orchestra leader – if the word orchestra applied to the eleven League of German Girls playing violin, oboe, flute, cello, guitar, piano, and glockenspiel.

"Luisa!" Rainer pointed her baton at one of the two flautists. "You keep missing notes. Have you been working on your circular breathing?"

The chagrined fifteen-year-old nodded.

"Take a deep breath," Rainer continued. "Close your eyes, envision the melody, and come in – not too strong – but like a bird landing on a delicate branch. And Gitta!" Rainer turned to the stout girl with curly brown hair at the piano. "You have to strike the keys with conviction." Rainer feigned piano strikes. "This number is a story of love and desire and the ache of it all. If we can't get it right here, how do we expect to do it for the National Socialist Women's League concert next week?"

She sighed. "And you, Marga! Where's your head today? You keep missing your entry. I expect more from my first chair and most skilled musician. There's a reason you're my *konzertmeister!*"

Marga sat up. "I'll give you my best, Frau Rainer. I promise!"

"Don't just say it! *Do it!*"

Frau Rainer faced her musicians. "Now, girls, concentrate. Relax and focus on your breathing, timing, and execution." She tapped the lectern and raised her hands. "From the beginning!"

* * *

"I don't think Frau Rainer was too pleased with us today," Portia said to Marga as they walked home from rehearsal.

A group of girls suddenly ran past them giggling. One turned and yelled teasingly, "Watch out, *Konzertmeister!*"

Marga scowled and shouted, "Go home and learn what a B-flat is, Trina! You were awful today!"

Trina stuck out her tongue and continued on, pigtails flying.

Portia turned to Marga. "That was harsh."

"But it's true," Marga huffed. "She missed it all through practice."

"Is everything okay with you?"

Marga frowned. "Everything's fine. Why?"

"You just seem distracted...like something's bothering you."

Marga huffed again as she switched her violin case from one hand to the other. "I don't know what you mean."

"It's the exam, isn't it?"

Marga slowed her gait and sighed. "It's all I've been thinking about."

"What are you afraid of?"

"I'm not afraid!"

"So, what is it then?"

"What if I pass?!"

"What if…?" Portia laughed. "You'll pass. You've never failed a test in your life. And, if you pass—it's your way out of summer labor service! You won't be picking potatoes or slopping hogs in the East."

"Don't you ever get tired of all that National Socialist jabber? Every week sitting through lectures about inferior races, the need to bomb our enemies—which is just about everyone—and this notion we should have as many children for the Reich as possible." Marga raked a hand through her hair. "If I pass that exam, Portia, who knows what they'll have me doing for the state?"

"You mean the Nazis."

Marga nodded.

"What about our fathers? They work for the state."

Marga's eyes narrowed. "They aren't Nazis, Portia!"

"What about Dr. von Braun? I saw him in his SS uniform once."

Marga shook her head. "How much choice did he have?"

"I'm afraid about as much as you do in taking that exam."

Marga embraced her violin case as if it were a life preserver keeping her afloat. "What am I going to do?"

"Only you know the answer." They resumed their walk. "On a brighter note…" Portia's tone lightened. "Someone's birthday is coming up."

"And…?" Marga drew out the word playfully.

Portia smiled. "And…I have an idea."

CHAPTER 26

Smoking a cigarette behind a dumpster, Janko ruminated. He'd monitored Hermann Goetz for weeks and suspected a connection between him and Freida Geisler. They weren't sleeping together, of that he was sure, but a relationship existed. He wondered about her presence at Peenemünde. He'd searched office rosters and telephone directories and found no listing for her, yet she kept an office in Building No. 4, base headquarters, behind an iron door. He'd asked a janitor assigned to the building about her. The Slovak had merely smiled and said she had the finest legs in the building and that she kept to herself. And, never allowed anyone into her office. Of interest to Janko, however, was the fact that her office phone had been installed by a technician flown in from Berlin.

He took a ponderous drag. Was she Kripo? Gestapo? Sicherheitsdienst? Or one of the many other security agencies infesting the Third Reich? He recalled the night in the officer's club. Only a woman of great influence and self-assurance could have assaulted an officer as she did.

A distant roar shook the ground and Janko turned his head. More testing of a weapon to destroy the Allies. He drew on his cigarette anxiously and his thoughts turned to Ullie, whom he'd recently learned was engaged to be married. He smirked. The young engineer had made a mistake using the teenage girl to deliver books to the village, and now Gerda Hewel posed another potential threat to their work. He recalled something his seamstress mother had often said: 'Too many loose threads ruin a sweater.'

A few days later, still nagged by suspicion, Janko acted. It was a rainy afternoon, and he carried a wooden toolbox into Goetz's dormitory building. Shaking water from his raincoat, he climbed to the second floor when a man abruptly came around the corner and asked, "Are you with maintenance?" He juggled a briefcase and fedora while cinching his tie. "I called about my hot water...It's kaput. Unit 210." He pointed over his shoulder. "Can you check on it?"

Janko nodded. "I'll take a look."

"Splendid," the man said before trotting down the stairs and out the door.

Continuing on his self-appointed errand, Janko knocked on Goetz's door. No answer. He let himself into the room and put his toolbox down by the door and went to a small desk in a corner. He checked each of its drawers, flipped through papers, and checked a file cabinet beside the desk. The obvious suddenly appeared before him – Goetz's small black notebook atop the desk. Perusing its pages, he sneered.

Goetz was clearly spying on the men he collaborated with.

Jan 14: Dr. von Braun speculates on thrust dynamics needed to enter moon's gravity.

Feb 10: Linkler and Haupt sketch out missile potential to fertilize crop fields.

Mar 6: von Braun...(others) discuss weight-thrust ratio to escape earth gravitational influence.

June 6: Toth and Heller discuss commercial use of missiles in space... Mention 'spaceships.'

Aug 3: Ullie Mainz...Often speaks with janitor – a Pole who more than once pocketed paper from Ullie's waste basket.

Janko jotted down the information and replaced the notebook. As he walked back to his maintenance shop, his mind was racing. Something had to be done; something immediate and drastic. But what?

Back in his shop, he sat on a work stool deliberating. Goetz had been keeping book on his co-workers – reporting to Freida Geisler – and mentioned *him*. It must have been easy to blackmail Goetz. She'd more than likely threatened his family.

It was but a matter of time before he and others were questioned. He reached for and opened a drawer beneath his workbench and retrieved a shiny length of braided stainless-steel cord he flexed between his mighty hands. Janko Novak had found the answer to his problem.

CHAPTER 27

Marga was washing dishes, her mother drying them alongside her, when the phone rang. Her mother dropped her dishtowel and ran to answer it.

"I understand…Thank you for calling and good night," Erna said.

"Who was it, Mama?"

"Frau Grimke."

Marga tensed.

"You failed your examination."

Marga looked out the kitchen window. "I'm sorry, Mama."

"Go to your room. I'll discuss it with your father when he gets home."

Drying her hands, Marga stepped to the swinging door leading from the kitchen.

"You don't seem surprised or upset even," Erna said.

Marga paused. "Because I'm not, Mama. I'm sorry." She pushed open the door and quietly exited.

* * *

It was late as Janko stood in his workshop studying a stainless-steel garrote glimmering under a lamp. He eyed its woven strands, calculating how best to apply it, pulling it taut and testing its strength. When he was finished, he tucked the garrote into his denim shirt pocket and reached for his cap. Turning off the light, he opened the door and breathed in the warm night air. A full moon peered through parting mid-August clouds casting a luminous silvery light. It was time.

* * *

A tapping on her window alerted Marga and she sprang out of bed.

"Do you have your swimsuit?" Portia asked in a hushed voice standing outside her window. Felix stood next to her clutching a wicker picnic basket.

Marga smiled and pulled open her shirt revealing her black bathing suit.

"Good!" Portia remarked and helped her climb through the window.

"Let's go," Felix said, cautiously looking around, and the three friends scurried off into the night.

Crossing railroad tracks and darting between warehouses, they followed a wooded path to a familiar spot by a lake where Portia laid out a plaid blanket and the picnic basket while Felix started a small campfire that soon cast a dancing light over their faces.

"So, what did you get for your birthday?" Portia asked, reaching into the basket.

"Mama baked a carrot cake and gave me a satin headscarf." She sighed. "It was one of hers, but she said I'm old enough to wear it now. Papa gave me a box of drawing pencils."

"Any frosting?" Felix asked.

"Ersatz," Marga replied referring to the imitation topping her mother had fashioned from improvised ingredients. "But it was good."

"Well, birthday girl," Felix said as he produced a bottle of Beck's beer from the basket. "I can vouch there's nothing ersatz about *this!*"

"Beer?" Marga watched Felix remove the cap and hand it to her. "Where did it come from?"

Opening her own bottle, Portia cleared her throat. "You mean to say, 'Thank you, Felix, how thoughtful of you.'"

Grinning sheepishly, Marga chuckled. "I apologize, Felix. You are very thoughtful. Thank you."

"To our birthday girl." Portia raised her bottle.

"To our birthday girl!" Felix echoed.

Taking a sip, Portia wiped her lips. "Still cold."

"I also have cigarettes," Felix announced digging into his shirt pocket.

"I'll have one," said Portia.

"Marga?" Felix asked, offering her one.

She shook her head. "I can't… Mother—"

"Mother, mother, mother," Portia snickered. "Just take a puff." She handed Marga her cigarette.

Marga took and examined it as if inspecting a bug before placing it between her lips. She took a puff, flashed a disgusted look, and began coughing.

Portia and Felix laughed.

"So gross!" Marga furiously fanned away the smoke.

Smiling, Portia reclaimed the cigarette. "Maybe this will be better." She reached inside the basket for a small apple tart wrapped in a napkin.

Marga clasped her hands. "You didn't!"

"I told Mama it was for you…She gave me the apple, some flour, and a pinch of cinnamon."

"That's so thoughtful!" said Marga, her smile lit by the fire.

"Wait!" Portia said producing a small pink candle she lit with her cigarette and stuck into the tart.

Marga squealed playfully. "You shouldn't have!"

"Make a wish and blow it out," Portia said.

"Yeah, I'm hungry," Felix echoed.

"None for you!" Portia declared. "It's too small, and it's *her* birthday."

"Don't be silly," Marga chided playfully. "We'll each have a bite—I insist."

Marga closed her eyes, made a wish, and blew out the tiny flame. Portia plucked back the candle and Marga took a bite. She nodded, smiled, and handed it to Felix, who did the same before handing it to Portia, who popped the remainder in her mouth.

"To good friends," Marga said, raising her beer in a toast.

They sat and told stories, gossiped, and enjoyed each other's relaxed company amid sounds of chirping crickets, belching toads, and the nights' buzzing sounds. Felix and Portia giggled as they tried blowing smoke rings. Marga laughed as she sipped her beer.

"Get her another one," Portia told Felix.

Marga pulled her knees to her chest as the effects of the beer and lapping flames warmed her senses. Glancing at the starry moonlit night, she sighed. "You've made this a memorable birthday. You're my best friends, and I'll never forget this."

* * *

Maneuvering through the darkness, Janko approached Hermann Goetz's dormitory. The engineer's window was illuminated, and Janko proceeded to the second floor.

Behind one of the doors, a radio was playing. Behind another, someone laughed. Focusing on his objective, Janko knocked on Goetz's door.

It opened.

"Dr. Goetz," Janko said.

Goetz adjusted his glasses. "Janko? What…what are you doing here at this time of night?"

Janko reached into his jacket and held up the sheet of paper on which he had copied Goetz's diary entries. He gave Goetz a few seconds to get the gist of it.

Goetz stiffened. "How did you get that?" He reached for the paper, but Janko pulled it back.

Janko then said, "We must speak," and pushed his way into Goetz's apartment.

Goetz shut the door and as he turned, Janko's garrote snared the engineer's throat.

* * *

A clock on the window sill read almost midnight as Harold entered the kitchen in his cottage. He wore his pajamas and slippers and eyeing the clock, realized he'd been asleep for two hours before waking up and deciding on a glass of water. Looking out the window above the sink, he noticed a full moon and for an instant, he wondered what it would be like to fly there in a rocket-ship. Reaching for a glass from an overhead cabinet, he turned on the faucet, filled the glass, and retrieved a bottle of bicarbonate. He poured a teaspoon into the water and drank it. With a belch, he put the glass down and balanced a hand on the counter. Looking out the window at the moonlit silhouettes of neighboring homes, a strange vibration began to slowly ripple through the counter, shaking his water glass and rattling the windowpane.

"No…!" He knocked over the glass and bolted from the kitchen. *"Erna! Marga! Get up! We're under attack!"*

* * *

"Quit it!" Marga shrieked as she and Felix splashed each other. The three friends were swimming in the moonlight, their faint laughter echoing across the lake.

"Are you having fun, Marga, dear?" Portia asked, her arms and legs churning beneath the water.

Marga slicked back her hair. "This is my best birthday ever! Why, look at that full moon! It's so bright, and the stars so…"

A thunderous growl from the sky swallowed her words.

"Bombers!" Felix yelled.

Crooked moonlit shadows danced over the silvery lake and surrounding forest. Explosions lit the sky.

"We're under attack!" he cried.

"Attack?" Portia yelped over the roar of engines and blaring of air-raid sirens. "By whom?"

"Just run!" he hollered, bolting for shore.

* * *

"Marga!" Harold threw open his daughter's bedroom door and flipped on the light. Her covers had been pulled aside and the window was open. She was gone.

* * *

Clawing frantically at the metal wire choking him, Goetz felt his strength rushing out of his body as the pressure tightened around his throat. Reaching over his head, he scratched and gouged at his assailant's face in vain but, within thirty-seconds, his arms dropped to his sides and his body slumped.

Hermann Goetz was dead.

* * *

Janko exited the dormitory as sirens and explosions erupted. Peenemünde was under attack and he began to run when the ground began shaking and breaking apart as if some great subterranean force were emerging. A thunderous explosion suddenly knocked him to the ground. He screamed as flames washed over him and he frantically waved his arms and legs beating out the fire burning his clothes and flesh. Around him, men screamed as they ran from the dormitory. Others jumped from windows. Regaining his feet, his clothes smoldering, Janko staggered away when a thunderous blast spun him around and into a cascade of fiery debris expelled from the collapsing dormitory.

* * *

Explosions tore through Peenemünde's residential quarter, setting houses, dormitories, and barracks aflame. Clad in wet swimsuits and tennis shoes, Marga, Portia, and Felix burst from glowing trees into the conflagration where cordite and phosphorus stung the air and a murky smokescreen slowly spread beneath parachute flares dancing in the wind like flaming jellyfish.

"Mama! Papa!" Marga stammered, dodging panicked residents running through the shattered, burning streets.

A hand suddenly snatched her arm, and a voice shouted, "Wait!"

Marga turned to see her neighbor. "Mr. Peters!"

His face blistered and streaked with soot, he stood barefoot in torn pajamas looking like a lost child. "I'm late for work! Has the trolley come?"

Steering him away from the burning homes, Marga grabbed a snarled bedsheet off a picket fence and wrapped it around him. "Sit here!" She urged him down onto a fallen telephone pole.

"Yes…yes," he babbled. "I'll wait here for the trolley!"

Wheeling away, her heart racing and limbs pumping, Marga ran until she was home. When she saw its blown-out windows and smoldering roof, she clutched her chest. "Mama!"

"Marga!"

She turned.

"Thank God!" exclaimed her father squeezing her tight.

"Oh, Papa! Where's Mama?"

"Marga!" Her mother cried out.

Turning toward the frazzled voice, Marga was slapped.

"Mama!" Marga clutched her cheek.

"Where were you?" Erna yelled grabbing her daughter's shoulders. "We thought the worst, child!"

"Mama…I!"

With the flames dancing in her eyes, Erna declared, "Listen to me!" She suddenly took on a puzzled look and sniffed Marga's face. "Have you been drinking?"

Marga flinched, anticipating another slap, but Erna shook her daughter. "We're at war, Marga and it's come for *us!*"

Marga's lips quivered. "Mama…I'm sorry…"

"The time for games is over. Do you hear me?"

Wiping a tear, Marga nodded.

A Volkswagen suddenly skidded to a halt, raising a cloud of dust and ash. "Toth, get in!" It was Wernher shouting to her father from behind the wheel.

Harold stuck his head through the passenger window. "Where to?"

"The central files building. It's burning—all our records! Let's go!"

Harold turned to his wife.

Erna nodded and yelled, "Go!"

Still wearing pajamas, Harold jumped into the car, and the two men sped away.

* * *

It was three days after the Royal Air Force raid on Peenemünde. The attack prioritizing the residential quarters in an effort to kill some of

Germany's most brilliant minds ironically left intact the test stands and production buildings. Holding her violin, Marga stood in a remote corner of a clearing where mounds of earth lined the edges of freshly dug mass graves filled with over 300 pine coffins. Her League of German Girls navy-blue skirt and cravat fluttered in the breeze as she held her violin and bow, awaiting her signal from a chaplain to play "*Treue Liebe.*"

Hundreds of mourners dressed in black stood somberly in the August heat under a halcyon sky. Many pressed handkerchiefs to their faces, tamping away tears as they grieved lost friends and loved ones. Adding to the misery was the stench of charred wood, broken sewer lines, and organic decay – from bodies still buried in rubble. Marga screened her eyes from the sun with a hand to her brow, listening to the final moments of the chaplain's eulogy laden with National Socialist undertones.

"In conclusion," he said, "I remind you that the Reich demands great sacrifices if we are to achieve our Führer's vision for a greater German society!" He closed his prayer book and removed his glasses. "Say a final prayer and keep in your hearts our most sacred tenet… *Ein Volk, Ein Reich, Ein Führer!*" He extended a Nazi salute and cried out, "*Sieg Heil!*"

A military brass band played the somber, "*Ich hatt' einen Kameraden,*" before Marga received her cue from the chaplain and she placed the violin under her chin, closed her eyes, and set the bow to its cords. A lump welled in her throat as she thought of her neighbor, Mister Peters, who'd died on the telephone pole she'd left him on.

After some final words by the chaplain and tossing of flowers onto caskets, Marga walked behind her parents as they left the service to their temporary home in a community of tents where Portia and her family were also staying. Felix's family had moved to nearby Wolgast, but she expected to see little of him, as his time would be divided between the Hitler Youth and the National Labor Service.

"Thank you for digging through what was left of our home and saving my violin, Papa," Marga said.

His fedora canted on the back of his head; Harold absently nodded.

"Did you save your jewelry box, Mama?"

"I did."

"And your book of sonnets?"

Erna looked over her shoulder. "Why do you ask?"

Marga shrugged. "I don't know...It just occurred to me. I know how you treasure it."

"It's a bible actually."

"A bible? Do you read it?"

Erna nodded. "There are times I take comfort in its words. It'll be yours someday."

"But you keep it locked away...in your hope chest...why?"

Erna's face stiffened. "To protect you and Papa, *Liebchen*."

"Protect us? How?"

"When is the last time any of your teachers discussed God or the bible?"

"Never, Mama. But it doesn't mean I don't believe. You and Papa baptized me a Lutheran...I'll always have that."

Glancing over her shoulder, Erna smiled.

Marga looked up curiously. "What is it, Mama? Your smile..."

"It's nothing, dear." Erna's head rose a little higher, and her step grew a little firmer. "I love you is all."

CHAPTER 28

Six months later, two stories beneath London's Treasury building, Harrison Brightwell, standing under the white glow of a slide projector, briefed five men seated around a conference table in the dark. "Our intelligence confirms the Germans have relocated their rocket-assembly program from Peenemünde to the Harz Mountains." A slide revealed the grainy image of a cave entrance. "Inside these old gypsum mines near Nordhausen, the Nazis have created an assembly line which, unlike Peenemünde, is impervious to aerial attacks." A new image revealed a half-dozen missiles lining a narrow, dimly lit, subterranean corridor. Brightwell stepped into the projector's light. "Which, by the way, they've renamed the V2."

"V2?" someone asked.

"V for vengeance," said Brightwell. "Dubbed by their propaganda minister, Josef Goebbels. Claims it projects the weapon's intent."

"Is there a V1?" another asked.

"Yes, the V1 is a ramp-launched, unmanned rocket plane. It's slower and flies like a conventional aircraft—but, unlike the V2, we actually have a chance of shooting it down."

The slide advanced to show gaunt men hunched over workbenches wearing filthy oversized striped coveralls. "And this is how they're building them…with forced labor. French, Dutch, Poles, Russians…They are literally working them to death."

An aerial reconnaissance image then filled the screen showing a massive concrete dome fused into a mountain. Brightwell cleared his throat. "This hardened silo has been identified in Saint Omer near the Pas de Calais…Putting their V2s within reach of London."

"And what are we doing about it, Brightwell?" asked a patrician voice.

"I can assure you, sir, that plans are underway to neutralize this facility."

The patrician voice pressed the issue. "Surely, the Germans have alternative means of delivery… a backup plan?"

The slide changed, revealing a spindly six-wheeled flatbed trailer.

"They do, sir. They're called *Meillerwagens*."

* * *

Captain Martin Schauffer rode in the front seat of an armored staff car as it led a convoy of military vehicles through a snow-covered Polish forest. Looking up from his window, he spotted a noisy flight of crows paralleling the winding line of smoke-belching trucks. Reaching a clearing, Schauffer flung open his door and began giving commands, prompting soldiers to set about with practiced efficiency digging slit trenches, uncoiling wires, erecting antennae, and firing generators while the groan of servomotors and murmuring hydraulics signaled the raising of a V2 from its cradling *Meillerwagen*. Set onto its launch platform, tanker trucks huddled around the rocket as men in protective garbs worked through frosty clouds of liquid oxygen being injected into the missile. Schauffer watched from a distance, evaluating his troops and was reminded the rocket could only be fueled standing upright to prevent the added weight of propellants from buckling the V2's thin metal frame.

"Herr Captain," said Sergeant Helmut Rudd. "The *Meillerwagen* performed well over the uneven terrain. The securing clamps and collars held the missile in place—no damage or slippage. She stayed snug in her cradle the entire way."

"Good news, Rudd. If these trailers can prove themselves here, they'll have no trouble in the flats of France and Holland. I'll include it in my report to von Braun."

Poised against a clear, winter sky, the V2 stood ready, venting frozen clouds of liquid oxygen as the final seconds to launch ticked off. Suddenly, with a flash of light and mighty rush of snow, a howling roar shook the forest and the 28,000-pound rocket shot skyward. With field glasses pressed to his eyes, Schauffer stood beside his staff car and watched as the missile climbed straight and true, gaining speed rapidly until it was but a flaming pinprick in the sky. He turned to a junior officer monitoring a radio and holding a stopwatch.

"How long from arrival to launch," he asked the junior officer.

"Fifty-seven minutes, Herr Captain."

Schauffer resumed looking through his field glasses and he smiled. "We just might win this war yet."

CHAPTER 29

Ullie stood holding a clipboard inside a tunnel deep inside the Harz Mountains. The clatter of sheet-metal presses, drills and generators echoed throughout cavernous passageways and narrow shafts, their chalky walls glowing from acetylene torches operated by men—forced laborers—in filthy, striped pajama garments, welding rivets in the assembly of V2 rockets.

"How does anyone breath in this hole?" Udo Dorner, a fresh-faced design engineer with a cowlick dusted in limestone, asked.

"You don't," Ullie replied, keeping his focus on his clipboard and a set of figures he was working on. "Stay down here long enough breathing-in these sulfites and you'll start looking like these workers."

"I feel like someone dropped a bag of chalk on me…Look at this!" said Dorner holding out his arms covered in a thin, white layer of dust.

"My advice is, take frequent breaks and get outside—clear your head and lungs."

"What about these guys?" Dorner asked, nodding toward the pale, sickly men in striped uniforms.

Ullie lowered his clipboard. "The lucky ones…" A sudden commotion of yelling guards drew his attention.

"What's going on?" asked Dorner, looking into a cavernous chamber lined with work benches, rail tracks, and V2 parts in various stages of assembly.

"Stop your work! Drop your tools and fall into ranks!" uniformed guards shouted in German, French, and Russian as they waved billy clubs and prodded men into the center of the cavernous mine shaft beneath a gantry crane forty feet above their heads. Within minutes, they were formed into a foul-smelling platoon totaling sixty men.

"My God, they're little more than scarecrows," said Dorner.

Ullie's pulse quickened and his stomach churned. He knew what was coming next.

"Maybe you should take a walk, Dorner."

"A walk…What're talking about?"

"Form up! Be quiet! Hands at your sides!" a gruff voice shouted in German to the assembled laborers.

"*Achtung! Achtung!*" a voice blared from wall mounted speakers as six men, their hands bound behind their backs, were shuffled before the prisoners prompting a discomfited murmur to rise from the ranks.

"Silence!" guards shouted in various languages as they walked through the ranks poking prisoners with their clubs.

"These individuals," the voice over the speaker announced in German, "are guilty of shirking and sabotage and are thus sentenced to death!"

More murmurs. Guards formed a line with raised clubs. The gantry crane suddenly clattered as it was positioned over the six men whose grimy, forsaken looks betrayed acceptance of their fates. The crane's iron crossbeam descended, and nooses were slipped over their victims' necks.

"For crimes against the Third Reich," the speaker pronounced, "you are hereby sentenced to death by hanging!"

The nooses secured to the crossbeam; a hydraulic rasp reverberated as the gantry rose. The condemned men's bodies straightened, then lengthened as their feet left the ground.

Someone shouted, "No!"

He was descended upon with clubs.

"Ullie!" Dorner stepped forward. "They're…they're…"

"There's nothing we can do!" said Ullie clutching Dorner's arm.

The hanging men flailed and jerked, like fish on the ends of hooks. Dark stains blighted their dingy pants, and a foul stench nipped the air. The men standing in ranks were made to watch until the last of the condemned ceased jerking and squirming. The six now hung like poultry in a shop window.

"Let this serve as an example," the loudspeaker crackled. "Lack of effort, sabotage…Resistance of any kind will *not* be tolerated!"

Staggering unsteadily on his feet, Dorner dropped to his hands and knees and vomited.

"It seems they failed to mention this at the production briefings," said Ullie, plucking a handkerchief from his pocket and handing it to his stricken comrade.

Wiping his mouth, Dorner regained his footing and uttered, "Bastards! Do they know about this in Peenemünde?"

Ullie faced him. "You should probably be asking, who in Peenemünde doesn't know?"

CHAPTER 30

With the temperature hovering at freezing, Marga shivered as she stood next to Portia on Peenemünde's train platform. A small, brass military band played *"Erika"* while dozens of family members viewed a platoon of fifteen young men, mostly seventeen-year-olds, in stiff, newly issued military uniforms, standing at attention. They would shortly board a train taking them to basic training and then to war. Despite a festive air manufactured by the music, an unspoken somberness muffled the spirits of those watching. It went unsaid that for many, it would be their last goodbye.

Marga and Portia kept their eyes on Felix who stood upright in the second rank. Pale and tense, he looked like the others around him—a boy being sent to fight in a man's war. The music halted and a smartly clad officer in an overcoat, peaked cap, and polished boots stood before the formation. Through frosty breath, he asked the young men to raise their right hands. They did, and the officer led them through an oath-swearing ceremony in which they pledged their lives to their nation and, most importantly, their Führer.

Die for the Führer? The idea sickened Marga.

The oath completed, the officer faced the crowd and announced the train would depart in ten minutes. He invited friends and family of the soldiers to say their final goodbyes. Marga and Portia waited politely but impatiently as Felix hugged his mother, who begged him to be careful, and shook his father's hand. A design engineer, Felix's father stoically advised him to listen to his superiors and not take unnecessary risks. Hearing these soft cautionary words, a lump formed in Marga's throat.

A whistle blew, and a porter shouted, "Five minutes to boarding!"

Marga and Portia advanced. "Herr Kleiner, Frau Kleiner, forgive our intrusion," Marga said. Tamping a handkerchief to her eyes, Felix's mother half-heartedly smiled and stepped back as Mr. Kleiner nodded and joined his wife.

Marga embraced Felix. "Take care of yourself," she said sniffing back tears. "Promise to write?"

"Any chance I get," he said.

Marga kissed his cheek and made way for a similarly tearful Portia who also hugged him. "Send us a picture in your uniform!"

He snorted a dry laugh. "So the two of you can throw darts at it?"

Portia clutched his shoulders. "Felix…Come back to us!"

Forcing a smile, he nodded.

A loud whistle sounded, and shouts echoed along the platform.

After they each planted a final kiss on his cheek, Marga and Portia stepped back. The last kiss and handshake came from Felix's parents.

Turning away, Marga unexpectedly met the gaze of Walter Mitz. *Walter?* Unlike Felix and his platoon of recruits yet to be trained as field soldiers, Walter and the men around him, wore helmets, field gear, and carried rifles.

Eyeing him curiously, she stepped through the crowded platform. "You're leaving?"

He straightened. "My SS unit has received orders to Berlin. From there we'll be deployed to the field and combat."

"Will you be back?"

He didn't reply.

Marga looked under the bill of his helmet. "Walter, I want you to do something."

"What?"

"Pray every day. Didn't you once tell me you were raised a Lutheran?"

He narrowed his eyes. "We don't pray in the SS."

She took his arm. "The SS can't save your soul, Walter. But God will. He'll sustain you."

He shook his arm free. "Do you think I need sustaining? I'm an SS man, remember?"

She remained unmoved. "There will come a time when you'll need more."

He grinned like young men do when hiding fear. "I think I'll stay alive long enough to come back and make you my wife. What do you think of that?"

"I think you'll need a better reason than that to stay alive."

"All aboard!" a porter yelled.

"Let's go, Mitz!" one his platoonmates called out as he boarded the train.

"*Auf Wiedersehen*, Walter," Marga said, brushing his sleeve and turning away.

Walter suddenly took her by the arm and drew her close. "*Auf Wiedersehen,* Marga Toth. Maybe when this war is over…"

Marga sensed his longing for something heartfelt between them. Something that he could take with him toward a dark and uncertain future. For a moment, she felt a sadness for being unable to give him what he desired. She gently squeezed his hand. "Maybe, Walter…Just be careful."

Marga returned to where Portia stood on the platform. Felix had boarded and his parents had drifted away.

"Don't cry," Marga said to Portia as she threaded her arm through hers.

"He made me promise not to," Portia said. "I'm going to miss him."

"Me too."

A steam whistle sounded and a bell clanged as the smoke belching locomotive chugged from the depot. Marga and Portia braced against a stiff, icy wind, wiping their tears and waving to Felix, who hung from a window, waving his cap until the train faded from view and only a thin black halo of smoke remained in its wake.

CHAPTER 31

Seated by an open window, her violin tucked between her shoulder and chin, Marga took in the sight of the patients in the Peenemünde hospital dayroom. The fortunate sat in robes and slippers. Others lay in traction. Some nursed horrible burns and wounds while many sported slings, crutches, and casts. As the music of Mozart began, she noticed it brought a smile to the lips of a young woman sitting in the front row whose eyes were bandaged and her hands scarred and deformed from horrible burns. Marga guessed the woman was still recuperating from the bombing raid almost a year earlier.

When Frau Rainer, who was conducting, glanced at her, Marga recognized her cue to stand. The music stopped. Marga slid her bow and began playing her solo rendition. She winced when she played one wrong chord and hoped no one in the audience had noticed. Reaching the song's crescendo, she sliced the bow fiercely, causing her bobbed hair to thrash over her face, and the music stopped.

The applause was enthusiastic. Smiling proudly, Frau Rainer extended an arm to her musicians. The young women stood, offering courtly bows and curtsies. A man with broken legs whistled. Another rapped his cane on the floor, and an appreciative nurse presented Frau Rainer with a bouquet of wildflowers.

From a corner, a man in a suit wearing the conspicuous arm-band of the National Labor Service stepped forward clapping. "I commend you, Frau Rainer," he said, as patients walked, hobbled, or were rolled back to their wards. "You've assembled a talented group." He glanced at Marga who, along with the other girls, were busy placing their instruments back into their cases.

"Thank you," Frau Rainer replied. "They've worked very hard. I see you're with the National Labor Service…Are you a patient?"

He smiled. "My name is Wolfram Helmuth, and I'm here meeting with youth group leaders, determining where Peenemünde's Hitler Youth and League of German Girls can be of greatest service in the coming year."

Frau Rainer looked at her girls. "It'll be a shame to lose this wonderful ensemble. I'm told they'll be picking potatoes somewhere."

He surveyed the young women folding chairs and stacking them against a wall. "Perhaps I can offer a solution." He turned to face Frau Rainer. "There are countless places throughout the Reich in need of morale boosting."

"You mean concerts?"

He pulled a card from his pocket and handed it to her. "I think a summer tour would be most inspiring. Hospital wards, factories… train stations."

"That sounds wonderful, Herr Helmuth, but expenses…"

"Leave that to me," he remarked, snapping his heels. "Just have your girls ready to play as they did today. I'll handle the rest."

CHAPTER 32

The effects of a two-day rail journey wore on Harold as he settled into a chair in Wernher's Nordhausen office, a few miles from the underground mines where the V2's were assembled. Since the attack on Peenemünde, he spent as much time here, in the Harz Mountains, hidden away from Allied bombers, as he did on the Baltic, where research and test flights continued.

"Cognac?" Wernher offered holding up a decanter.

"Sure," Harold replied.

"Two days is a long time to be cooped up on a train," Wernher said, handing Harold his drink.

"The track was damaged outside Dessau, and we weren't cleared beyond Blankenburg for six hours."

Stepping behind his desk, Wernher asked, "And how are Erna and Marga?"

"Erna is running a tight ship in our little cottage in Wolgast."

"How are you liking it?"

"It's modest but the roof doesn't leak, and the mice stay outside. Not to mention, after six months living in a tent camp, a solidly built home is welcome. And, if the bombers return to Peenemünde, we'll be safe outside its perimeter."

Wernher nodded and sipped his drink.

"As for Marga," Harold continued, "she's on a band tour."

"Our Marga?"

"Part of a health, welfare, and morale program promoted by the labor service to distract the war-weary masses with Chopin and Mozart."

"We could use such distractions here," said Wernher before downing his drink.

Harold cleared his throat. "Speaking of distractions, Wernher…I've been meaning to ask you."

"Ask me what?"

"I've spoken to some of the men."

Wernher was lighting a cigarette. "Go on."

"The working conditions in the mines, Wernher. I'm told…"

Shaking his head, Wernher fidgeted with a letter opener on his desk. "Harold, we're currently forced to deal with some inescapable realities."

Harold sat forward. "Wernher, men are beaten… and worse, I'm told!"

"My immediate responsibilities are to manage engineering issues. We're on a tight schedule!"

"Men are being killed, Wernher!"

"Harold, the workers, the guards—overall security—all belong to Himmler and the SS!"

"Surely, we have some say!"

Wernher scowled. "Our job is to produce rockets, Harold!"

"And ensure they're properly built. What can we expect from vehicles assembled in drafty caves by men with guns to their heads?"

Wernher stubbed out his cigarette, snatched the telephone off its cradle, and thrust it at Harold. "Go ahead! Call Himmler! Better yet, the Führer!"

"So we become party to what's happening in those caves?"

"Give me a solution!"

They stared at one another.

Harold shook his head. "My point remains, Wernher. These rockets just can't be slapped together like toasters."

"And they're not." Wernher hung up the phone, stood up, and stepped to the window. "Harold, I agree, conditions *are* lacking but…" He turned to a credenza, grabbed a folder, and began flipping through its pages. "Here." He handed Harold a document. "Read the second sentence."

Harold saw it was time-stamped at the Wolfschanze, Hitler's Prussian headquarters. He read aloud. "Henceforth, the Führer expects a minimum production of five thousand rockets per month." He looked up. "Five thousand?"

Wernher folded his arms. "Read on."

"Failure to meet production goals will be considered a dereliction of duty, and violators will be subject to immediate discipline." He looked at Wernher and tossed the file jacket on the desk. "How long before we get them to the field?"

"Reports from Blizna are encouraging. I'd say summer. September at the latest." Wernher waved the document. "Which is why, Harold, any objections to how Himmler is managing labor issues in those caves will fall on deaf ears."

"But without us, Wernher, it all comes to a halt. Perhaps if we speak up."

"And how many of the others do you think would follow you?" Wernher shook his head. "Given his way, Himmler would take full control of our program—make it entirely an SS operation."

Harold scoffed. "Imagine, Germany's highest technological research program under the thumb of a chicken farmer."

"I have it on good authority he's raised the matter with the Führer. If not for Albert Speer convincing the Führer otherwise…"

Harold sneered. "Speer is looking out for Speer and his ministry of armaments. He's just as much to blame."

"Better working under him than that butcher Himmler."

Harold studied his glass, then shook his head. "Wernher, you and I know… Damn it! Forget monthly rocket quotas! We're living on borrowed time!"

Folding his arms, Wernher jerked an uncertain smile. "If you're saying the war is lost, I know this much. I don't plan on spending the rest of my days working for the Russians."

"What do you plan to do?"

Wernher's cool Nordic eyes met Harold's. "I've decided to go into the insurance business."

CHAPTER 33

Colonel Pringer's mind raced as he crossed the Danish border north of Flensburg in a Mercedes driven by an army private. Perhaps he was being lured into a trap. Rumors persisted of disgruntled officers working to unseat the Führer and negotiate a surrender with the Allies. Countermeasures to entrap such traitors were constant. But he had to take the chance and his thoughts returned to one night—nine years earlier in Moscow...

"*Tovarich!*" Major Pavel Petroshenko bellowed, removing a cigar from his jowls and raising a shot glass brimming with vodka. Russian and German army officers raised their own glasses and echoed, '*Tovarich!*' before downing their own drinks.

"You!" Petroshenko wrapped a burly arm around Captain Gerhard Pringer and said through an interpreter, "You are one of us and we are one of you!"

The major refilled their glasses.

"*Prost!*" Pringer snorted a toast.

A plump brunette wearing a colorfully embroidered sarafan and valenki boots sashayed through the raucous Red Army officer's club playing "Kalinka" on her accordion. Men cheered and hooted. Several grabbed at her fleshy bottom.

Petroshenko suddenly stood and growled, "Silence!"

The music stopped and the room quieted.

Glassy-eyed and balancing on the back of a chair, Petroshenko surveyed the sweaty faces staring back. "Our time with our esteemed allies"—he pressed a fist to his mouth and belched— "has come to an end." His words were echoed in German by an interpreter. "Initially, I like many of you, harbored feelings of distrust toward a former enemy. As a young—very young—private at Tannenberg, I learned to despise our Teutonic neighbors. But, I also grudgingly learned to respect their mettle as soldiers and tacticians." He raised his glass to Pringer. "But now, what we have learned and shared, between once bitter enemies, will serve our nations—for years to come!"

"*Prost!*" hollered a group of German officers.

"*Vashe zdorov'ye!*" countered the Russians raising their glasses before draining their vodka.

Pringer stood and hugged Petroshenko. The accordion's trill resumed, and Russian officers shoved aside tables and chairs to perform improvised versions of the *Hopak* dance.

"There's something different about you," Petroshenko said, settling alongside Pringer. "You see beyond the limits of fascism." The Russian refilled their glasses.

Pringer snorted a laugh and said through his interpreter, "Fascism…Communism…It's all the same really. The only difference is who's in charge."

Petroshenko nodded and fired a cigarette. "However, I foresee a time when our ideologies will conflict."

Pringer frowned. "Then why does Stalin continue to welcome us?"

"He sees opportunity. In exchange for allowing your army to violate the restrictions of the Treaty of Versailles by conducting field exercises in Russia and beyond Europe's watchful eyes, your generals—Guderian, von Rundstedt, Boch—have significantly improved our officer corps and taught us to think like Prussians."

"What an irony it would be then for our nations to find themselves in a conflict over ideologies—Fascism versus Communism."

Petroshenko narrowed his eyes. "If and when, it might behoove one to have a friend on the other side."

Sitting back, Pringer studied his Soviet counterpart before offering a toast. "To friends, then." He raised his glass. "On the other side."

That was 1935 Pringer reminded himself. A lot had changed since then. Germany had invaded the Soviet Union in 1941 and laid waste to its land and people. But in the 3 years since, Russia had fought bitterly to push their German aggressors back and the Nazis now fought a losing, two-front war.

Pringer looked out the sedan's rear window. Only the darkness followed. Settling back into his seat, he thought of the cable he'd received two days earlier in Berlin. He should have ignored the communiqué. But Germany's days were numbered, and his role as a member of the SS, responsible for the war's greatest atrocities, would be revealed. Rumors already persisted of post-war tribunals. But Petroshenko had the power to save him and Pringer hoped that having a friend, 'on the other side,' would pay its dividend. What remained to be answered – the price.

The Mercedes turned right, and Pringer sat up straight to see a white-washed two-story farmhouse barely visible in the headlights. He tensed as he clutched the fountain pen in his pocket and wondered how the cyanide would taste if this turned into a Gestapo sting operation. He then felt for the butt of his holstered Luger sidearm. He could try shooting his way out but realized he wouldn't get far. The cyanide was his best option, quick and to the point.

The sedan halted and the driver opened his door. Pringer hesitated before stepping out into the cool Danish night. Straightening his uniform, he adjusted the bill of his cap and braced his nerves. As he climbed onto the wooden porch, the front door opened and a young man in civilian clothes came out, motioning toward Pringer's Luger. With one hand still clutching his fountain pen, Pringer unsnapped the holster and handed over his weapon.

The young man directed Pringer inside and into a dim parlor with creaky floorboards. Another man stepped from the shadows. *"Tovarich,"* he said. "It's been many years." His Russian words were translated by the younger man.

Squinting through the darkness, Pringer beheld Major-General Pavel Petroshenko, but he was dressed like a farmer. The Russian extended his hand.

Relieved, Pringer eased his grip on the fountain pen and shook his old friend's hand.

"Sergei, *bistro, bistro!*" Petroshenko said to the man who'd taken Pringer's gun. Sergei left the room and promptly returned carrying a tray of smoked herring, pickled relish, and vodka.

With Sergei as interpreter, they sat by the fire sipping vodka and caught each other up on the events of the years since their last meeting. Captured twice by the Germans, Petroshenko had amazingly escaped both times, but his brother was killed at Sevastopol and his son was maimed in the Pripet Marshes. Pringer tried as much as possible to nurse his drink while he listened carefully for hints as to why he'd been lured to the remote farmhouse.

As he chewed, Petroshenko waved a hand. "Colonel, I recall our many chess matches in the field by campfire." The general smiled with greasy lips and wagged a finger. "For a Teuton, you played well, but alas the game of logic, cunning, and reason belongs to my people."

"As I recall," said Pringer wiping his mouth, "I won my fair share of matches."

Petroshenko nodded. "You did, but never consecutively. I learned your method and was prepared the next time." Petroshenko washed his herring down with a slosh of vodka. Sucking his teeth, he nodded and prepared another serving. "In any chess match, there's a moment when the outcome is established"—he met Pringer's gaze— "from which point, the contest becomes an academic exercise."

"I have a feeling you're using chess as a metaphor for the reason of my being here," said Pringer.

A smug-looking Petroshenko smiled.

"You're saying Germany has lost the war and you want me to work for your side."

"No." Petroshenko swallowed a morsel and chased it with vodka. "I want you to work for *me*."

Pringer remained silent.

The Russian general poured them another drink.

"Your record in the SS—not to mention, the *Einsatzgruppen*, your merciless roving death squads—makes you a prized target." Petroshenko propped his elbows on the table. "As we speak, there are committees deep in the bowels of Soviet bureaucracy planning mass trials and executions. Public ones to satiate a war-ravaged nation's rage."

"What are you asking of me?"

"A time will come when, perhaps working from within the crumbling pillars of the Third Reich, you may be useful."

"And if I choose to cooperate with the Americans?"

Petroshenko laughed. "You'd best have quite a prize, Herr Colonel. You once remarked that fascism and communism were in essence, the same, the difference being who's in charge." Petroshenko sat forward. "I, as does my government, understand you and can overlook your actions. What your people did to ours…" He shrugged. "Our government has done just as bad and worse to its own. Now, the Americans…?" He shook his head. "Their newspapermen will eat you alive before turning on their own officials for harboring a war criminal." He made a tsk-tsk sound. "No, you'll work for me if you want to avoid the hangman."

Pringer looked into the fire. Petroshenko was right. His days in a German uniform—an SS one no less—were numbered. He was a proud man and hated having his hand forced. Had Hitler and the fools around him not blundered at critical junctures of the war, per-haps his and Petroshenko's rolls would be reversed. But they weren't and he had to make a choice.

Petroshenko's chair creaked as he sat back and drained his vodka. He burped and wiped his lips. "Now, Herr Colonel, I've given you much to think about. But you're an intelligent man…I'm sure you'll make the right choice. In the meantime…May I interest you in a friendly game of chess?"

CHAPTER 34

Arno Huff loitered on the fringes of Berlin's Tiergarten whose once-green wooded scape with meandering trails and cool secluded ponds were now scarred by shattered trees, gaping bomb craters, and strategically placed flak batteries, searchlights, and ammunition dumps. He wore slacks, a knitted pullover, brown leather jacket, and a Gatsby cap—the latter a signal to clients he was available. He observed people trundle past, their hats slung low, shoulders stooped, eyes averted. Many carried baskets and water jugs. Their clothes and shoes were threadbare, and most looked exhausted. But surely, someone would want what he provided.

His stomach growled, and he ached for a cigarette. He glanced at a pocket watch and decided he'd wait ten more minutes before calling it a day. The snap of a twig startled him. He turned around to see a young soldier in a field-gray uniform.

"Have you a light?" the soldier asked, holding out a cigarette.

Though he was too thin for his uniform, Arno found him attractive. He pulled a box of matches from his pocket. The soldier smiled and drew close. Arno struck a match. The soldier leaned in and brushed his cheek against Arno's hand holding the match. He took a quick drag and exhaled. "Thanks."

"My pleasure," Arno answered, blowing out the match.

The soldier drew on his smoke and looked around. "Are you waiting for someone?"

"You might say that." Arno tugged at his cap and smiled.

The soldier faced him. His blue eyes cool and sincere. "What a shame."

"Why is that?"

The soldier balked. Arno sensed he wanted to say something.

"May I?" Arno reached for the cigarette between the soldier's lips. He took a firm drag and handed it back.

"I don't know how to say it…" The soldier looked around warily.

"Are you looking for a friend?"

The soldier tensed.

Arno tugged the bill of the soldier's cap. "I might be able to help."

The soldier dragged on his cigarette and tossed it. "I only have five marks."

Arno rubbed the soldier's arm. "I think we can come to an understanding. What's your name?"

"My name…?"

"You have a name, don't you?" Placing his arm around the soldier, Arno led him toward a thicket and reached for the soldier's belt. "You are going to tell me your name, aren't you?"

The soldier looked from side to side, smiled and said, "My name is—"

Whump!

A fist caught Arno's jaw. Stunned, he staggered back and was set upon by men bursting from the surrounding woods. They threw him down, kicked him, punched him, and then handcuffed him. Feeling his lip swelling up, Arno faced the soldier who'd betrayed him. A thin, bloodless smile crossed the young man's face. His eyes, moments earlier shy and trusting, were now cold and menacing.

"Arno Huff," said one of the men holding his identification papers. "You're under arrest for lewd and deviant behavior."

"It's hard labor for you!" said another, shoving him toward a black sedan.

His legs weakening, Arno was about to faint. But he managed to blurt out, "Wait! I can give you something!"

The man yanking his cuffs flashed an amused smile. "I'm not your kind!"

"I mean something real! Involving state security!"

The man shoved Arno against the car. "What are you talking about?"

Arno felt ill. His head swam. An inner voice begged him to stop, but he pressed on. "I…I know of a spy ring!"

* * *

Ursula answered her telephone on the first ring. She listened intently, then closed her eyes. She thanked the caller and hung up. Bowing her head, she leaned her weight on the phone. She had always known this moment would come.

She thought of Ullie. *Spy rings are like musical chairs…eventually the music stops.*

Reaching into a metal box inside a closet, she removed a gasoline-filled light bulb. She extinguished the living room's overhead light, then climbed a stepladder and unscrewed the bulb. In its place, she gently inserted the one filled with gasoline.

Stepping to the bar, she poured and downed two shots of scotch. From a cabinet she removed a vile filled with white powder, which she sprinkled on the back of her hand. Snorting it brought a rush of euphoria that energized her senses.

The screeching sound of tires outside her front door let her know the time had come. She peeked from behind a curtain to see four men spilling from each of three sedans. Dressed in suits and fedoras, several brandished handguns. One carried a club. Around their necks, swinging on chains, she recognized their silver Gestapo badges. She stepped to the fireplace and used the toe of her shoe to open the gas lever, triggering a soft, hissing sound. Turning for the couch, her head pleasantly buzzing, she reached into a pewter pillbox and removed a glass ampule.

* * *

Having just flown into Berlin, Freida sat in the passenger seat of a Mercedes coupé rushing her to the posh address on Unter den Linden. They dodged bomb craters and a string of torched trolley cars before pulling up behind several vehicles outside a white townhouse with a fenced yard and a weeping Japanese maple. Bolting from the car, Freida strutted through an open gate.

* * *

Her eyes and throat irritated by the smell of propane; Ursula sat in the dark waiting on the sofa. She slid the glass ampule between her teeth.

* * *

"Break it open!" Freida shouted at the group of men clustered around the front door. One threw a shoulder to no avail. A second reared his boot and smashed it open.

* * *

Her senses numbed, Ursula bit into the ampule, and the taste of bitter almonds flooded her mouth. Her heart stopped instantly.

* * *

Charging into the living room, someone demanded, "Lights!"

Another yelled, "I smell...gas?"

"I found it!" a man blurted and flicked a wall switch sending 110 volts of electricity into the gasoline filled lightbulb.

* * *

The explosion blasted Freida off her feet, hurling her shoes into the street. Her face burned and blistered, her clothes torn and smoldering, she lay motionless in the yard under a fiery glow.

CHAPTER 35

Two stories beneath the treasury building, Harrison Brightwell showed his identification to a Royal Marine guarding a metal door and was allowed to enter a claustrophobic anteroom. There he encountered another fortified door that he opened by entering a code into a mechanical keypad.

"Hello, Mrs. Sherbourne," he said to a petite thirtyish brunette in a trim Women's Royal Navy Service uniform standing over an open file drawer.

"Major," she said looking over her shoulder. "How is it outside?"

Turning to another locked door, he remarked, "I forgot that you spend twelve-hour shifts in this mole hole."

"I'm starting to understand how Ann Boleyn and Catherine Howard felt in the Tower of London."

"At least you'll keep your head at day's end," he chuckled.

"I fear someday the war will end and I'll still be here, forgotten."

"No chance of that, love." He pushed open the adjacent room's door. "Even down here, you'll hear the party horns from Piccadilly Circus. In fact, you'll be the first one I take for a glass of champagne."

"In that case," she slammed shut the drawer, "a nice bottle of Krug, 1926, will do just fine."

"Sounds expensive," he replied.

"I'm worth it," she said winking.

Closing the door, he turned on an overhead light illuminating an even more claustrophobic room with a wall-mounted chalkboard inscribed with code names, operational statuses, and remarks. He folded his arms and read the name at the top of the list.

It was LARK, or Tomas Fromme, formerly assigned to the radar station at Würzburg Riese outside Peenemünde and now working somewhere above the Arctic circle in Norway.

Next came SPARROW, or Ludwig Mintzer. A red X appeared in his status box, meaning he'd been compromised. If he wasn't dead, he might wish he were.

CROW, or Arno Huff, had last reported six days ago. Though not unusual for operatives behind enemy lines to fail to report on time, it didn't bode well considering recent events.

He eyed the chalked letters for OSPREY and the accompanying red X beside it. He'd never met or spoken to Ursula Pohl but kept an old magazine with her seductive, smiling image advertising Stoewer automobiles. Future generations would owe her a debt of gratitude.

He then drew an X beside HAWK, or Janko Novak. It had been confirmed he'd perished in the Peenemünde bombing.

Brightwell moved on to FINCH, or Dr. Ulrich Mainz, the only remaining member of the Peenemünde spy ring – Brightwell's last hope. Turning to a map of Germany, he eyed where the Peene River swept northward around Usedom Island and Peenemünde's sandy stretches to meet the Baltic. He rubbed his chin pensively.

Where exactly are you, Dr. Mainz?

CHAPTER 36

The darkness his unwitting ally, Ullie navigated between sandy dunes overlooking the Baltic.

He had to work quickly. Hours earlier he'd received orders reassigning him from Peenemünde to a mobile missile battery on the North Sea where he'd serve as a technical advisor.

He'd received word of Ursula's fate and wondered how many others had been arrested and tortured. Had it been Tomas or his wife Sylvie who had betrayed them? He dismissed the thought. If it had been either of them, he'd already be in Gestapo custody. Perhaps it was Tomas's Berlin contacts. How many were there? He'd never know.

He was racked with guilt over feeling grateful Ursula had died. If tortured, she might have betrayed him. He uncorked a pocket flask and took a swig of schnapps. Gerda's laugh haunted him. He took solace that she'd died instantly, among forty women killed by an RAF bomb's direct hit on their dormitory that fateful night a year earlier. She'd borrowed a dress for their upcoming nuptials. Even though it was not a wedding dress, she'd refused to let him see it. She'd insisted on keeping the camera, convincing him no one would suspect her of espionage. He looked at her differently thereafter—she must have truly loved him to have taken such a risk.

After taking another nip, he wiped his mouth and pocketed the flask. Then he knelt over a gnarled piece of driftwood, pushed it aside, and began digging until he felt an oilskin sack. Pulling it from the sand, he opened it. Relieved that it hadn't been found by someone else or gotten wet, he removed a binder containing a stack of typed documents—the V2's most vital technical data.

Setting aside the bag, he reached into the hole for a second sealed oilskin bag containing a square cracker tin. When he opened it, a cluster of wires and a pair of headphones spilled out. He then raised and inspected the shortwave radio transmitter inside—checking its knobs, frequency dial, and telegraph key. Everything appeared to be in order. He placed the transmitter on the ground and flipped a toggle switch causing a tiny light to go on. He felt a sense of relief and then recalled the last time he'd met Ursula, at Berlin's Anhalt Station at Christmas, her sable hat dusted with snow. As she handed him a suitcase with the transmitter, she'd told him of the premonitions she'd had of their operation being compromised. He'd played down her fears and told her she was imagining things. She then kissed him, like many other couples that snowy night, saying good-bye to one another. He couldn't help but notice a somberness in her beautiful eyes, as if knowing they'd never meet again.

Taking another swig from the flask, he shook the memory and carried the transmitter to the top of a dune and faced the sea. He set the radio to a frequency provided by Ursula. She'd assured him it was continuously monitored by British agents, a little more than 100 kilometers away in Sweden, and by roving Royal Navy submarines off the German coast. Opening a small plastic bag, he quickly assembled a small diamond-shaped kite and attached it to the transmitter with a long wire. When he launched the kite upwards, it caught the breeze and hovered overhead. Putting on the headphones, he closed his eyes and taking a calming breath tapped a coded message on the telegraph key before shutting off the transmitter.

After retrieving the kite, he broke it apart and jammed it along with the headset and cracker tin into the oilskin bag. Then he clambered down from the dune, stuffed the bag into the sandy hole, filled it in, and covered it with the driftwood. Brushing his hands free of sand, he clutched the document case, climbed back atop the dune, and once again faced the sea, wondering if his message had been received and what, if any, effort would be made to extract him and his cache of records. His senses dulled by the liquor; Marga came to mind. He took another, bracing swig. He hated to involve her, but he needed insurance, and she was his best bet. With gusto, he took a final nip before rearing back his arm and heaving the flask into the night. Then with the documents tucked under his arm, he turned his back on the Baltic, knowing it was perhaps for the very last time, and set off.

CHAPTER 37

Her violin tucked between chin and collar bone, Marga focused on her sheet music as she played Mozart's "Symphony 40" for the patrons in the Adlon Hotel's lavender-scented dining room. Striking a final note, she lowered her bow and yielded to the flutes and oboes. As she balanced her violin on her knee, she stared longingly at a platter of roasted pheasant whisked past the musicians by a waiter in a prim white jacket.

As the first flautist was finishing her solo, Marga lifted her violin and got ready to play, counting out the beats until she would rejoin the number, when a familiar face stood out. He was sitting at one of the tables in the far corner of the room with a bottle of wine and a long stem crystal glass. *Ullie!* Her hand with the bow went slack, and she failed to come in at the violin's entry point. Realizing her error, Marga rushed her stroke and played out of tune, which drew an icy stare from Frau Rainer. Marga closed her eyes momentarily to reorient herself and find her rhythm.

Once she was calm and back in sync with the other musicians, Marga snuck a peek over her sheet music at Ullie, who sat alone beneath the glow of an Art Deco sconce. Dressed in a black dinner jacket with a matching bowtie, he looked more handsome than ever before. Their eyes met, and she smiled. He didn't smile back but downed his drink, stood, and waved a small white envelope. Her eyes followed him through open French doors leading into the spacious lobby and to the front desk where he handed the envelope to an attentive elderly clerk in a tailored suit.

Twenty minutes later, the Peenemünde League of German Girls ensemble hit their final notes and rose to acknowledge the applause. A customary bouquet of flowers found its way to Frau Rainer along with an invitation for the girls to dine at a private table. Marga excused herself and headed to the front desk where she asked the clerk if someone had left an envelope for her.

"Are you Fräulein Toth?" he asked, peering down at the envelope with her name written on it.

"I am," she said excitedly. "I'm Marga Toth."

He handed her the envelope and she headed for her room on the second floor. Clutching Ullie's envelope, she was dizzy with anticipation and once in her room, she closed the door, dropped her violin case on her bed, and tore open the envelope.

Marga,

You look and sound great. Your parents would be very proud. Please come to Room 414 at nine…Alone. – Ullie

Marga's smile almost sprained her cheeks. She reread the note. *He thought she looked great and invited her to his hotel room – Alone!*

Catching her breath, she looked in the mirror and ran her fingers through her hair. *You look awful!* She glanced at a clock on the nightstand. She had an hour to prepare.

When she stepped out of the bathroom after her shower, Portia was sitting on one of the double beds.

"So, what was the big rush?" Portia asked as she kickd off her shoes.

"How was dinner?" Marga asked, ignoring Portia's pointed question.

"We had thin but good horse steaks seasoned in some kind of mushroom sauce. They also had these little pearl onions and chopped potatoes." She suppressed a burp. "It was amazing."

Containing a smile, Marga sat on the edge of Portia's bed. "Ullie's here."

Portia straightened up. "What do you mean…here?"

"I mean in the hotel!"

Portia covered her mouth.

"He left me a note at the front desk." Marga couldn't help but let a girlish giggle escape her lips.

Portia's face brightened. "That's why you skipped dinner!"

Marga stood and retrieved the note, which Portia quickly snatched from her hand.

"Hey!" Marga reached for the note, but Portia was holding it high over her head.

"'Marga, you look and sound great,'" Portia read aloud. "'Your parents would be very proud. Please come to Room 414 at nine… Alone – Ullie'" Portia grinned. "*Alone?*" She laughed. "Ooh, Marga, come to my hotel room…*Alone!*"

"Stop it!" Marga protested, jumping for the note.

Laughing, Portia handed it back and fell onto her bed. "So… what are you going to do?"

Clutching the note, Marga blushed. "I…I don't know."

"You don't know?" Portia raised up. "Is that why you spent twenty minutes in the shower?"

Marga looked at the note. "I guess I should go…right? I mean, it would be rude not to."

Portia rolled her eyes. "Don't be a twit! Go!"

Marga leaned into the mirror, felt her cheeks, and reached for a hairbrush.

Portia sidled up to her, flashing a sly grin. "I know what you're thinking."

Marga met Portia's gaze in the mirror. She frowned. "Don't even say it."

"Oh, please!" Portia clutched Marga's shoulders. "It hasn't crossed your mind? Marga, you're eighteen! There's a war on! Tomorrow holds no promises!"

"What are you saying?"

Portia spun her around. "I think you should follow your instincts."

"What if I don't know what they are?"

Portia reached into the closet for a powder-blue dress with white polka dots, short puffed sleeves, and a cloth belt. Of Marga's three dresses, it was the smallest and did the most to accentuate her figure. "This will do," said Portia holding it up.

Ten minutes later, her hair combed and shimmering, Marga exited the bathroom. Extending her arms, she turned from side to side. "How does it look?"

"You mean, how do *you* look?" Portia exclaimed.

"Well?"

"You look great! I can just imagine what Ullie will think!" Portia plucked a barrette from her head and clipped it to Marga's hair. "There…" She stepped back to study her. "It gives you a little glamor."

Looking in the mirror, Marga smiled. "It does, doesn't it?"

"And here," said Portia pressing a thin glassine packet into Marga's palm.

"A condom?"

"Mama gave it to me. She said I am a big girl and sometimes things happen."

Marga handed it back. "Nothing is going to happen!"

"Don't be a ninny!" Portia reached for Marga's clutch purse and stuck the condom inside of it. "Take it…just in case."

As she approached Ullie's room, Marga checked her breath and rehearsed what she would say. *Hi Ullie…Hello Ullie…Hi, how are you, Ullie.* Reaching his door, she paused. *What am I doing?* She turned and considered retreating but held firm, settled her nerves, and knocked.

The door opened.

Marga smiled. "Ullie…"

"Marga," he said welcoming her. He'd removed his dinner jacket and tie. He wore his button-down shirt open at the collar and sleeves rolled to his elbows. "Thanks for coming."

She entered the room laced with the masculine scents of after-shave, liquor, and a half-smoked cigar.

"Let me look at you," he said closing the door. "You're all grown up."

Her nerves fluttering, she answered, "Do you think so?"

He nodded, sliding his gaze over her. "Most certainly. And you played beautifully tonight. Your parents would be very proud."

Her expression brightened. "Have you seen them?"

He shook his head. "Not in a while. As of late, they have us moving about quite a bit."

Marga looked around the room. Toiletries cluttered a bureau. A bottle of cognac and two glasses sat atop a writing desk next to a leather briefcase, and clothes spilled from an open suitcase on a luggage rack. Her eyes then turned to a partially unmade double bed. A hint of moisture formed on her brow and her heartbeat quickened.

He nodded to the bed. "Let's sit and talk."

Marga sat on its edge, crossing her ankles and clutching her small purse over her lap.

He sat down next to her, and their knees brushed. The sudden contact whet her senses.

"Marga, we don't have much time, and I have something very important to ask of you." He cleared his throat. "I debated this but…I think it first occurred to me that day in the office when you brought your father his lunch."

Her heart twittering, she said, "I remember. And I have to admit…I thought the same thing."

"I just want you to know—what I'm about to say—I've given it considerable thought and…" He gently touched her hand. "I'm hoping you'll agree to it."

"It's okay, Ullie." She sat upright, hoping to project a sophistication she didn't feel. "I know why you asked me here."

"You do?"

She nodded assertively. "I want you to know that I feel the same way." Her mind racing, she leaned forward and moistened her lips. "I'm a woman now, Ullie. You may kiss me." She closed her eyes, tilted her head, and positioned her lips in anticipation.

Ullie knit his brow. "Pardon me?"

"It's okay...you may kiss me." She resumed her pose, eyes closed, lips carefully drawn.

"Marga..." He cleared his throat. "I think there's been a misunderstanding."

She opened her eyes. "Mis...misunderstanding?"

"Marga, I'm fond of you, but..."

Oh, my God! She covered her mouth.

"Marga, are you alright?"

Dropping her purse, she pressed her hands to her burning cheeks.

"Oh, Marga...you thought..."

"Please, don't!" She looked away, tugging at the hem of her skirt.

"Marga, I'm so sorry. I asked you here because I need your help." He stood and retrieved the cognac. He poured himself a splash and turned to her. "I'd offer you a drink but—"

Her heart racing, she raised her chin defiantly. "I'll have a drink if you're offering."

"Are you sure?"

"Yes," she said without hesitation.

He poured a splash and handed it to her. She eyed the liquor, met his gaze, and downed it in one swift gulp. Then she doubled over coughing.

Ullie dropped on a knee, took her glass, and gently patted her back. "Easy there," he said. "It takes some getting used to."

"Oh, Ullie!" She pressed her hands to her face sobbing. "I've made such a fool of myself!"

"Hush," he said embracing her.

"I'm sorry. You must think I'm such a…child!"

Still kneeling, he took her hands and looked into her eyes. "Marga, I'm flattered. You're a very special girl and nothing you do or say will ever change that."

"Really?"

"Really." He pinched her chin playfully. "Now, I do need your help. Not as a child, but as a brave young woman."

Accepting a handkerchief, she tamped her nose and cleared her throat. "What kind of help?"

"I need you to memorize something of great importance."

"Memorize?"

He poured himself another drink. "Marga, the Allies are going to win this war. But, before that happens, the Führer's henchmen will destroy as much of the Third Reich as possible, including our research at Peenemünde."

Puzzled, Marga stood and folded her arms. "I don't understand what it has to do with me?"

Turning for the briefcase, he removed a stack of papers and tossed them on the bed.

"You want me to memorize all of that…now?"

"It represents the V2's most vital technical data—years of painstaking research."

She thumbed the documents.

"The complete set of plans could fill a room but, what you have in your hands, if it were lost, would take years to regain." He stepped to a window and peeked out its blackout shade. "Not long ago, a V2 crashed in Poland on a test flight. It was smuggled in pieces to England." He faced her. "Despite having the rocket laid out before them, the Allies couldn't fully reverse-engineer its functions." He smiled with pride. "Even the Americans failed."

"So, why not smuggle them out?"

He sighed and sank his hands into his pockets. "I plan to."

She looked at him a long moment before clearing her throat. "I see. So why have me memorize this?"

He swigged his drink and wiped his mouth. "In case I don't make it."

"What about Dr. von Braun? Papa? The others?"

He remained silent.

"You mean…they may not make it out either." An image of her father and Dr. von Braun being shot by a firing squad flashed through her mind.

"Marga, nothing is guaranteed. What you have there represents mankind's path to the stars. You might be the only one who makes it out of this miserable war with that information." He poured another drink. "Think of it. Years of research stored in your pretty little head."

Marga fingered the documents.

"Please, Marga. It's important."

"Does Papa know?"

He shook his head. "About this, it's only you and me."

Marga took a deep breath and imagined what her father would think of her being the keeper of the work to which he'd dedicated his life. She knew the answer.

"Okay, Ullie…Where do I begin?"

CHAPTER 38

Private Hanno Foche stuck a spade into the charred, ashen ground where one of Peenemünde's women's dormitories had once stood. It had been a year since the air raid but the clearing of rubble continued. Raising a spade-full of dirt mixed with broken masonry and shards of glass, Foche dumped the refuse into a wooden wheelbarrow, repeating the process until filling and pushing it to a dumpster where another group of soldiers unloaded the debris.

Striking something metallic, Foche reached down and curiously dug his fingers through dirt and crumbled brick. Feeling something, he pulled out a thumb-sized, rectangular metal casing with a small square lens. It looked like a tiny camera. Blowing dirt off of it, he curiously eyed the black, faded lettering on its side – Minox.

"Foche!" a sergeant's voice barked. "What have you there?"

Puzzled, Foche handed the object to the sergeant.

"Where did you find this?"

"Right there." Foche scratched the ground with the toe of his boot.

Inspecting the damaged but intact micro-Minox camera, the sergeant turned to the young private. "Good job, Foche!" He slapped his back. "You just earned a three-day pass!"

CHAPTER 39

S eated by an open window at the Hohenlychen SS hospital north of Berlin, a breeze caressing her hairless, bumpy scalp, Freida cradled a box with salvaged items from the Peenemünde women's dormitory that had been obliterated by a 500-pound bomb the night of the air raid.

"This is all that was found?" she asked the young SS officer who'd brought her the box. "I was told there was more."

"There was great damage to the building," he replied. "It burned to the ground—most of its victims incinerated."

Retrieving a cracked hand-mirror, she studied her scarred face. Her lips appeared to have been removed, melted, and reattached to her mouth while her nose and an ear had been reduced to pink fleshy nubs with perforated openings. A puckered scar blighted her cheek, and a black patch covered her now hollow left eye socket. She stared into her lone blue eye encased by uneven lids fashioned from skin grafting. Never having appreciated her natural beauty until now that it was gone, she brushed off remarks that she was fortunate to have survived compared to the five Gestapo agents who had not.

She put down the mirror and picked up the small dented micro-Minox camera and slowly turned it over between her fingers.

She thought of the microfilm images found in the binding of the book *Tales of the Caribbean* – all taken with the same model camera.

The officer handed her a folder. "You asked for background on the four women from whose room this debris was found."

Freida took the file and read the short list of typed names: Erika Spuntz, Marika Haas, Gerda Hewel, and Marta Klein.

"All secretaries… with clean records," said the officer. "One of them, Gerda Hewel, was engaged to an engineer."

Freida's eye narrowed. She didn't believe in coincidences. "Which one?"

"Dr. Ullie Mainz of the Technical Design Office. His information appears in the file."

Flipping the page, her memory jogged by the name once mentioned by Hermann Goetz, Freida read the brief biographical sketch of Mainz. He certainly was young, bright, and potentially altruistic.

She handed him the folder and said, "You're dismissed. And relay my appreciation to Colonel Pringer for bringing this new information to my attention so quickly."

He nodded, snapped a salute, and left the room.

Left alone, Freida's mood soured. Somehow, that camera was connected to her spy hunt at Peenemünde. She grimaced as she struggled to her feet and balanced herself on the window sill. She was wasting time. The traitors within von Braun's team were still active and she wasn't going to catch them convalescing in a former sanitarium.

She reached for a telephone on her nightstand and waited for a woman's voice to come on the line.

"Yes, Fräulein?"

"Get me Dr. Fiske. I want an immediate discharge!"

"But…Fräulein, your condition…"

"Do it now!" Freida barked and slammed down the phone.

* * *

Four days later, having secured her medical discharge, Freida balanced on a cane in her Peenemünde office. She sipped a cup of coffee and studied a wall chart with a dozen photographs and names, many connected to one another with threads of yarn linking potential conspirators in her hunt for spies. She narrowed her eye to view a photo of Ursula Pohl. The explosion at the former model's townhouse instantly flashed through her mind. She wiped a hand over her uneven face and glanced at her desk, cluttered with bottles of medications and pain pills. *Oh, what I would have done to you in a Gestapo torture chamber.*

She turned her attention to a photo of Gerda Hewel. Had she believed Mainz when he convinced her it would be safer if she hid the camera for him? How crafty of him to let his faithful, unassuming fiancée take the risk. No one would suspect a secretarial typist.

Freida pressed a finger against the glossy image of Arno Huff, the homosexual caught soliciting in a Berlin park. He'd betrayed numerous lovers, including Ludwig Mintzer, who, like Ursula Pohl, had swallowed a vile of poison as the Gestapo kicked in his door. She'd heard he set his gramophone to play a Marlene Dietrich record at the highest possible volume. *Silly queer.*

She opened a folder to a photo of Hermann Goetz with a detailed image of the garrote fused into his charred throat. *Nicely done. The work of a professional.*

Retrieving another photograph, she looked at the twisted remains of a man crushed beneath a heap of bricks outside Goetz's dormitory. On the back of the photo was a name—Janko Novak / Janitor and prisoner of war. Turns out the janitor worked in the building in which Mainz and Goetz had both worked. She tapped her lips. Goetz had informed her that Peenemünde's scientists were as interested in space flight as they were in weaponizing rockets. "Perhaps more so," he'd said. She held up Janko's photo. Did he kill Goetz to protect Mainz?

Suddenly, a searing pain electrified her face. She reached among the medication bottles on her desk for a metal tube labeled, Pervitin—a methamphetamine—and shook loose two pills. She swallowed them and within minutes, the pain ebbed and her focus sharpened.

A perusal of Ludwig Mintzer's phone records showed that he didn't use his phone often, but when he did, he called other men—homosexuals mostly, many of whom were now in concentration camps. Running a finger down the page, she noticed he'd called the radar base at Würzburg Riese, a scant ten kilometers west of Peenemünde, several times. She dug out a list of outgoing calls from Ullie Mainz's Technical Design shop and checked off in red pencil a series of calls placed to the same number. Shuffling through papers, she found the slip with the subscriber information for the Würzburg Riese number and squinted as she read, GENERAL TRUNK LINE – CAFETERIA.

Was she to believe a cook or kitchen worker was involved? Hardly.

There were also call records for the payphone outside the Technical Design shop. She noted four calls placed to the same

Würzburg Riese number. She flipped more pages. Payphone records outside Ullie Mainz's dormitory revealed the same—more calls to the now-familiar cafeteria number.

Her coffee spilled, and she cursed it. She was still getting accustomed to using her reconfigured mouth. Wiping stains off a photo of Arno Huff, she recalled that he'd confessed that Ludwig Mintzer had provided him stolen Peenemünde documents but didn't know their source. But of all her suspects, only Mainz had had access to them at their source. Freida eyed the phone records and pondered. Huff never mentioned Mainz—only Mintzer. And Mintzer died before he could be interrogated. So, who was his contact? Seeing that both Mintzer and Mainz called the radar base, she reasoned Mainz must have photographed the missile plans, gave them to someone at Würzburg Riese who got them to Mintzer who gave them to Huff. She sighed. She couldn't prove Mainz's involvement, but she didn't care, for there was enough suspicion to question him in a manner she was confident would yield the answers she sought.

CHAPTER 40

"How certain are you?" Pringer asked. Through the phone, Freida could hear air raid sirens wailing and flak guns thumping outside his Berlin office.

"I have the camera that was found among Gerda Hewel's possessions. What could a secretarial typist have been doing with such a thing? Her work didn't afford her opportunity to photograph classified documents. On the other hand, her fiancée, Dr. Mainz, had access to everything!"

Freida switched the receiver from one ear to the other. "I've also established a connection through telephone records that someone in Mainz's office dialed members of Ursula Pohl's spy ring. That bastard Polish janitor killed my informant to protect someone. I'm betting Mainz. Colonel, let me question him."

Pringer cleared his throat. "You may, but take caution. He works for von Braun, who has powerful friends, like Albert Speer."

"The Minister of Armaments is subject to the law like everyone else," she protested.

"I know, but he can pick up the phone and speak directly to the Führer. You're aware of Herr Hitler's recent directive giving the highest priority to the missile program. Harassing members of his overworked rocket team will draw a response."

"I understand, Herr Colonel, but keep in mind it'd be a shame if it were later discovered that a traitor was under our noses all along and we failed to act." She sighed. "I don't have to tell you the consequences."

"Very well. You'll find Mainz in Holland."

"Holland?" Freida scowled. "What's he doing in Holland?"

CHAPTER 41

I t was the final days of summer, and the laughter rang out from the wooded lanes within Haage Bos, a cool, leafy sanctuary in The Hague. Beneath an expanse of mature silver maples, old men on park benches read newspapers, played checkers, and chatted quietly while amused mothers watched a young man in a top hat and over-sized checkered blazer captivate a young audience by juggling three colorful balls while tooting a nursery song on a kazoo.

Suddenly, the growl of diesel engines shook the forest. Squawking pigeons took flight. Board games and conversations ceased as rumbling trucks, armored cars, and a tarp-covered *Meillerwagen* invaded the scene.

Shrieking children sought their mothers who snatched their hands and whisked them away as soldiers spilling from vehicles barked at gawking bystanders to leave. A swift-moving platoon removed the *Meillerwagen's* tarp to reveal a rocket lying on its side. It took only fifteen minutes for the noisy hydraulic motors to raise it up until it loomed like an imposter among the surrounding trees. Energy, motion, and purpose surrounded the V2 in preparation for launch as wires and cables and antennas were strung and raised. Inside a command vehicle, acting as a launch control center, a missile officer wearing headphones, tuned and calibrated instruments as the V2's pressure and temperature readings flashed across a bank of glowing gauges.

At the missile, tanker-trucks filled its aluminum fuel tanks with its volatile propellants and Ullie worked a slide ruler to calculate time, distance, and fuel consumption. Once completed, he set a compass heading and aligned one of four tail fins with the target azimuth. He then pocketed the slide ruler and gave one of the tail fins a final tug before declaring the rocket ready for flight. As he walked away, he turned to inspect the V2's riveted metal exterior with a cartoon of a gleeful Felix the Cat holding a shiny spherical bomb with a lit fuse. He envisioned how a child might smile at the whimsical caricature and considered the painful irony that this technological marvel was slated to, within the next ten minutes, claim such innocent lives.

Vehicles withdrew into surrounding woods, and the missile men took cover. An officer in the command vehicle peered through a periscope while another maintained his undivided attention on a glowing instrument panel. Shielded behind the hood of a truck, Ullie watched through binoculars and listened to a radio as the final seconds were counted down. "*Drei…zwei…eins!*"

Inside the V2, sodium permanganate and hydrogen peroxide combined to charge a steam turbine that activated turbo pumps injecting liquid oxygen and ethanol into a combustion chamber igniting 25,000 tons of thrust. Eyeing the rapidly ascending rocket, Ullie checked his stopwatch and calculated what would happen in the coming minutes. At 25 seconds, a sonic boom thundered over the North Sea. At 54 seconds, a program motor initiated a gentle 49-degree vertical tilt of the missile, setting it on an arcing trajectory across the English Channel. At 65 seconds, hurtling at three times the speed of sound, an accelerometer cut the engine. The V2 had reached an apogee of 55 miles – 288,000 feet. Within the radio compartment's silent, airless void, an electrical circuit armed the glass-insulated one-ton Amatol warhead, and like Icarus reaching for the sun but faltering, the rocket nosed over and spiraled earthward, burning through the atmosphere at 3,600-feet-per-second like an arrow shot from the sun.

* * *

Emogene Hobbs, a cheerful six-year-old with curly amber locks and hazel eyes, crouched on the sidewalk in the shadow of the modest rowhouses. She licked her lips as her tiny hand traced hopscotch squares. An eyeless teddy bear sat propped on the curb.

"Emogene, you watch out for cars!" her mother cried from a kitchen window that overlooked the street in the East London neighborhood.

"Yes, Mummy!" Emogene answered over the bark of a small, scruffy terrier tied to the steps of a neighbor's walkup. She stood and clapped chalk from her hands before straightening her threadbare magenta dress, which matched her scuffed Mary Janes. "How's that, Mister Jeepers?" She bent toward the teddy bear and gave him a kiss on the top of his soft brown head. "Don't worry. You can play too. I'll carry you when it's your turn. Polly and Willa won't mind."

Just then, a butterfly landed on her shoulder. She craned her neck to view the delicate creature when a swirl of wind ruffled her hair and caused her to squint. What sounded like the crack of lightning shook the sky and tickled her skin. She looked up, but Emogene Hobbs never knew the sound ricocheting off the pavement to be the sonic boom from a V2, launched minutes earlier from a shady park in Holland.

* * *

From Bromley to Enfield to Harrow, sirens howled, and Londoners gawked at the bulbous cloud of smoke and crystalized ash spiraling over their war-torn city. Harried telephone operators fielded frantic calls reporting ruptured gas lines, munition explosions—even a plane crash. National Fire Service crews arrived to razed buildings, mounds of shattered bricks, and a massive smoldering crater. Extinguishing flames and digging through rubble, they discovered a previously unseen oddity—traces of ice within the crater. Puzzled, they went about their grisly work oblivious to the phenomenon derived from frozen moisture accumulated over the V2's metal skin during its voyage through earth's alternating atmospheric layers.

And, atop a nearby sloping roof, a fireman found an eyeless, singed teddy bear, identified only by a silk tag with a child's script – Mister Jeepers.

* * *

In his subterranean Whitehall office, Harrison Brightwell sat at his desk reading official reports of the mysterious blast and immediately dismissed speculation of gas line or munition explosions. He took a deep breath and sat back. A sinking feeling slowly enveloped him.

V2s had come to London.

CHAPTER 42

Seated beneath a pergola on a patio with sweeping views of the Black Sea, Pavel Petroshenko listened to General Smirno Gurovsky, of the Soviet High Command, address four senior members of the Soviet military including a NKVD General representing Russia's security services. They sat around a long table stacked with platters of smoked meats, caviar, and sliced fruits. Reaching for a plump fig between bottles of Stolichnaya, Petroshenko let his gaze wander the spacious lawns, orchards, and gardens that once belonged to a Romanov prince. Sounds of laughter drew his attention to a nearby swimming pool where naked women basked in the Crimean sun sipping champagne and exemplifying the decadence of entitled senior Soviet officials far distanced from Russian battlefields and their Moscow superiors.

"I spoke with Major General Tulokov from Comrade Stalin's staff," said Gurovsky as he took a drag from a Turkish cigarette. "He informs me that plans are being finalized for Europe's postwar borders."

"I presume our allies agree with Comrade Stalin's intentions," said NKVD General Yuri Nagorov who wore the Order of Lenin on his lapel. He helped himself to a cup of boiling water from a samovar.

Gurovsky narrowed his eyes. "Comrade Stalin realizes the Americans have no stomach for further conflict beyond defeating the Axis powers. As for Churchill and de Gaulle…" The general shrugged. "What can they do?"

Petroshenko cleared his throat and asked, "Are we to extend our borders to Alsace-Lorraine then?"

"Of course not," Gurovsky muttered, crushing out his cigarette and promptly lighting another one. "But Comrade Stalin insists we maintain our hard-earned territorial gains in Central Europe to provide a buffer between us and the West. Never again will our enemies encroach upon Russia's borders. But it's imperative that we have a strong bargaining position." Smoke leaked from Gurovsky's nose as he engaged the stares of the men around the table. "We're all familiar with Germany's advances in the sciences. Of particular interest to Moscow…their ballistic missile research. If the Americans beat us to this technology, it could impact Comrade Stalin's bargaining position. This is significant because we know the Americans are secretly working on a new…miracle weapon."

"Miracle weapon?" asked Admiral Leonid Vasiliev of the Red Navy's Black Sea Fleet.

For an instant, Petroshenko was reminded of his and the admiral's time as cellmates during the purges of the Soviet officer corps in the late 1930s. Vasiliev chewed smoked herring with what Petroshenko knew to be false teeth. Despite having been beaten unconscious during interrogations accusing him of being a spy against the Soviet Union, Petroshenko was grateful that at least he'd kept his teeth.

"Something never before seen and of immense power," said Gurovsky. "It's being developed in the desert—Los Alamos, they call it." A shallow grin contorted his portly face. "We have assets keeping us informed."

"And getting Germany's missile technology will offset this miracle weapon?" Petroshenko asked.

Gurovsky's face darkened. "If they somehow couple this new weapon with Germany's missile technology, there's no telling what leverage they'll have over us."

"You mean forcing us back to our pre-war borders," commented Nagorov.

Gurovsky exhaled a cloud of smoke. "There is to be another summit of Allied leaders. Churchill will make his usual blustering demands concerning our territorial gains—in particular, Poland's autonomy—it's why this whole war started to begin with. While Roosevelt, unaware of what we know about his Los Alamos project, will feel emboldened to push for America's interests."

"You mean force Comrade Stalin's hand into concessions," said Petroshenko.

"We cannot allow our esteemed leader to be embarrassed on the world stage." Gurovsky's face stiffened. "We have emerged from this conflict a great power and we plan to remain as such. Therefore, Comrade Petroshenko, I'm assigning you the responsibility of getting this missile technology. You're to oversee a network of operatives tasked with securing Germany's top scientists and their cache of documents. Once we achieve victory, they'll work for us, and their research will be the foundation of our own ballistic missile program."

Gurovsky mashed his cigarette into an ashtray. "You leave tonight. In the meantime, have a swim, a lunch of smoked eel and caviar then…a quiet afternoon retreat with one of our lovely guests. Remember, Comrade Petroshenko, your efforts will be closely watched—no less by Comrade Stalin himself—for your actions might well impact Russia's fortunes in post-war Europe's political landscape." He set his eyes firmly into Petroshenko's. "Do not fail us."

Watching Admiral Vasiliev chewing, Petroshenko nodded.

CHAPTER 43

The smell of fresh paint lingered in Brigadier General Stanley Melton's Pentagon office nestled within a recently completed inner ring of the 150-acre building. Flipping through a stack of intelligence reports under the amber-glow of a banker's lamp, he nursed a half-smoked cigar before glancing over a pair of low-slung reading glasses and asking Army Major Dan Whitcomb, "How are my friends at Wright Field these days?"

Melton had spent three years assigned to the Army's Technical Data Branch at the Ohio military base where most recently, a rebuilt pulse-jet engine, similar to ones developed at Peenemünde for the V1 flying bomb, had been successfully reverse-engineered and test-fired.

Seated opposite the general's desk, Whitcomb answered, "Colonel Sharpe sends his regards."

"Sharpe? Heck of a wide-out on that '29 team. Tough son-of-a-bitch." He reached for his cigar and took a quick puff. "Speaking of which," he dug around his desk for a thin volume titled, *Army Football – 1944.* "We got a heck of a squad this year. With Blanchard and Davis…" He laughed through a cough. "No one is getting past us! Not even the squids!"

The major smiled. "I don't suppose so, sir. Though, in all fairness, many of America's greatest gridiron talents are currently indisposed around the globe."

"Excuses, Major." The general sucked his cigar and expelled a great white cloud. "You aren't an academy man. Remind me of your alma mater."

"Rensselaer—"

"Of course," snorted the general, "R-P-I...electrical engineering. It's why you're here and brings me to the point." He set aside the Army football prospectus and clasped his hands. "As you're aware, the Krauts have made significant advances in various technical fields but none as promising as in rocketry. I'm putting you in charge of an elite team of experts to secure this technical data. This means the V1...V2...All projects on the drawing board. And, I don't have to tell you, their engineers and scientists are at the top of our list of people we want to get our hands on."

Whitcomb shifted in his seat. "I suppose, sir, that we're collaborating with the—"

"Fuck the Russkies!" the general growled. "The French and Brits too! Your job is to move fast and track down these brainy jokers before anyone else gets to them! What we do in this new-fangled, five-sided maze of a building is plan for the next war. I don't have to tell you who our next threat will be."

Sitting forward, General Melton leaned on his elbows. "And, Major, if we don't get the goods, you damn well better make sure the other side doesn't either. Am I clear on that?"

Meeting the general's steely gaze, Whitcomb cleared his throat. "Three bags full, sir."

CHAPTER 44

Freida strutted into Peenemünde's SS barracks where a young duty officer straightened behind a reception desk, his eyes drawn to her disfigured face and black eye patch. She had been used to attention of a very different sort. But it didn't matter now. All that mattered was tracking down Germany's traitors.

"Who's in charge?" Freida demanded.

"I am," said the officer. "Lieutenant Sturm at your service."

She tossed her credentials on the counter. The officer glanced at her cropped photo alongside a Sicherheitsdienst stamp. "Sturm, I need you to contact your counterparts in Holland." She produced a photograph. "I want this man, Dr. Ulrich Mainz, promptly arrested."

Sturm looked at the photo. "Do you know his whereabouts?"

She frowned. "He's assigned to a missile battery somewhere along the North Sea."

"Those batteries are mobile, Fräulein, and constantly on the move."

She slammed her fist on the counter. "Why don't you start by cabling your counterparts in Amsterdam…Rotterdam…wherever-dam. But find him! And if you can't, perhaps a posting to our collapsing Eastern front would be a more suitable assignment for you!"

Snapping to attention, Sturm replied, "I'll cable Amsterdam immediately, Fräulein!"

CHAPTER 45

Gerhard Pringer stared out the window of his sedan as it sped away from Wewelsburg Castle and where he'd been lectured for the previous hour by SS-Reichsführer Heinrich Himmler. It had been Pringer's second visit to the 17th century Renaissance-style fortress with high walls and turrets overlooking a sleepy medieval village.

Though a committed Nazi, Pringer found the castle an unsettling reminder of the maniacal mindset of Himmler and his vision for the SS, Germany, and a new world order. He'd created special chambers for ritual ceremonies imbuing mystical powers upon its participants and Himmler took pride in showing him its 12,000-volume library where scholars would one day study Aryan and Teutonic literature and folklore. It was one thing to gain political power through skewed lies and twisted theories of racial superiority, Pringer thought. It was another to actually believe them.

Watching the rolling Westphalian hills and ripe valleys rush past, Himmler's words rang in his ears. "Your orders, Brigadeführer Pringer, are simple! Seize all records and documents from the Nordhausen rocket assembly caves and destroy them all!"

"But Mein Reichsführer…"

"Every last scrap of paper, Pringer...*Burned!* And, as for von Braun and his men...I want them put someplace quiet—where, when the time comes, they can either be ransomed or..."

"Or...?"

"Don't play the fool, Pringer! If they fail to be of any value to us, they'll be disposed of. Do I make myself clear?"

Two hours later, as his twin-engine Ju-88 dropped its landing gear on approach into Berlin's Tempelhof Aerodrome, Pringer had devised an alternative plan.

* * *

Under the cover of darkness, technicians from Wernher's research team loaded suitcases and file boxes onto flatbed trucks and idling cars outside his Nordhausen office he was abandoning. Lugging a suitcase, he turned toward the sound of an approaching vehicle. Harold's compact two-door Peugeot with extinguished lights rumbled forward and screeched to a halt. The driver door was flung open, and Harold exited like a coiled spring.

"Wernher, I got what I could! Maybe with another truck..."

"Harold, it's too late for all that!" Wernher stepped toward the open trunk of a Mercedes sedan. After handing his suitcase to the driver, he reached into his coat pocket for a map, which he gave to Harold. "We'll meet in Garmisch-Partenkirchen. The details are written in the margins. I suggest you memorize them and then burn the map."

"On the Austrian border," said Harold, tilting the map toward the hazy moonlight. "Then what?"

"Trust me," Wernher replied, patting Harold's shoulder. "Have you spoken with Erna?"

"She's on her way to her sister's in Dannenberg."

Wernher walked around the side of the sedan to an open rear door and placed one foot inside. "Good. It's imperative she gets as far west as possible. The Russians could use her to get to you."

"She knows."

"And Marga?"

Harold shook his head. "Last I heard, headed for Holland."

Wernher grinned. "Perhaps in Allied custody by now, eating Baby Ruth bars and listening to jazz records."

Harold sighed. "If only."

"I'll see you in Garmisch then."

They shook hands, and Wernher went to close the door when Harold stopped and asked, "Wernher…We will have something to offer? The Allies, I mean."

Wernher closed his door and through the open window replied, "Trust me, old friend. Now, get a move on it."

＊ ＊ ＊

Siegfried Voss stood in a dark, Thuringian forest outside a mine shaft dug through a craggy outcrop of boulders. "You have all of it?" he asked the driver of the truck that had just rumbled out of the darkness and sat idling.

"To the last paperclip."

"Very well." Siegfried removed a stick of dynamite from his coat pocket. "Once the mine is sealed, nothing goes in or out."

"As Doctor von Braun requested," said the truck driver.

The order given, a group of men in the back of the truck removed their blindfolds and unloaded dozens of wooden boxes, which they then trundled aboard creaky rail cars into a water-tight chamber at the bottom of the abandoned mine.

Once completed, the men boarded the truck, replaced their blindfolds and the truck departed. Left alone once more, Siegfried jammed the stick of dynamite into the boulders over the mine entrance, lit the fuse, and scrambled for cover before a powerful blast shook the night, sealing the mine and the cache of Wernher von Braun's V2 rocket secrets.

Blowing on his hands for warmth, Siegfried began his late-night hike through the woods and thought, that with any luck, he'd be home by first daylight in time for breakfast

* * *

Miles away from the small mine where Wernher's documents lay hidden, Nordhausen's underground V2 assembly complex sat silent. Tools, uniforms, shoes, documents, typewriters, empty liquor bottles, and sundry debris lay scattered throughout ransacked workshops and offices. Trashed sheet-metal presses, generators, bundles of wiring, and scrapped aluminum tanks sat beside abandoned missile sections in shadowy corners and access tunnels. Near the main entrance of the subterranean structure, twenty-six sealed wooden crates sat under armed guard.

It was midday when a convoy of military vehicles rumbled to a stop outside the evacuated complex. A wiry junior officer with large sunken eyes jumped from a *Kubelwagen* staff car and craned his neck skyward toward hundreds of white contrails from Allied bombers headed into the heart of Germany. Cursing under his breath, he strutted to a sergeant standing with a machine gun strapped to his chest. "Sergeant!" He thrust a quick-arm salute and flashed a hand receipt. "Is everything ready to go?"

Reviewing the document, the sergeant nodded. "Have your men follow me inside, sir."

* * *

Gerhard Pringer waited anxiously at a rail depot on the outskirts of Berlin for the Nordhausen train delivering the twenty-six wooden crates containing all of von Braun's V2 documents. Checking his watch, he glanced toward two cargo trucks that would transport the crates to a Spandau warehouse to await Petroshenko's arrival with the Red Army. Gazing skyward, he envisioned being rewarded with a modest pension and a small farm in appreciation for his accelerating the Soviet Union's missile program by a decade. He'd take a wife, a simple woman for cold nights and a desire for old-fashioned values of home and hearth.

A distant whistle sounded, and Pringer cast his eyes on the horizon toward a thin trail of smoke signaling the train's approach. Adjusting his holstered Luger, he steeled his mind. His future was on that train, and no one or anything would jeopardize it.

* * *

Preparing to enter a sauna at his private club in Berlin's Charlottenburg suburb, Pringer had just taken off his bathrobe when the telephone rang. His first instinct was to ignore the ill-timed call, but he relented and answered.

"Pringer here!"

"Herr Brigadeführer, this is—"

"What is it Schempke? Where are you?"

"In the Spandau warehouse. The crates, sir…"

"What about them?"

"Sir, they're…they're…"

"They're what, man?"

"Junk, sir!"

"Junk?"

"They're filled with papers, phone books, newspapers—tools even!"

Pringer seethed. "Have you checked every crate?!"

"No…no, sir, but…"

"Check every last one, damn it! And call me back!"

CHAPTER 46

Devon Farrington lay in a semiconscious slumber. What seemed like a distant knocking, perhaps a lover's faint tapping on his door, tweaked his curiosity and prompted a lazy smile. He shifted under the warmth of Egyptian cotton sheets and tucked an arm beneath an overstuffed goose down pillow.

The knocking grew louder, and the sound of a voice interrupted his bliss.

"Major Farrington, sir," Isabella's butler announced. "A communiqué has just arrived for you." Farrington opened an eye, the dormant circuits in his brain quickly reestablishing his whereabouts—the plush, fragrant bedroom of Lady Isabella Canforth's Yorkshire estate. Farrington rubbed his eyes, and the snowy-haired butler in tails and white gloves came into focus. He was holding out an envelope, which Farrington took.

"Will that be all, sir?"

Sitting up, Farrington sliced open the envelope and nodded, "Thanks, Ben."

"Mr. Tobin, if you'd please…sir."

"My apologies, old boy." Farrington smiled. "That's all, thank you."

Farrington was certain the cable was from Harrison Brightwell, as no one else knew his whereabouts. He read the brief message:

Major Farrington. Report immediately to Section Headquarters. Matter Most Urgent.

–Brightwell

Farrington rubbed his chin stubble and sighed. *It was too good to have lasted.*

"Darling," Isabella Canforth's aristocratic voice chimed as she entered the bedroom through French doors leading from a patio. She carried a small bouquet of jasmine and yellow daffodils. Her hair was pulled up, and she wore a silk kimono cinched at the waist. "Do you like them?" She sat on the edge of the bed and allowed him to smell the flowers. "From the greenhouse."

"As fragrant as you, dear," he said kissing her hand.

Smiling, she traced a hand over his strong, unshaved jawline before raking her fingers through his mane of tousled hair. She rose for the dresser and a crystal vase into which she placed the flowers. "The courier…for you?" She met his eye in the mirror.

Swinging his feet to the floor, he waved the cable. "For king and country, dear."

"You have to go then." She sighed. She went into the bathroom, filled the vase with water, and placed it on the nightstand. "I know better than to ask, but…you'll be sent into harm's way?"

"Perhaps you can accompany me—to London, at least. I recall how pleased we were with the room service at the Dorchester."

"If only," she sighed with a smile. "But I'm hosting the Yorkshire Lady's Auxiliary Committee in two days. We country matrons have to do our part for the war effort too."

"A pity," he said, standing to button his trousers when her hand intervened.

"Before you go my darling, let us enjoy your flowers…for king and country."

CHAPTER 47

"Farrington, I'm sending you to Holland," Harrison Brightwell announced beneath a halo of blue tobacco smoke hovering over his desk. "On an exfiltration."

"An exfil?" Farrington brushed invisible lint off a knee sitting opposite his boss.

"A German, non-English-speaking asset."

"So, my tourist's German will come in handy."

"Six years in Hamburg as an attaché's son should have provided you a better command of the Hun dialect," said Brightwell annoyed. "This chap is a scientist with a briefcase full of technical secrets. It's vital we get him."

"Where to? The Hague? Rotterdam?"

"Amsterdam," said Brightwell, frowning. "And there isn't to be a repeat of that debacle with the Italians in Benghazi!"

"Brighty, I told you. It was Giana. The lovely secretary with emerald eyes who lured me into the desert. If you'd you seen the curves on that Mediterranean beauty..." Farrington grinned. "Well, you had to be there. Besides, old boy, I handled the situation."

"Situation? She led you into an ambush of Italian commandos!"

Farrington smiled. "Ask the five, or I should say, three still alive, how it all went."

Brightwell maintained his frown.

"To show her I harbored no hard feelings, I drove her home. A peck on the cheek my sole reward. I can still hear her as we parted beneath a strawberry moon. 'Ciao Bello!'"

Brightwell shook his head. "Well, here's how this operation is going to go. You'll parachute into Holland, behind enemy lines, where you'll link up with Dutch Resistance. They'll get you to Amsterdam where you'll collect our man. You'll then be led to a landing zone for extraction by Lysander."

Furrowing his brow, Farrington toyed with his watch. "Remarkable flying crates those Lysanders…Why not simply have the Dutch scoop him?"

"Because the powers that be want it handled by one of our own! We don't want the Dutch getting any funny ideas. There's too much at stake. Therefore, I'm sending you, old boy, my best operations man."

"I'll remind you, Brighty. I'm technically on furlough." Farrington inspected his fingernails. "Perhaps as recompense, the Crown could see to a modest extension of it upon my return? I hear there's a twelve-to-one ratio of Wrens to chaps at the naval school in Liverpool."

Smirking, Brightwell sat forward. "Naval auxiliary women should be the last thing on your mind, Devon. However, get that bloke back here and I'll make it an even ten days!"

CHAPTER 48

Low ragged clouds skimmed the airfield at RAF Manston as Devon Farrington waddled across the tarmac under the weight of a bulky parachute harness and kit bag toward a four-engine Halifax bomber. Sergeant Billy Surry assisted him into the cramped interior aglow in red lighting.

"So, you're the reason we're dashing this hay wagon across the Channel on a night like this," the sergeant commented. "We'll be in the soup all the way, but between the darkness and clouds, it just might keep our arses from getting blown out of the sky."

"I forgot my swim trunks," Farrington quipped as he sat down against the fuselage wall. "So, a splash in the Channel is out of the question."

"You're Farrington?" a gruff voice hollered through a bulkhead leading to the cockpit. Farrington turned and squinted through the dim interior. "Aye-aye!"

"I'm Lieutenant Wordsley. I'll be flying you tonight. Our time to the drop zone will be thirty-six minutes. You'll receive ten-, five-, and one-minute warnings. At five minutes, Sergeant Surry will get you positioned over the drop hatch."

"The old Joe Hole," Farrington said, referring to the opening through which parachutists dropped from the Halifax.

Wordsley pointed a fur-lined glove at him. "When I give the signal, you jump. Questions?"

Farrington grinned. "Will you be serving highballs?"

Shaking his head, the pilot smiled and snapped on a rubber oxygen mask. "It's a shame we're wasting all the clever ones on suicide missions."

The Halifax rumbled to life, taxied through the darkness, and roared into the overcast. Climbing through turbulence, Farrington checked his parachute straps and fastening clips, pulled a semi-automatic pistol from a holster, chambered a round, and then felt for the combat knife strapped to his chest—essential were he to land in trees.

Eyes closed, he rested against the plane's vibrating metal skin when Sergeant Surry slapped his knee, flashed all ten fingers, and shouted over the engines, "Ten minutes!"

Nodding, Farrington gave a thumbs-up.

Suddenly, a jarring explosion catapulted him through the night sky, ten minutes too early. Tumbling end over end and fighting for breath, he yanked the parachute's ripcord. It sprung open. When he reached overhead for the steering toggles, he saw flames dancing over his silk canopy.

As he broke out of the clouds, the inky silhouette of fields, hedgerows, and drainage canals appeared below. He dropped fast and landed hard, his legs buckling and body twisting over soggy turf. Snatching at metal latches, he freed himself, and the flaming chute drifted away, frittering into a smoky haze.

Muddied and dazed, he staggered to his feet. He shed his attached gear and looked around, trying to orient himself when a wave of nausea flooded his senses and he collapsed into an unconscious abyss.

CHAPTER 49

Twenty-one-year-old Pieter Bakker coasted on his bicycle over the Singelgracht Canal and down a narrow street in Amsterdam's Jordaan District. Sandy-haired and athletic, he stopped outside a narrow three-story brick apartment building blighted with boarded windows and anti-German graffiti. From beneath the brim of a fisherman's cap, he looked around, tugged at the collar of his olive-green reefer coat, and slung a leather satchel over his shoulder.

Lifting his bicycle up a set of steps, he entered the building and glanced at three mailboxes numbered 1 through 3. A strip of tape on box 3 was his signal to come to the apartment. He tucked his bicycle under the stairs and sauntered up to the third floor.

"Alma," Pieter greeted a young woman silhouetted against a window in the living room of her apartment. She didn't smile and appeared anxious. The small room was unkept. Seat cushions were strewn about, and a chair lay on its side. Broken glass littered the floor, and empty crockery and baking powder were scattered over the counter of an adjacent galley kitchen. Pieter surveyed the scene, concerned. "Alma?"

Alma's gaze cut over to the partially open bathroom door. It was then Pieter noted her cut lip. Their eyes met, and Pieter bolted from the room. The bathroom door smacked open, and three men charged after him. Pieter bounded down the stairs and out the front door when a forearm caught his jaw and he crumpled to the curb.

CHAPTER 50

Devon Farrington slowly awakened. Enveloped in darkness, he lay on a bed of straw, bound by his hands and blindfolded. The smell of manure and hay hung thick in the air and somewhere below him, a cow or perhaps a horse munched straw. A barn door suddenly squealed open. He lay still, listening to what sounded like footsteps climbing a ladder. Hay rustled and floorboards creaked. A foot suddenly poked him.

"I'm awake," he said.

His blindfold was removed, and he sat up, squinting under a lantern's glow. Batting his eyes, he saw a young blond woman staring back.

Clearing his throat, he said through a forced grin, "Is this The Ritz, by chance?"

"What's your name?" the woman asked, betraying a Dutch accent.

He smiled. "You first, doll."

Reaching into her boot, she drew a double-edged knife and turned it from side to side so that it gleamed under the lantern's opaque light. "Have you ever severed a hog's balls?" She met his eye. "There's a particular way I like to do it."

Eyeing the blade, Farrington proffered a thin smile and replied, "I'm sure you do. The name's Farrington…Devon Farrington, British Armed Forces. Now, if you are who I think you are, it's your turn."

A second set of footsteps then creaked on the ladder rising to the hayloft. A bearded man in his late twenties toting a sub-machine gun approached. The man and woman exchanged quick words in Dutch, and the man drew his own knife, which, like the woman's, was long and sharp and accustomed to use.

"My name is Yorick," said the Dutchman. "This is my sister, Anna."

She gave a nod.

Yorick continued. "A British plane crashed last night a few kilometers to the west. There were no survivors."

"I was on it," said Farrington.

Yorick tapped the butt of his knife against his thigh and asked, "You were recently at a country estate. What was your host's name?"

Smiling, Farrington glanced at Anna. "You mean, what's my lover's name?"

The brother and sister stared at him unmoved.

His hands still bound, Farrington plucked a piece of straw and stuck it in his mouth. "That would be the irrepressible Lady Isabella Canforth."

The siblings glanced at one another, and Yorick flicked his knife, slicing the rope around Farrington's wrists. "We're to get you to Amsterdam," he said. "She'll be your guide. She's good at what she does."

Farrington admired Anna's sensitive blue eyes and plump lips. His eyes dropped to the holstered pistol cradled against the soft outline of her breast. Smiling, he asked, "And that would be…?"

Yorick scowled. "You have a cavalier manner, Mister. You should know…Our brother Pieter is missing. He went into the city to make final arrangements for your assignment. We got a report the police found a body matching his description in a canal."

Farrington shook his head. "I'm sorry."

"We're working on confirming it," said Yorick, pulling a pistol from his waistband and handing it to Farrington. "If you run into trouble"—he motioned to Anna—"don't let her be taken alive. I assure you she'll make sure you aren't."

Farrington smiled at Anna. "How reassuring."

"I'll have some food brought up," said Yorick. "In the meantime, get some rest. You leave after dark."

CHAPTER 51

"Hold still," Marga said as she peered through a box camera preparing to snap a picture of Portia and Ilse Stahl posing before Rembrandt's three-story brick home. A sign nailed to the weather-beaten front door read *GESLOTEN* – Dutch for closed. Dressed alike in their navy-blue skirts and League of German Girls' butternut winter jackets, the red and white youth league patches emblazoned with swastikas on their sleeves served as inescapable reminders of where they'd come from.

"Now, one of you," said Portia switching places with Marga. "Smile!" She snapped a picture.

"Mama will be so excited!" Marga bubbled as she took back the camera.

Ilse looked at a small map. "Let's do a little more sightseeing and then head back to the train station."

Portia glanced at her watch. "Relax, the train leaves at five. That gives us an hour, with time to spare."

Marga pulled a corn muffin wrapped in wax paper from her jacket pocket. Breaking off a piece, she offered some to Portia and Ilse, who both shook their heads.

"It tastes like sawdust," Portia remarked.

"In case you haven't noticed," Marga replied, "there isn't much to eat here."

"We'll be in Berlin the day after tomorrow and Karlshagen soon after," said Portia. "Mama salted away a leg of lamb for my return. You're both invited."

"I'll be there!" Ilse exclaimed as they walked along a canal.

"Me too," said Marga taking in the splendor of the Renaissance, Baroque, and Georgian brick homes with their plunging gabled roofs, lead-glass windows, and ornate chimneys. Before long, they were traversing Dam Square and found their way to Nieu Wendijk Street. Its medieval architecture housing quaint shops that once welcomed the world's tourists were now boarded shut. Despite the elegance fashioned over centuries by its wealthy mercantile class, Amsterdam felt staid, tired, and grubby. Mended laundry hung from windows. Garbage lay in alleys. Thin horses pulled creaky carts, and hunched pedestrians in threadbare clothes avoided eye contact, one woman going so far as to cross the street avoiding them.

"Did you see that?" Marga remarked. "That woman…"

"What about her?" Portia asked absently.

"She…"

"Come on!" Ilse waved to them as she trotted toward a canal bridge. "This will make a great shot!" She snapped a picture of Marga and Portia against a backdrop of colorful houseboats.

"Where shall we go next?" Ilse asked. They huddled around a weathered city map mounted to a light pole when a young man's voice called to them in broken but viable German. "Are you girls lost?"

They turned as two men in dark fatigues and caps with shouldered rifles approached. Armbands identified them as belonging to the para-military arm of the Dutch National Socialist Movement or NSB.

"We're just orienting ourselves," Ilse spoke up, sweeping a hand through her wavy auburn hair.

"Perhaps I can help," said the tall young Dutchman as he adjusted his field cap.

Still smiling, Ilse asked, "Have you a cigarette?"

The two Dutchmen exchanged smiles, and the tall one produced a pack and shook a cigarette loose for her.

"You?" He offered Marga.

"No, thank you."

"I'll have one," said Portia, helping herself.

"You're sure?" he again asked Marga.

She shook her head as she shielded her eyes against the setting sun.

Taking a deep drag, the sentry remarked to Ilse, "Your friend doesn't say much."

"Marga, dear," said Ilse. "Say hello to…?"

"Morten," he said.

Marga politely smiled, then walked away, her attention drawn to a building in the distance.

"Shy girl," he remarked to Ilse.

"What exactly is that place?" Marga pointed toward a high barbed-wire fence partitioning the city. "That building…with turrets and spires. It's so…curious."

Morten stepped alongside her. "It's the Jewish Quarter and that building is called the Waag. It's famous and the oldest in the city." He sucked on his cigarette. "The plaza around it has served as a market for centuries."

"And now it's a ghetto?" Ilse asked.

"You can smell it when the wind blows," Morten replied. "Word is, they'll all be gone soon."

"Gone?" said Marga.

With smoke pouring through his nose, Morten nodded.

Portia cleared her throat. "I know! Marga, take a picture of us!"

"What...?"

"*Schnell, schnell!*" Portia snapped her fingers as she and Ilse huddled together with the two Dutchmen.

Marga aimed the box camera. "Smile," she said and took the picture.

"Now, one of us!" Morten exclaimed, motioning Marga over to him.

"Go," Portia said, taking the camera. Marga stood alongside the sentry, who wrapped an arm around her. As Portia snapped the picture, Morten firmly squeezed Marga's buttock.

"Hey!" Marga yelped spinning around.

He chuckled. "Now, Fräulein, you'll always remember that photo!"

Marga tugged at her skirt and moved away from him. "Shall we go?" she muttered to her companions.

"Oh, come. Let's stay and chat," said Ilse. She leaned toward Marga's ear and whispered, "He really likes you."

Marga smirked. "Stay and chat then. I'm taking a closer look at that Waag place."

"Where is your friend going?" Morten asked.

Drawing on her cigarette, Ilse shrugged. "She's being a real tourist."

As Marga crossed the canal, her stomach growled, and she dug out the corn muffin. Approaching the barbed wire fence, the shabby buildings within the enclosure, many abandoned and missing windows and sideboards, stood out to her. Men in frayed coats and hats stood around like hobos, tending small fires, while skinny children ran around the former market's open spaces kicking a ball while chased by a scruffy brown terrier.

Chewing her muffin, Marga admired the Waag's brick turrets and slate-tiled buttresses. She was reaching for her camera when a young voice said to her, "Care for a tour, Fräulein?"

Marga looked down to see a boy and young girl peering through strands of rusty wire.

"You speak German?" Marga asked.

"*Ja!* Our mother is from Hamburg. I'm Josef, and this is my sister, Karla. I'm twelve…she's ten."

Marga found it hard to smile at the girl. She looked smaller than her age. Pale and thin, her eyes large and resigned, she wore a faded tan coat with wooden peg buttons that, like her brother's, had a yellow star stitched to its lapel. Marga followed the girl's saucer-like eyes to her corn muffin.

"Here," said Marga, holding forth the muffin.

"What are you doing?" Ilse shouted as she approached.

Marga turned. "She's just a child."

"They're urchins!"

"She's hungry—look at her!"

"Marga, step back," Ilse demanded. "They have lice, and God knows what else!"

"Halt!" a man shouted.

They turned. An NSB officer fast approached.

The girl in the tan coat suddenly snatched Marga's corn muffin and took off running with her brother at her heels.

"Halt!" the NSB officer yelled as his hobnail boots clattered over ballast stones. The fleeing siblings never broke stride and disappeared between two buildings.

Storming forward, the NSB officer grabbed Marga's arm. "You're under arrest!"

Portia came running over. "Arrest?"

"Let me go!" Marga cried, jerking her arm free.

The sentry blew a whistle, and soon two more guards rushed over.

"She handed contraband through the wire!" said the officer.

"Contraband?!" Marga protested. "She...she took my corn muffin!"

"You're coming with us," the officer said.

"You can't arrest her," Portia cried. "We have a train to catch!"

"Step aside!" the guard said, pulling Marga by the arm.

"Portia...?"

"Marga...!"

A security guard blocked Portia's path and in a surly voice announced, "Be a good Fräulein and go catch your train!" He glared at Ilse. "Both of you!"

"But...but..." Portia stammered.

"Go!" the guard shouted, pointing his nightstick off in the distance. "And don't come back!"

CHAPTER 52

As he stood gazing in the mirror over the sink of his Amsterdam hotel bathroom, Ullie was haunted by thoughts of the V2s he'd helped launch over the past few days. *How many had died? How many homes and lives had been destroyed?*

The images of soaring rockets were interrupted when an envelope slipped from the hallway under his door reflected in the mirror. Toweling his face, he snatched up the envelope from the floor and opened it. Inside was a single slip of paper with a message typed in code.

AN7GH UT5YH OP3MB JU8LP WS2HN WH7BV PQ6TY RV0PO KX2BN

He quickly reached for his shoes and detached a rubber heel, prompting a cipher key to drop into his hand. Carefully correlating letters and numbers from a grid, he deciphered the message.

12 - Δ Hazen/Eland – 2100 – Green Scarf – 10 x 3 – Tulips – Yuletide

He didn't dare smile, afraid that he had misunderstood the message: Starting the 12th of the month…tonight. He was to be at the corner of Hazan and Eland Streets at 9 P.M. The contact, wearing a green scarf, would wait ten minutes before leaving and would repeat the process over three nights. The challenge and passwords were Tulips and Yuletide.

Ullie's sprits soared. *Thank God! They're coming for me!*

Suddenly, there came a knock at the door.

Ullie tensed. "Who is it?"

"Hotel management," replied a man's voice in German.

Ullie quickly gathered his message and cipher.

Another knock. "Dr. Mainz, please open the door."

Ullie darted into the bathroom, balled up the incriminating evidence, and dropped both items into the toilet. The sound of rattling keys alerted him, and he flushed the toilet.

"Dr. Mainz!" A man charged into the bathroom with a second one following behind him. Both had silver Gestapo badges dangling around their necks.

"You're under arrest!" The first man said, grabbing Ullie's arm.

"On what charges?"

"We'll decide once we've chatted. Come along."

Ullie shrugged his arm free. "I'm to join my missile battery in the morning…in Amstelveen. We're staging for an offensive into Belgium."

The Gestapo agent took hold of his arm and chuckled. "I'm sure everything will be cleared up by then, Herr Doctor."

"Wait!" the other man said. "What's this?" Ullie saw the envelope that had contained the message was still lying on the floor. The observant one picked it up and waved it in Ullie's face. "What was in this?"

Ullie cleared his throat and shrugged. "It was under the bed. Remind me to speak with housekeeping."

Through a dubious frown, the man pocketed the envelope and said, "Get dressed, Herr Doctor. We're taking a ride."

* * *

They drove through Amsterdam's silent, drab streets to a squat brick police station with rusted iron bars on its windows and a black SS banner over the entrance.

"Who have you brought us now?" asked a dour mustached desk sergeant in the black para-military uniform of the NSB. He spoke German with a noticeable Dutch accent and sat behind a wooden pulpit overlooking the cramped foyer where Ullie stood sandwiched between the two Gestapo men.

One of the Gestapo agents reached up and handed the desk sergeant a form. "This man is to be held until retrieved by representatives of the Sicherheitsdienst."

The desk sergeant raised a pair of reading glasses and eyed the form. "How long will he be with us?"

"A day or two. No one is to talk to him or..." The Gestapo man cleared his throat. "Let's just say we want him to remain healthy. Understood?"

The desk sergeant smirked then turned to a corporal seated behind a desk in the corner and instructed him to place Ullie in Cell B.

The corporal took Ullie by the arm and led him through an iron door and into a cellblock with three small jail cells.

On entering, Ullie's eyes adjusted to the dim lighting. Suddenly, a soft and familiar feminine voice spoke to him. "Ullie?"

He turned.

"It *is* you!" Marga blurted out, clutching the bars of her cell.

"Marga? What are you doing here?"

"Quiet!" the corporal exclaimed. He shoved Ullie into the cell next to Marga's and slammed the door shut. He pointed at Ullie and then at Marga and then placed a finger over his lips.

They waited until the corporal left, closing the cellblock door behind him.

"Ullie!" She thrust out her hands through the bars of her cell.

"What in the world are you doing here?" he asked, reaching out and clutching her hands.

"Oh, Ullie, I don't know! I gave children some cornbread… They took it from me and ran. They were Jewish—it's a crime to give them food. Though, if you'd seen them…so pale and skinny…I felt so sorry for them."

"Did anyone come for you?"

Marga withdrew her hands and sighed. "Our train was to leave at five. I heard a steam whistle headed east. I'm sure it was them."

"Don't lose hope. I won't be here long. Perhaps I can get you out."

"Wait! What are *you* doing here?"

He lowered his voice. "Marga, do you recall the Adlon…What I had you memorize?"

"Oh, Ullie…They know!"

"Listen to me. I don't have time to explain but I'm to be extracted."

"Extracted?"

"Beginning tonight, at nine, for three nights, a contact will appear at the corners of Hazan and Eland, remain for ten minutes, and then depart. If you can, get there! The contact will have a green scarf. Say the word *tulips*. They should answer with *yuletide*."

She pressed her face against the iron bars in a desperate but unsuccessful bid to see him. "What are you talking about? Tulips... yuletide?"

"It's a challenge and password."

"What about you?"

"If I make it and you don't, I'll come back the next two nights—I promise."

"Ullie..."

"Remember Berlin, Marga. What you know...it's importance!"

"But...!"

The sound of the cellblock door opening drew their attention.

Ullie quickly remarked, "Hazan and Eland, nine o'clock. Someone wearing a green scarf. You say, 'Tulips.' They answer, 'Yuletide.' If they fail to say it...run!"

The cellblock door clattered open, and the corporal entered followed by a uniformed military officer in a peaked cap and great coat.

"Herr Doctor!" said the officer, stepping around the corporal. "Are you alright?"

"I'm fine."

The corporal inserted a key into Ullie's cell door and swung it open.

"Let's go," said the officer. "We have missiles to launch."

Ullie stepped out of the cell. "How did you get me out?"

"Let's just say a certain general intervened on your behalf. Now come, I have a car waiting."

"Wait," said Ullie, turning to Marga who was peering out from her cell. "I know her family, and she's here on a terrible misunderstanding. I'm bringing her with us."

Marga straightened and smiled.

The officer clapped Ullie's shoulder. "I see your interest, Herr Doctor. Unfortunately, we're needed immediately in Amstelveen. Perhaps on the way back?"

Ullie turned to Marga. "Remember what I said."

Clutching her cell bars, she nodded and Ullie was led away.

CHAPTER 53

"Here you go…Fräulein!" It was Morten, the young sentry Marga had met earlier with Portia and Ilse. He slid a metal bowl under the cell door and handed her a dented spoon.

Marga picked it up and sniffed the bowl. It made her nauseous. She placed it back on the floor.

"Circumstances have changed, haven't they?" he said smugly.

"You're…Morten?"

"And you're Marga, with the nicest butt I've ever squeezed."

She frowned as she clutched the cell bars. "Morten, what's going to happen to me?"

"The charges against you are serious. Aiding Jews is a grave crime. It's why there's a fence, you know." He removed a pack of cigarettes from his pocket and shook one loose.

She clutched the bars tighter. She had to get him on her side. "But I didn't do anything!"

He lit the cigarette, blew smoke to the side and shrugged. "Perhaps, but a court may see otherwise. They're always looking for someone to make an example of…you know, a warning to others. You'll need someone to speak on your behalf."

Marga felt a surge of hope. "Would you?"

Grinning, Morten leaned his face through the bars. "Perhaps we can discuss it."

Marga eased back, deflated as she understood his implication.

He lowered his voice. "How about we go for a walk. I'll show you around. There's a good enlisted club where they still serve meat."

Still wary, Marga asked, "Why do you care what happens to me?"

He took a puff and smiled. "I believe you. Those little urchins took advantage of you."

"I…I don't want to get into any more trouble." She stepped away from the door.

He shrugged. "Suit yourself. By the way, they cut the lights at eight and…I see you don't have a bucket."

She was puzzled. "Bucket? What bucket?"

He seemed to relish telling her, "To relieve yourself."

The thought churned her stomach, which suddenly growled. She glanced at the fetid bowl of slop on the floor and envisioned herself sitting in a cold dark cell, hungry, with a bucket of her own… It seemed to make sense to take a chance on going with him. "You're sure I won't get into trouble?"

Morten placed his face between the bars. "I'll speak with the desk sergeant." He winked. "We're old pals."

* * *

"It's cold," Marga said. She hugged herself to keep from shivering as they walked the dark and deserted streets.

"Here," he said removing his field jacket and slipping it over her shoulders.

She pulled it tight. "Thank you."

He lit a cigarette. "You aren't going to try and run, are you?"

"Why would I do that? You were kind to get me out for a few hours." Even as she said it, Ullie's contact at the corner of Hazan and Eland came to mind. It then occurred to her that she had no idea where the two streets met. She grew anxious. Suddenly, she recalled the map mounted to a light pole she had referenced with Portia and Ilse. Come to think of it, she'd seen several across the city; likely holdovers from a time when tourists flocked to Amsterdam.

He gestured toward a gabled two-story brick building. "Here's the place."

They entered a dim café choked by the smell of beer and cigarettes. Most of its few patrons were young men in black uniforms like Morten's.

"Have you ever tried Dutch beer?" he asked as they sat at a table littered with crumbs, spilled beer, and overstuffed ashtrays.

Marga shook her head, pushing aside an ashtray.

He signaled for two mugs of beer. They appeared promptly, overflowing their suds onto the table.

"Good…?" He asked.

She nodded. "Fabulous."

Morten ordered them seared flank steak with mashed potatoes.

"I…I don't have any money," she said.

He smiled. "Relax…You're with me."

He waved to a group of young men in uniforms at a nearby table with whom he exchanged a few quick words in Dutch and they laughed. Marga suspected they'd shared a crude wisecrack at her expense.

The waiter returned with their dishes. Despite small portions, the food looked and smelled good. Not having eaten a proper meal in over a day, Marga savored the first bite.

"Do you like it?" Morten asked, one cheek bulging with mashed potatoes.

Marga nodded.

They finished in less than five minutes. Still hungry, Marga licked her fork.

He lit a cigarette and ordered more beer. "Do you like dancing?"

She shrugged. "I guess…I've haven't had much practice."

He glanced at his watch. "There's a small dance hall nearby. Let's try it."

She shifted anxiously in her chair. "I don't know. Maybe we should go back."

He tickled the back of her hand. "It's early. Do you really want to return to that dreary cell?"

She pictured herself sitting in the cold darkness beside her bucket.

He took a hearty swig and wiped his mouth. "You know? You might be here longer than you think."

"How so?"

"Even if you're released, train service is intermittent. The Allies frequently bomb the tracks, and the Resistance plays havoc with them." He smiled drawing on his cigarette. "It's why we shoot them on sight. Besides, seats are reserved for essential personnel. Are you essential?"

"My ensemble…they made it."

"They were on government orders. Bands often are." He shrugged. "A musician traveling alone is of less value than a soldier— or a head of cattle, for that matter. And that's supposing you're found innocent. If found guilty…"

Marga swallowed. Ullie's instructions thundered in her head. Somehow, she had to get to the corner of Hazan and Eland by nine. "This dance hall. Is it close by?"

He twitched a grin. "Just around the corner."

He paid the bill and they left. But after they rounded the corner, they continued walking for three more blocks, their footsteps echoing off the darkened buildings along a canal.

"I thought this place was close by," Marga said.

Someone suddenly whistled. They turned. Three men in black uniforms were walking toward them in the shadows. One hollered something in Dutch. Another smacked his lips with an exaggerated kiss.

Marga looked away. She sensed trouble.

"Come this way," he said, steering her toward a dimly lit footbridge over a canal tainted by the scent of brackish water.

The shadowy outlines of an amorous couple on the opposite end of the bridge drew Marga's eye. Her pulse quickened. "Morten, maybe you should take me back."

"Relax," he said, playfully pinning her against the rail.

"What are you doing?! Aren't we going dancing?"

He drew near. "Shhh…"

* * *

The Fa 223's growling engine and whumping rotor blades echoed off Amsterdam's Nieumarket Plaza as Freida jumped to the ground and strode to a waiting staff car. She was driven to a holding facility, where she descended cement steps into the basement followed by two Gestapo agents in trench coats.

"The room on the right," said one of the agents as they walked down a corridor.

Freida stepped into a cold, barren room with cement walls and a single lightbulb hanging from the ceiling. She raised her foot to find a tooth stuck to the bottom of her ankle boot. She shook it loose.

"You should keep a cleaner room," she snapped. "This place is filthy." She sniffed the air. "It smells like urine and vomit. Have you no pride?" She turned toward the man who was the reason for her visit. Stripped to the waist, his face swollen and bruised, Pieter Bakker sat in a rickety chair with his hands tied behind his back. His eyes were closed, as if he was in a trance. His breath was wheezy and shallow, and he stunk.

Freida stood over him. "Pieter…?"

He tilted his head back and groaned.

She gently stroked his head, smearing her fingertips with blood. "Pieter…" she drew close to his face. "Would you like to go home?"

The Gestapo agent at her side translated her words into Dutch.

He groaned.

"Pieter!"

He flinched.

"For whom do you work?"

He coughed and shook his head.

Freida stomped the heel of her boot into his bare foot.

He shrieked.

"Pieter!" she clutched his face. "I can help you, but you must tell me what I want to know!"

He winced. Tears rolled down his cheeks. He coughed, and pink spittle foamed over his lips.

"Pieter, it's time to go home...Yes?"

He nodded at the translator's words.

"Will you tell me what I want to know?"

A long pause followed. Freida gritted her molars and prepared to stomp his foot again, when Pieter muttered, "Yes..."

"Good," Freida said reaching into her jacket and retrieving a green scarf. "Let's start with this."

* * *

"Morten, no!"

"Relax," he muttered tightening his embrace.

Marga turned her head from side to side, avoiding his greasy lips. "I thought we were going dancing!"

His hand found her breast and he laughed. "You're my prisoner, remember?"

"Stop it!"

He pinned her against the rail, his breath thick with beer and cigarettes. He drew closer and said, "Kiss me."

Recoiling, Marga twisted her face away.

Yanking her close, he pressed his lips into hers and squeezed her breasts until they hurt.

"No!" Marga growled as she thrust a knee into his swollen crotch.

Morten staggered back. A flash of anger lit his eyes, and he lunged. Marga ducked—he sailed over her—falling headlong over the side but somehow, he managed to grab hold of a vertical rail support, leaving him dangling twenty feet over the canal.

Marga turned to run but he snatched her ankle. She fell to her knees then onto her stomach. Her heart racing, she clawed the ground—envisioning herself being yanked into the murky water where he might drown her.

"No!" she cried, raising her other leg and bashing her heel into Morten's clutching hand to no avail. Grunting and writhing, she repeatedly kicked him until he finally let go but he managed to hang onto the footbridge. Determined to be rid of him, she coiled her leg, like a cobra about to strike, and smashed her foot into his clutching fingers. He screamed and fell into the water.

She heard splashing and Morten shout, "German bitch!"

Scrambling to her feet, her limbs shaking, Marga regained her senses and began running, as fast as she could, into the night.

CHAPTER 54

Marga stood in the shadows opposite the corner of Hazan and Eland Streets with Morten's jacket firmly around her, blowing on her hands for warmth. She looked around anxiously and wondered if anyone had followed her after she'd spent several minutes studying a map on the side of a bus stop kiosk locating the place described by Ullie.

A clock tower pealed nine bells. She scanned her surroundings. *Ullie, where are you?*

A figure appeared at the corner. Marga held her breath. *Ullie?* She cautiously approached. *Yuletide…Yuletide…Yuletide.* She slowed her gait. It wasn't Ullie. Feeling vulnerable, she glanced at an adjacent alley and the nearest escape route.

"Who are you?" a woman's voice asked in German. She stepped from the shadows, and a streetlamp revealed her disfigured face, a black eye patch, and a green scarf around her neck. "Where's Mainz?"

Marga caught her breath. "I…I don't know. Ullie told me to come. He said starting at nine…"

The woman drew her pistol and cocked the hammer.

"Wait! I have the same information!"

She looked Marga up and down. "Where is it…your pockets?"

Marga took a calming breath. "I have it memorized."

"Memorized?" The woman lowered the gun. "Who exactly are you?"

"My name is Marga. Marga Toth and…"

"Go on."

Marga lowered her voice. "Tulips…"

A puzzled look crossed the woman's face. "What?"

"Tulips." Ullie's words rattled in Marga's head. 'You say tulips— they answer yuletide. If they fail to say it…run!'

Smirking, the woman raised her gun but was interrupted when a radio crackled from the shadows and an excited voice jabbered through its speaker. "It's Mainz! He's on the train platform!"

The woman swung a walkie-talkie to her face and shouted, "Get him!"

A sudden breeze fluttered the green scarf over the woman's face.

It was the break she needed and Marga bolted into the alley running hard.

CHAPTER 55

A steady wind swirled through Amsterdam's Central Station rail platforms where screeching iron wheels, clanging bells, and hissing jets of steam competed with loudspeakers announcing arrivals and departures. Standing alongside the uniformed officer who'd secured his release, Ullie glanced at an overhead clock. 9:05 p.m. He looked down at his document case and thought of Marga... *Had she somehow made it to Hazan and Eland?*

The shriek of a porter's whistle drew his attention to the approach of three men in trench coats and fedoras, their silver Gestapo badges swinging around their necks. He recognized two of the men who'd arrested him hours earlier in his hotel. One pointed at him.

A Dutch voice announced through an overhead speaker, "Now arriving on Track 5 from Delft..."

He was sure they were there to re-arrest him—'Spy rings are like musical chairs,'—Ursula's voice played in his mind. 'Eventually the music stops.' Clutching his leather case, Ullie jumped from the platform onto the tracks and ran.

"Halt!" a Gestapo man shouted.

Ullie's hat flew off as he hurdled over iron rails and plunged into oily steam clouds making it difficult to see where he was going. His only thought—to escape.

A gunshot echoed. People screamed. Porters dropped their bags. Everyone ducked.

"Arriving...Track 5...Train 421 from Delft," announced the speaker.

"Halt!"

More shots rang out.

Surrounded by the clatter of iron wheels and ringing bells, Ullie darted through the billowing steam when a searing light bleached his eyes. Stunned, he stood frozen in place, clutching the leather case to his chest. He braced as the train rolled forward, its whistle blaring before everything went black.

CHAPTER 56

Bursting into a plaza, her heart pounding and limbs shaking, Marga spied a green door leading into a four-story brick building. Her footsteps echoing, she raced for it and shouldering open the door, charged up a set of stairs.

Fast-moving footsteps echoed below her as she reached the top floor. Suddenly, she heard the voice of the disfigured woman from Hazan and Eland. "Cover the plaza! Hans, come with me!"

Marga flung open a door leading onto a steep tiled roof with a wooden walkway running the length of the long, narrow ridge-line. She trotted along the walkway until she reached the roof's edge. Balancing herself, she eyed the distance to the neighboring building and cursed her luck—it was too far to jump. Suddenly, the door leading onto the roof flew open. Marga ducked as the woman with the green scarf and the man presumably named Hans charged forward.

"Wait here!" she heard the woman say. "In case she doubles back!"

Marga stooped and scrambled down the angled roof as the woman's footsteps rattled the walkway.

"Marga! You have nowhere to go!"

Marga stooped behind a brick chimney, then descended to the roof's edge. Clambering along gutters, a tile dislodged and crashed onto the plaza. Men in overcoats, their guns drawn, ran toward the sound.

The overcast abruptly parted, and moonlight flooded the rooftop.

"Marga!" the woman shouted.

Marga bolted, breaking and dislodging tiles until she reached an angled cornice overlooking the plaza. Looking around desperately, she scrambled for the ridgeline. A man's silhouette suddenly appeared above her, and she crouched behind a clay stovepipe chimney.

"You're trapped!" the woman bellowed 20 feet beneath her, balancing precariously on the edge of the building. She aimed a flashlight at Marga, momentarily blinding her.

"Come up!" Hans hollered from the ridgeline. He brandished a gun.

Marga looked at him, then at the woman, then at the neighboring building.

"I know what you're thinking!" the woman yelled as she inched forward. "You'll never make it!"

Rising to flee, Marga slipped. To break her fall, she grabbed onto the chimney, which broke free in her arms just as the woman was charging up the roof's incline. Bracing herself, Marga flung the chimney and knocked the woman off her feet, sending her tumbling over the roof's edge.

"Hans! Help me!" the woman shouted as she dangled from a copper gutter four stories above the plaza.

Hans slid down to help his accomplice while Marga clambered on all fours toward the ridgeline and its wooden walkway.

"Shoot her!" the woman yelled.

Hans wheeled and fired. The bullet smacked into something behind Marga. It had just missed her.

Halting at the edge of the roof, Marga stared at the chasm between her and the neighboring building. Her heart pounding, she stepped back to calculate the distance when she stumbled over a discarded plank.

Grunting, she lifted the heavy twenty-foot plank. It smacked with a loud clap onto the opposite ledge, bridging the fifteen-foot gap between the two buildings. She gave it a good shake, wiped sweat from her brow, and stood on the plank. Behind her, she could hear hurried, uneven footsteps rattling over the roof tiles. Taking a deep breath, she looked straight ahead, extended her arms at her sides, and began to walk forward careful not to look down at the alley 50 feet below. She could feel the board waddle with every careful step.

Suddenly, a gunshot echoed from the plaza. The board jerked and splinters flew out, hitting her face. Marga crouched down and clutched the board. More shots rang out. She rose to her feet and ran across the bouncing plank, tumbling onto the flat asphalt roof. Jumping up, she grabbed the board and sent it crashing down below before zigzagging across the roof as gunshots sounded behind her.

Marga soon reached an exit door and tried the knob. It wouldn't budge. She threw her weight into the door, but it held firm. Swiping hair from her eyes, she looked about frantically. A wooden toolbox sat tucked against a cornice. She dropped to a knee and dumped out its contents. A pry bar bounced off her foot. Snatching it, she jammed its tapered edge into the doorjamb and yanked. Wood cracked but the door held. Cursing, she tried again, forcing the pry bar along the edges. Finally, the splintering of wood announced deliverance.

She threw aside the pry bar and shoved open the door only to find herself in a pitch-black landing with the tops of metal handrails barely visible. She grabbed them and raced down a set of steps to a landing where light shone from under a door. *Please be unlocked! Please!* She grabbed the doorknob with both hands and fiercely twisted. It turned easily, and she stumbled through the doorway into a drafty, dimly lit corridor.

Spotting a stairwell, she ran down its steps when a stampede of footfalls and excited voices echoed from below. She wheeled around to return to the corridor and noticed a wall-mounted garbage chute. Ripping off Morten's jacket, she yanked open the hatch and flung it through. Suddenly, footsteps rattled on the stairs leading from the roof.

Feeling faint, Marga trotted along the corridor, which was lined with apartment doors. She tugged at a doorknob—it was locked. She tried another—nothing. *Oh, please!* Her knees weakened. She snatched another knob—it turned! She pushed her way inside and closed it behind her.

"Lara?" a woman's voice asked.

Marga froze as she faced a small woman in her forties who stood in the middle of a small, modestly furnished apartment. Shouts and jogging footsteps echoed in the hallway. The rattle of doorknobs followed Marga's trail.

"Quick!" said the woman motioning for Marga to follow her into the bathroom.

Despite the woman speaking Dutch, Marga understood her gesture and hurried after her. The woman pulled back the shower curtain, pushed Marga into the stall, and pulled the curtain shut. She turned off the light and closed the door.

Two men burst through the apartment door. "What's the meaning of this?" the woman demanded.

"Have you seen a girl?" one of them asked excitedly.

Acting drunk, the woman wrinkled her face and clapped her hands to her hips. "No, but I see you…" She burst out laughing.

The second man leaned over a counter and peered into the tiny kitchen before stepping around the woman to open the bathroom door.

"Hey!" the woman protested. "I'll tell Uncle Adolf on you!"

The man flipped on the bathroom light, looked around, and then snatched the shower curtain when a man charged into the apartment and yelled in German, "Come! She's crawled down the garbage chute!"

The men rushed out the door and were gone.

Marga waited, trying to calm her breathing when suddenly, the shower curtain ripped open and the woman, her eyes alight and harried, stood facing her.

CHAPTER 57

"My name is Marga."

The woman dipped a dishcloth into a bowl of water and wiped the soot from Marga's cheek as they sat on the sofa together. "I'm Jana. You're safe here."

"You speak German," Marga commented.

"My husband. He came during the last war and never left. Besides, I've had five years of occupation to practice."

Feeling awkward, Marga took the cloth and dabbed the scrapes and scratches on her hands and shins. "I'm sorry for barging in…I should go."

"You'll stay until it's safe for you to leave." Jana looked Marga over. "By the way, how old are you?"

Marga straightened up. "Eighteen."

Jana sighed. "She'd have been just about your age…"

Marga studied Jana's small delicate face creased with thin lines and asked, "Who would?"

Jana's smile betrayed regret. Her lips parted to speak but she stopped herself. She stood up. "You'll forgive me, dear, but you're a bit of a mess."

Marga looked down at her torn skirt and sooty hands and knees.

"There are towels in the bathroom. Help yourself."

"I…I really couldn't impose."

"I'll say it bluntly then. You need to wash up."

Jana went into her bedroom and came back with a light-blue wool skirt with a matching jacket and a white blouse, all of which she handed to Marga. "Now go."

When Marga had finished showering and came out of the bathroom wearing the clean clothes, she found Jana in the kitchen making eggs.

"Those clothes fit you well."

"I can't thank you enough." Marga ran her hands over the lovely fabric.

"You must be hungry."

"I couldn't impose."

Jana shook her head and placed the sunny-side-up eggs on plates with soda crackers. "Eat," she said, handing Marga one of the plates. "It's not much, but it'll keep us going."

They ate silently on the sofa. Marga looked around the modestly appointed apartment. The room contained two chairs, a sofa, coffee table, floor lamp, and small slant-top desk. An inexpensive watercolor of a cityscape with orange-tiled roofs, the kind bought from a sidewalk artist, hung on the wall. Squinting, Marga read the word ROTTERDAM etched along the bottom.

A battered violin case beneath the desk caught her attention.

Marga cleared her throat. "Can I ask you something?"

Jana nodded as she dipped a cracker into the egg yolk.

"When I came in, you thought I was Lara."

Jana's expression flattened. She wiped her mouth and reached into a small wooden box on an end table for cigarettes and matches. She offered one to Marga, who declined. Jana lit her cigarette. "She was my daughter. She'd be seventeen now. Her brother, Mateus, fifteen."

Marga set down her plate.

"They were home that day. My husband too…he was a book-keeper. We lived in Rotterdam." A distant, nostalgic glimmer played in her eyes. "I was out shopping when this strange humming filled the sky. People began running and screaming." Jana's hand quivered as she drew on her cigarette. "I didn't know what to do. Someone pushed me inside a building where we crowded into a cellar and listened as our city collapsed around us."

A knot formed in Marga's throat. She recalled theater newsreels hyping the conquests of France, Holland, and Belgium with images of victorious German soldiers goose-stepping through defeated cities, touring museums, climbing the Eiffel Tower, and snapping photos of Holland's tulip markets.

"I made it home days later. After the fires died, there was nothing left." She took a final drag and crushed out her cigarette. "The bastards flattened our city."

"I'm…sorry," said Marga, ashamed.

Jana fell into a trance, staring deep into the past.

"I notice you have a violin."

Jana looked at it and shook her head. "It was Lara's."

"I play," Marga said.

"Do you?" Jana stood and retrieved the battered case. "It was one of the few things I salvaged from the ashes of our home." She held the case with reverence.

"May I?" Marga asked reaching for it.

Jana hesitated before handing it to her.

Placing it on her lap, Marga ran her hand over the scratched and blistered case, as if feeling its traumatic past, before opening it and releasing the faint odor of smoke. The instrument had survived unscathed. She removed it from the case. A sheet of music lay folded beneath it. Marga pulled it out. Pachelbel's "Canon in D."

Jana wiped a tear. "She was learning it at the time."

"Would you do me the honor of letting me play it for you?"

Jana hesitated before she nodded.

Marga laid the sheet music on the coffee table, tucked the violin beneath her chin, and gently moved the bow across the strings. She tweaked the violin's pegs, strummed the strings again, made another adjustment, and then proceeded to play a slow, melodic rendition of the song.

Tears welled up in Jana's eyes as Pachelbel's classic resonated from Marga's fingers. After strumming the final note, Marga lowered the instrument.

Wiping her eyes, Jana smiled. "Lara would have liked that very much."

"I believe our departed love ones watch over us, so I'm sure she did," said Marga returning the violin to its case.

Jana lit another cigarette, took a drag, and asked, "Now, dear, what's your story? You're a long way from home, and the Gestapo wasn't chasing you for an overdue library book."

Marga averted her eyes. "I…I don't want to burden you."

Jana sat back and folded her arms. "Well, seeing as I took you in, I think I'm entitled to some explanation."

Picking at the sofa fabric, Marga gathered her thoughts, and then briefly summarized the story of her traveling orchestra and the events that led her to Jana's doorstep.

"Are you a spy?" Jana asked directly.

Marga's pulse quickened. Was she being set up?

"You're not the only one taking risks. You brought the Gestapo to my door. I harbored you. I might as well be dead."

Marga bowed her head.

Jana then sighed and placed a hand on Marga's knee. "It's okay, dear. I won't ask you to put either of us in any more danger."

In the distance, a church bell tolled, and Jana checked the desk clock. "Let's get to bed." She brought Marga a pillow and blanket. "It's not the Savoy"—she nodded to the sofa—"but it'll do. Sweet dreams, dear."

CHAPTER 58

Marga awoke to an empty apartment. Jana's bedroom door was open and there was no sign of her.

She looked out a window to find a gray and sullen skyline, the once-great city of Amsterdam looking especially bleak. Canals once vibrant with commercial and pleasure craft were now empty and like their surrounding neighborhoods, neglected. In the distance, shabbily clad people were rummaging through mounds of refuse, digging and scraping for firewood or anything of possible value.

Marga got dressed. Studying her reflection in the bathroom mirror, she thought her face looked thin and her straw-colored hair lacked its usual luster. She noticed a pimple on her cheek and picked at it. Her stomach growled. Hunger suddenly became more pressing than vanity.

Hours passed. Marga dozed on the couch. She played the radio softly and listened to censored reports of fighting in France and Belgium.

When she finally heard a key jangling in the front door, Marga's heart jumped.

"Hungry?" Jana asked as she closed and latched the door. She held up a paper sack.

"I'm fine," Marga lied, sitting up and fixing her hair.

Jana stepped to the kitchen and removed a small bundle of wax paper from the bag. "This is almost impossible to come by." She held up two silvery fish. "Shad. A friend of mine fishes the channel. They're small but meaty. I'll make soup from the heads."

Marga approached the kitchen. "I hope you didn't..."

Jana raised her brow. "Go through the trouble for you?"

Marga felt foolish. "I'm sorry...I meant to say, you're very kind, thank you."

Preparing the fish, Jana announced, "I needed a reason to go out. No one goes for walks unless there's a purpose—food, water, firewood. Someone is always watching."

"I'm sorry to put you at risk."

Jana glanced over her shoulder. "It served its purpose. You leave tonight."

"What do you mean?"

"No questions, dear." She lit the stove and placed the fish into a frying pan. "It appears the Germans aren't the only ones looking for you."

"I...I don't understand. Who else could possibly...?"

The fish sizzling, Jana shook the pan. "Our friends, the British."

Marga immediately thought of Ullie. "Did you learn if...I mean, is there anyone else?"

Sprinkling brine crystals over the fish, Jana shrugged. "I don't know but"—she turned to Marga—"they definitely want you."

* * *

Embraced by night's velvet cloak, they strolled past the red brick stock exchange on Damark Street and then St. Nicholas Church. They paralleled the Oudezzijds Voorburgwal, a tree-lined canal with some of Amsterdam's finest gabled homes before reaching a footbridge overlooking the Zwanenburgwal Canal where Jana pointed to the nebulous outline of a boat.

"Are you a friend?" Jana called out toward the water in a hushed tone.

"A friend of Jehovah," came a reply.

Jana turned to Marga. "Down you go."

"And you?" Marga asked, clutching the violin case Jana had given her.

Jana touched Marga's cheek. "I'll be right behind you."

The boat shoved off and followed the narrow waterway to where it fed into the breadth of the North Sea Canal. Gliding through a moist chilly mist, it reached a row of moored houseboats and was tied up to one with a green light on its prow.

The boatman helped the two women disembark. Jana told him to wait for her. She then escorted Marga along a narrow side deck to the door of the houseboat. She knocked.

* * *

Seated in a corner concealed in shadows, Farrington dozed when there came a knock on the door of the houseboat. He reached under his buttoned coat and gripped the butt of his semi-automatic pistol.

Standing by the door, Anna gave him a look.

"Open it," he said.

Drawing her pistol from a shoulder holster, Anna tucked the weapon behind her and opened the door.

* * *

The door opened and a blond woman stuck her head out.

"Is Marigold here?" Jana asked in Dutch.

The woman stepped back and motioned her and Marga into a large, narrow room lit by an oil lamp and two candles. Heavy cloth curtains covered the windows.

"Have a seat." Marga was startled by the sound of a man's voice as he emerged from a shadowy corner into the light. His German betrayed a hint of an English accent.

The woman replaced her pistol into her shoulder holster and motioned Marga and Jana to a banquette with a table on which sat an empty wine bottle and two glasses.

The man asked Marga, "What's your name, Fräulein?"

Marga turned to Jana.

Jana nodded.

"My name is Marga Toth and…Oh, please! Can you tell me if Ullie is safe?"

"Right now, *you* are my assignment," he said.

"But I'm only here because of him. He's the one you really want."

The man shook his head. "I have to go with what I have, and you're it."

"But do you know what's happened to him?"

"All I can tell you is, he never showed. You did."

Jana gently stroked Marga's shoulder. "Promise me you'll make beautiful music with that violin."

Marga smiled. "I'll always treasure it. Thank you. You've been so kind."

Jana faced the two strangers and gave a nod.

Turning for the door, Marga took her arm. "Are you going to be alright?"

Jana touched her cheek tenderly. "I always find a way, dear. You take care of yourself. And if you're ever again in Amsterdam..." She kissed Marga's forehead and exited the houseboat.

* * *

Farrington returned to his corner and sat down. Marga settled on the banquette.

Anna paced the room anxiously and suddenly announced, "I'm going out."

"Out where?" he asked her in English—confident Marga couldn't understand them.

She shot him a stern glance. "Yours isn't my only business on this trip."

"It's not part of the plan," he reminded her.

She looked at Marga. "The plan is working fine." She again pulled the semi-automatic pistol and retracted the magazine before locking it back into place. "You two should rest."

Farrington stepped forward. "Anna, you could be stopped and questioned." He shot Marga a sudden look. He'd just revealed Anna's name and sensed the girl had picked up on it. He chided himself for his carelessness. If they were caught by the Germans, a name, even a first name, with a physical description, could cause serious problems.

He turned to Anna and shook his head. "No, it's too risky."

"I got you here, remember? I'm Dutch, I know my way around."

"Perhaps I should go with you."

"No!" She paused. "I'll be fine."

"Yorick told me about your youngest brother… his disappearance."

Anna gave Farrington a hard stare. "He most likely drowned in an irrigation canal. I warned him against taking shortcuts."

"But you aren't sure."

"Like I said, yours isn't my only business at hand." Anna returned the pistol into its holster and put on her coat. "I shouldn't be more than an hour—two at most." She turned for the door.

"Anna…"

She turned.

"Be careful."

* * *

Marga watched Anna leave. The man poured himself a shot of Jenever, a Dutch gin. He took a sip and faced her. "You aren't carrying much." He nodded to her violin case. "Is that what we're all risking our lives for?"

"No…no, sir."

"No?" He stepped into the oil lamp's glow.

"I have information."

He gave her a curious look and shrugged. "Where is it?"

"I have it memorized."

"Is it a formula?"

"I'm not at liberty to discuss it."

With an amused look, the man downed his drink. "Very well." He put down his glass. "Time for a little business." He stepped to a small leather kit bag, unzipped it, and retrieved a wrapped condom.

Marga sat up and fixed her gaze on the small package.

The man ripped open the wrapper and removed the condom.

"What…what's that for?" she asked. The realization that she was alone with a strange man suddenly hit her. Looking around for something to defend herself with, she snatched the empty wine bottle off the table and held it at her side.

Wrinkling his brow, the man reached into the kit bag and removed a cigar-sized metal cylinder. "If I don't do this, we won't be going anywhere."

Marga backed against the wall staring at him as he tugged and stretched the condom. She bit her lip and tightened her grip on the bottle.

He seemed puzzled. He looked at her, then at the condom, and then at her again. Suddenly, he laughed.

"Don't come near me!" Marga squealed, brandishing the bottle.

He slipped the condom over the cylinder and gave a twist and the condom began to fill up with air like a balloon. Next, he stood on a chair, reached for the ceiling, and pushed open a small hatch.

Eyes wide, Marga watched him tie a long string to the inflated condom before attaching the opposite end to a small square case she deduced was a transmitter.

"Time to let them know we'll need a ride home," he said.

Marga sat forward, fascinated.

He released the condom which floated up through the open hatch. "Our antenna," he told her tugging on the string. He then flipped a switch on the small box activating a light and he began tapping out a message in Morse code: -... .. .-. -.. / .. -. / .... .- -. -..

The message sent, he shut off the transmitter, pulled a pocketknife, and cut the string. The inflated condom soared into the night sky and he closed the hatch.

Chagrinned, Marga put down the wine bottle. "I apologize. I thought…"

Suppressing a grin, he reached for the Jenever and poured another shot. He motioned to the violin. "Is that a prop or do you play?"

"I do."

He sipped his drink. "What do you know?"

"What would you like?" She opened the case.

"How about, 'Carmen Etonese'?"

"Sorry, I don't know that one."

He chuckled. "I wouldn't think you would. It's my school song…Eton. How about 'Blue Danube.'"

Tucking the instrument under her chin, Marga passed the bow over the strings. She tweaked a peg, set her jaw, and began to play. Despite the violin's need of tuning, the notes flowed gracefully.

The man closed his eyes and appeared to be listening intently.

As the final note floated across the room, Marga looked at him.

"Bravo!" He clapped and smiled. "That was wonderful."

Replacing the violin into its case, Marga looked at the British agent. She liked him. His easy manner and quiet confidence made her feel safe.

He glanced at his watch. "Now, I suggest you get some sleep. I'll wake you in a few hours."

Clearing her throat, she asked, "I apologize, sir, but I don't know your name."

"Call me...Abe."

"Abe?" She wrinkled her brow. "Is that your real name?"

He smiled shaking his head. "No. It's just...the less you know..."

"I understand." She removed her coat, bundling it over her violin case to fashion a pillow. Stretching onto the banquette, she yawned and said, "*Gute Nacht, Herr Abe.*"

He finished off his Jenever and wiped his mouth. "Good night, Fräulein."

CHAPTER 59

Abe spirited her away after midnight in a long, narrow boat. Seated in the stern, he paddled quietly past quays, docks, and jetties. Sitting low in the bow clutching the gunwales and her violin, Marga gazed at Amsterdam's darkened skyline set against the bright flashes and faint rumbles of distant artillery on the horizon. With her jacket raised over her cheeks, she breathed in the cool, humid air and gazed at shimmering stars peeking through passing clouds.

For a moment, she caught sight of the moon and thought of her father, Dr. von Braun, and, of course, Ullie. She worried he had been arrested. She prayed for him and longed to hug him tight—and more—the next time they met. It allowed for a faint smile and blunted her fears at being drawn farther into the night and the unknown.

* * *

Farrington brought them ashore. He led Marga through marshy reeds and over a grassy embankment. He halted them along a drainage ditch and knelt, listening to the night. Suddenly, he cupped a hand around his mouth and made a bird-like sound. Within seconds, it echoed back from the darkness.

"Follow me," he whispered. They advanced, through marshy soil and a watery drainage ditch when three figures appeared before them, each cradling a machine gun.

"Where's Anna?" Yorick asked.

Marga gripped her violin as if she might have to use it as a weapon.

"Your sister said she had other business in town," said Farrington. "I couldn't wait around."

"You left her?"

"She broke protocol…I wasn't taking any chances."

"She shouldn't have!" Yorick glanced at his watch. "Come, it's almost time."

They hopped a stone wall, and crossed a shallow canal and a hedgerow before reaching a broad clearing on which small lamps formed an impromptu runway. Scanning the silvery overcast, Farrington turned to Marga. "Here's what's going to happen. An airplane is going to land. When I say 'Go,' follow me and stay close. These planes don't always stop. You might have to run alongside, grab a ladder, and climb into the rear compartment. I'll help you."

"But my violin," she said.

"If it's a problem, dump it. These pilots have nerves of steel, but they're squirrely. Any sign of trouble—they're gone."

"They're coming!" Yorick announced as the drone of a distant aircraft grew closer.

"Tell your sister, no hard feelings," Farrington said to him.

"Good luck," Yorick replied, and they shook hands.

* * *

Watching the exchange, Marga's limbs rippled with adrenaline. This was it. Her saga would be over shortly and she'd wing her way across the English Channel to safety.

The growl of the single-engine Lysander echoed over the field as it sank from the sky. Touching down, the engine changed pitch and it decelerated.

"Let's go!" Abe pulled Marga by the arm.

She followed him, trailing the three men who'd appeared out of the darkness. Suddenly, the rattling staccato of machine gun fire and muzzle flashes burst from a nearby hedgerow.

"*Ambush!*" Abe shouted. He turned his body to shield Marga.

"*Run!*" The bearded man cried out. He wheeled around to return fire when a salvo of bullets threw him into Abe's arms and the two men collapsed in a tangle of limbs. Marga staggered back. They appeared dead. Terrified, she turned and started to run.

"Halt!" cried a voice from the darkness. Shots rang out.

Marga stopped and threw out her arms in surrender. Just then, a bullet smashed her violin case, leaving her clutching only its handle. In the distance, the Lysander's engine roared and the plane took flight. Her heart sank.

"Yorick!" Anna shrieked, running out of the darkness. She fell to her knees and cradled the bloody head of the man who lay atop Abe. She sobbed hysterically.

"Hello, Marga." The tone was sarcastic, the female voice familiar.

Marga, now trembling, squinted into the beam of the flashlight being shone in her face.

"You could have saved us a lot of trouble and lives if you'd just surrendered on that roof," said the woman holding a revolver. Marga gasped. It was the disfigured woman with the green scarf from the corners of Hazan and Eland—who'd chased her across roof tops and now foiled her escape at a murderous price.

Anna jumped to her feet and shouted at the woman holding the gun when a gunshot lit the night and Anna collapsed.

Marga screamed and covered her face.

The flashlight revealed the now-still body of Anna, who lay with a smoking hole in her head, atop the bearded man, who covered the body of Abe.

Sickened, Marga dropped to a knee and vomited.

"Come, dear," said the woman sweetly, as she holstered her pistol. "We have things to do and little time to do them in." She turned and walked away.

Still kneeling and now shaking, Marga wiped her mouth when footsteps crunching through the frosty ground walked towards her and a man's voice asked, "Are you coming, Fräulein?"

Marga looked up. It was Morten. Her heart sank further.

He crouched and drew close. "You thought you outsmarted me." His tone dripped with mockery. "Now, once again, you're my prisoner...And we..." he stroked her cheek, "have unfinished business." He stood and offered his hand. "Let's go."

The whine of a spooling turbine engine filled the night as Marga was led toward a wingless airplane with a pair of twirling rotors.

"What is this thing?" Marga asked.

"Get inside!" the woman shouted over the rushing sound of rotor blades.

Sitting on the cold metal floor next to Morten and across from the woman, Marga clutched her skirt as the noise around her reached a deafening pitch. The strange craft rose to a hover, dipped its nose, and lurched skyward.

An hour later, they landed on the lawn of a deserted Dutch caretaker's house. It was guarded by six Dutch SS men who clustered around a truck and a black Steyr sedan. They smoked cigarettes and welcomed Morten into their group. Marga was led inside the house and into the parlor. Cold and damp, it was lit by a single candle and littered with broken glass, empty food tins, and cigarette butts.

"Sit," said the woman pointing to a wooden stool in a corner. "And don't move."

Marga stepped to the stool. A sudden rush of angst swept over her and she spun around, facing her tormentor. "Who are you and why are you doing this to me?"

The woman smirked, making her disfigured face even more deformed. Her lone eye narrowed and she reached into her jacket for a set of credentials and flashed them in Marga's face.

Marga read the name, Freida Geisler printed beneath a photo of a serious but beautiful woman. Stamped in bold letters alongside it—Sicherheitsdienst.

"Do you know what I do?" Freida pocketed her credentials.

Marga shook her head.

"I hunt spies and traitors, like Dr. Mainz."

Marga scowled.

"And, traitors like you…Marga."

"Me?"

"Save it! You knew what brought you to that street corner." She clutched Marga's face. "Now sit in that chair…And not another word from your pretty little mouth or…I swear…I'll break it."

CHAPTER 60

"You know Dr. Mainz was killed?" Gerhard Pringer's voice rattled through the telephone receiver Freida clutched to her ear.

"An unfortunate accident, Herr Colonel."

"You mean, General."

Freida smirked. "Congratulations."

"I'm told this girl has information…the same as Mainz."

What?! Freida gritted her teeth. *He knew! But how?* She took a calming breath. Even so, there was nothing he could do to stop her now.

"Where are you?" he asked.

Freida considered hanging up. She had divorced herself of Pringer and the Sicherheitsdienst. The Third Reich was through. And for its crimes and their perpetrators, harsh justice awaited. She glanced warily at the silhouettes outside in the darkness and wondered if somehow, one of them had tipped-off Pringer. In the same way he'd learned about Marga, he might still foil her plans.

She decided to remain in the fold—for now. "South of Ahaus," she told him. "Near the rail line."

"Ahaus?"

"We flew here. I'm currently securing fuel for the helicopter."

"Helicopter? Freida, listen to me! I'm pulling out a map." Paper rustled in the background as he got his bearings. "Get to Münster. Catch a train to Bremen. The rail lines to Hamburg are still open. *Get there!"*

"I don't understand, Herr General?"

"You don't need to understand! You just need to follow orders—*my* orders! Bring the girl to me!"

She thought about how to respond.

"Freida…? *Freida…?"*

Pringer's shouts faded away as she lowered the receiver and hung up.

✶ ✶ ✶

As artillery rumbled in the distance like an approaching storm, Freida looked at the frightened eyes staring back at her. So blue. Someone, somewhere believed they were the prettiest eyes they'd ever seen. Perhaps her mother or father. For an instant, Freida wondered what it would have been like to have parents to dote on her… to have buttoned her coat on cold, snowy days. Perhaps they'd have worried when she was late getting home from school or hiking the Black Forest. She wondered.

Freida noticed a twitch over Marga's temple. The girl was scared. She gently tugged the ends of Marga's hair. She was certainly Aryan and therefore redeemable. Besides, this silly teenage girl was her best, perhaps only, chance to save herself.

"You're frightened," Freida remarked.

Marga nodded.

"Don't be. You're worth a lot more to me alive than dead."

"What…what are you going to do with me?" Marga's voice quivered.

"I'm going to take care of you, which means you're going to do exactly as I say. *Ja?*"

Bracing herself, Marga cleared her throat and asked, "Where's Ullie?"

Freida looked at her.

Marga waited in anticipation.

"He's of no concern to you."

"I heard the radio that night. He was on the train platform. You ordered him arrested."

Freida scowled.

"Oh, please tell me! Is he alright?"

Freida twisted her deformed lips into a smirk and cupping Marga's chin, drew close to her and said, "He's dead."

CHAPTER 61

Pringer yanked open a file cabinet and flipped through folder tabs. His mind raced as he worked feverishly, pulling and checking files before pitching them aside. He thought of Petroshenko's recent coded communique instructing him to secure all documents pertaining to ballistic missiles. It was within his reach—especially now that he had a lead on the girl with the photographic memory harboring technical secrets. After the failure to secure V2 records from Nordhausen, and with von Braun and much of his team on the run, his best hope to avoid the hangman's noose lay in Marga Toth. The overhead lights suddenly flickered and dust rained from the ceiling. Berlin was under attack again. But he kept up his search. After an hour, the floor was littered with files.

Finally, he found it—a file titled SAFE HOUSE INDEX. Opening it, he ran a finger down neatly typed columns to the entry NORTH RHINE –WESTPHALIA. He stepped to the wall map and found Ahaus. If she'd lied, there'd be no finding her. But perhaps, just perhaps, she'd been a dutiful subordinate—at least up until she'd hung up on him. Maybe she really was where she'd claimed to be. He checked the list for safehouses south of Ahaus and close to Allied lines.

He zeroed in on a typed entry for House No. 8, a single-room cabin nestled in a wooded stretch of Wesel, 60 kilometers south of Ahaus. Stabbing it with a finger, he reached for the telephone.

"Colonel Filber! This is SS-Brigadeführer Pringer! I need your fastest plane for departure within the hour!"

"General, even if I—"

"Listen to me, Colonel!" Pringer smacked his desk. "I can have you, your wife, and two sons arrested from their Dahlem home in less time than it'll take for you to comply with my request!"

The colonel cleared his throat. "Fine, General. I have a two-seat Me-262 on standby at Gatow. However, I must tell you, if Field Marshal Göring were to call—"

"It's a jet aircraft, no?"

"Yes, twin engine."

"How fast does it fly?"

"Almost 500 kilometers per hour."

"I need to get to the vicinity of Münster—approximately 400 kilometers from Berlin. It could drop me and be back in less than two hours."

"General…it's not that simple. There are numerous considerations."

"Such as?"

"The pilot must chart a course, plot weather, and account for landing conditions. Not to mention, many of our airfields, particularly along our western borders, have been damaged and their runways are unusable."

"Your planes have instruments, Colonel. They can fly through weather and darkness. Besides, I don't intend to land at an airfield."

"Where do you plan to land, sir?"

Pringer shifted a map on his desk, carefully studying the lines drawn over it. "I was thinking the Reich Autobahn."

"The…the highway?"

"Oh, come, Colonel. You know damn well the Autobahn and other roadways have been used for some time as improvised runways. It was part of the reason they were built!"

"I understand, but there are thick clouds from here to the North Sea. A visual landing would be challenging, let alone an instrument approach. And onto the Autobahn?"

"This is a matter of utmost urgency, Colonel." Pringer glanced at his watch. "Call the airfield. I'll be there in less than an hour!"

"But, General!"

"You have your orders, Colonel! Now, follow them!"

CHAPTER 62

The rumble of the helicopter shook the house as it flew off into the night. Marga hoped that Morten was gone with it. She sat slumped on her wooden stool, her eyes and nose red from crying over Ullie, when Freida entered the room, stamped the night's chill from her feet, and announced, "Let's go."

Marga didn't move and simply stared at the floor.

"Did you hear me? Let's go!"

Marga looked up. "Why did Ullie have to die?"

Annoyed, Freida stood over her. "Because he was a stupid man!"

Marga shot to her feet. "He was no such thing!"

Freida slapped her. "You little sniveling mouse. You think choices have no consequences, but they do! Dr. Mainz paid for his choices with his life. Did you think you were simply going to steal one of our nation's most vital secrets and skip happily across the English Channel and give it away?"

Her cheeks burning, Marga retorted, "Isn't that what you're doing?"

"You were doing it to betray your country! I'm doing it to stay alive!"

"I'm happy to betray this country and its twisted leaders!"

Freida slapped her again even harder, then jabbed a finger into Marga's chest. "We're leaving, *now!*"

Marga followed her outside where a man in a Dutch NSB uniform, like the one worn by Morten, placed gasoline cans into the trunk of the Steyr sedan. Freida stuffed a canvas-covered wooden box with rattling glass bottles beside them.

Freida ordered Marga into the rear seat. She then spread a map over the car hood and studied it by flashlight with the man in the NSB uniform. Eventually, they folded up the map and got into the vehicle—he behind the wheel; Freida, clutching her holstered pistol, next to Marga.

The engine started and the sedan began to move.

"Do as I say from here on," Freida said turning to Marga. "And you just might live to see your next birthday."

CHAPTER 63

Inside a hangar on Berlin's western fringes, Major Ernst Rathenow was getting ready for his flight by studying a wall map of Germany and the route he'd overfly—from Berlin to Westphalia near the Dutch and Belgian borders. Behind him mechanics readied the Messerschmitt Me-262B for flight. Thirty-four feet long with a 40-foot wingspan and twin turbo-jet engines, it was the world's fastest airplane capable of soaring at 540 miles-per-hour. Rathenow had been one of the first in his squadron to transition from propeller-driven fighters to the jet and was now one of the *Luftwaffe's* most experienced pilots in the aircraft.

A wall-mounted telephone beside a metal locker abruptly buzzed.

"Rathenow," he answered.

"Major," said a meteorologist calling from the airfield's base operations. "You'll be in the clouds from here to the Dutch border. Hannover reports 2,000-meter ceilings, half-kilometer visibility, and their radio beacon is intermittent."

Scribbling notes, Rathenow asked, "And Münster?"

"There it's a 1,000-meter-ceiling with a quarter-kilometer of visibility. Pretty much the same to the French border."

"What about winds?"

"Not much in this soup unless you get over 20,000. Winds aloft are north-northwest at 50 knots."

"And the portable landing lights I requested?"

"A sergeant in Münster is wrangling them along with a radio beacon for your approach."

"Anything else?" Rathenow tucked his pen into a jacket pocket.

"A case of Beck's if you manage an instrument landing on the Autobahn in this weather. Good luck, Major."

"I like mine ice cold," Rathenow chortled.

He hung up and turned to the mechanics pushing his plane from the hangar. "Hold it!" He trotted toward the jet and ducked beneath its belly where he gave the external fuel tank a good shake. "You inspected for leaks, Udo?" He faced the mechanic kneeling beside him.

Wiping his hand over oil-stained coveralls, Udo nodded. "Double-checked seals and gaskets, and you're topped off with as much gas as this pig can carry, Herr Major!"

Brushing his hands, Rathenow emerged from under the jet and patted the plane's aluminum exterior. "Udo, this piggy is taking me to market…and hopefully back."

Udo thumped its wing. "If it doesn't, Major, it won't be for lack of fuel."

A door leading into the hangar suddenly clattered open and Colonel Filber escorted a general-officer towards Rathenow and his aircraft. The general carried a small travel case and had a Luger pistol holstered at his side. He sported a long, dark, leather coat and polished dress boots. The silver death's head insignia on his peaked cap glimmered under the hangar lights.

"Major Rathenow, this is SS-Brigadeführer Pringer," the colonel said as he handed Rathenow a slip of paper. "You are to fly him as close to this vicinity as possible."

"You'll land on the Autobahn," Pringer said without hesitation.

"I'll do what I can," said Rathenow.

"I'm told you're the best in this squadron," Pringer remarked.

"Perhaps, because I'm one of the few left alive, sir," said Rathenow.

"Let's hope that doesn't change tonight." Pringer glanced at the aircraft. "Now, Major, lead the way."

Rathenow adjusted dials and switches on the glowing instrument panel while Pringer settled into the cramped rear seat. Each wore a helmet connected to an intercom, and despite them each having their own plexiglass canopy, Pringer could reach and touch Rathenow. As a light rain fell, they taxied toward a darkened runway where a final transmission from Gatow's control tower cleared them for takeoff.

The roar of engines filled the cabin and in less than a minute, they were airborne.

* * *

Sinking back in his seat, Pringer reached down and felt the butt of his Luger. A troubling thought had rankled his senses since his decision to pursue Freida and her prize. If he failed to find the girl with the missile secrets—he might as well be dead. He pulled the Luger and let its weight rest in his hand.

There was no coming back.

CHAPTER 64

Marga awoke when the sedan stopped outside a whitewashed cottage in the woods. Freida got out and motioned her inside. Stepping from the vehicle, Marga eyed the clapboard structure that was little more than a hunting cabin nestled in a clearing surrounded by thick forest. They entered the cottage and Freida lit a kerosene lamp, which she placed on a fireplace mantel on the rear wall. The floorboards creaked beneath Marga's cautious footsteps as she stepped around swarms of dead insects and yellow newspapers littering the floor. Two chairs and a rickety table provided the room's only furniture.

The driver came in with Freida's canvas-covered wooden box and set it on the table. "Top off the gas tank," she told him.

He nodded and exited the cottage.

"Have a seat." Freida pointed to one of the chairs, and Marga sat down in it. Freida reached into her jacket pocket for a small aluminum tube labeled Pervitin and shook two white pills, tossing them into her mouth. It was the third time Marga had seen her take these pills—they seemed to make her even more aggressive than usual and lent her lone blue eye a wild look.

"You haven't told me where we're going?" said Marga.

Freida ignored her as she did something out of Marga's view inside the wooden box that rattled with glass bottles.

The sound of the sedan's trunk closing drew Freida's attention. She turned to Marga, drew her revolver, and ejected its cylinder. Bringing it close to her eye, she gave it a quick spin before slapping it back into place. "Stay here," she said.

She couldn't see them, but Marga heard Freida and the driver exchange words. The driver laughed. Suddenly, *one…two…three* gunshots rang out.

Marga ran outside.

"Get inside!" Freida barked. She was standing over the driver, who lay face down on the ground, a halo of blood pooling around his head.

Marga couldn't bring herself to move. She just stood and stared at the dead man.

"Inside!" Freida yelled, the crazed edge in her voice matching the unhinged gleam in her eye.

Feeling as if she might faint, Marga stumbled into the cottage and retreated to the fireplace. The front door flew open, and Freida stalked inside. "It's over," she announced, proceeding to empty the spent shells into the fireplace.

Marga stared at her in disbelief.

Freida turned to her. "Do you know why I prefer revolvers?"

Marga forced herself to shake her head.

"They never jam." Freida said it casually, as if offering up a cooking tip. She pulled a box of bullets from her jacket and reloaded before closing the cylinder and holstering the weapon. "You're shaking." Freida touched Marga's cheek. "I'm not going to hurt you."

"Why…why did you do it?"

"He'd served his purpose."

"But…you just shot him."

Freida curled a crooked smile. "I did…didn't I?"

CHAPTER 65

Cruising at 400 knots at 9,000 feet, Major Rathenow eyed his instruments and strained to hear the faint series of pulsing dots and dashes emanating from a portable navigation beacon positioned along a remote western stretch of the Reich Autobahn. A sudden continuous audio pulse in his headset signaled him to begin his approach. His pulse rising, he dropped his landing gear, checked the airspeed, altimeter, heading, and stopwatch—he'd have one-minute and twenty seconds to break out of the clouds. If the lights of the improvised landing strip failed to appear in that time, he'd apply engine thrust, raise his landing gear, and initiate a climb.

Turbulence shook the jet as it descended. "Twenty seconds," Rathenow announced over the intercom to Pringer. "If we don't break out of this soup, I'm aborting the approach."

"Nonsense!" Pringer snapped. "You must land!"

Rathenow checked his altimeter…2,000 meters. He wouldn't—couldn't—go below 1,000.

"Can't do it, sir. At this speed, this close to the ground, we'd never recover in time."

"I have a gun at your head, Major. Do not abort the landing or I'll splatter your brains!"

Rathenow turned his head and bumped it into the weapon's muzzle. "Don't be a fool!" He glanced at the dials. Ten seconds remained at 1,200 meters of altitude. He tightened his grip on the controls. "One thousand meters! Time's up!"

Pringer shoved his arm forward and cocked the hammer. Rathenow gritted his teeth and cursed his luck. They continued dropping. The altimeter broke 500 meters, then 400…300!

The overcast abruptly broke and a string of amber lights, glowing like pearls in the night, appeared. Rathenow adjusted his controls, swooped onto the Autobahn and the jet bounced onto the slick asphalt, hydroplaning through mist and pelting rain until shuddering to a halt.

CHAPTER 66

Shards of early-morning light filtering into the cottage woke Marga from an uneasy slumber by the fireplace where she lay on a thin, tattered blanket. As she attempted to rub a faint headache from her temples, she realized her right wrist was handcuffed to a three-foot chain affixed to the mortar. She stood up and looked around the cottage. Freida was nowhere in sight. Drawn window shades prevented her from looking outside where the trill of birds harkened a new day. She recalled the previous night. Freida had given her tea. She must have spiked it with some sort of sedative. That would explain her mild hangover.

A wooden bucket, a tin of crackers, and a canteen were within arm's reach. She sighed and wondered how long she'd be left alone—to anticipate her fate—when an odd ticking sound drew her attention to the small table in the middle of the room.

On it sat two brown bottles—probably the ones she'd heard rattling inside the wooden box Freida had placed into the sedan's trunk. Wrapped with wire around the bottles were four red cylindrical tubes and... *What is that?* It looked like an alarm clock. Squinting, she read the clock's face to see the time. 7:24 A.M. She then noticed the alarm was set for 6:00.

A slow, numbing sense of doom creeped over her as she realized the four sticks were dynamite and this crude bomb would explode in ten and a half hours!

CHAPTER 67

Freida drove the Steyr sedan through the forest with a map at her side identifying the last known U.S. Army positions beyond Essen. Halting at the edge of a field, she looked around warily. Once she left the forest's protective cover, she'd be exposed to snipers, artillery, and air attack. After taking a settling breath, she retrieved a white handkerchief, held it out the window, and eased off the clutch.

* * *

Major Dan Whitcomb dozed on a folding chair inside a field tent, his muddied boots propped on an adjutant's desk, when an orderly burst in. "Sir! You have an urgent message from Brigade S-2! A scientific asset has been identified and you're wanted immediately!"

An hour later, Whitcomb sat in the back of an L-2 Grasshopper observation plane as it buzzed fields, forests, and dusty ribbons of armored columns before circling a field headquarters and gently settling to earth.

A Jeep pulled alongside the Grasshopper, and a young officer jumped out.

"Major Whitcomb! Captain Tenney, sir! I'll be your escort!"

"Lead the way, Captain," said Whitcomb as he tossed a kit bag in the rear seat and climbed aboard.

* * *

Whitcomb had been given her name and briefed as to what she had to offer as he entered a tent where Freida relaxed drinking Coca-Cola under the watch of two American military police officers. He was followed by a lieutenant colonel and a corporal, who would serve as his translator. The lieutenant colonel ordered the MPs to wait outside, and they exited and closed the tent flap behind them. Whitcomb perused her credentials. The photo had been taken in the years before her disfigurement. He looked at her and then at the photo and appeared confused.

"It's been a cruel war," she said bitterly.

"Sicherheitsdienst?" he said.

"Ah, you speak German?"

The corporal translated her words.

"Ask her where the girl is?" said Whitcomb.

The interpreter complied.

Freida toyed with her empty Coke bottle. "I made it clear. I want guarantees."

"It's out of the question," Whitcomb said, shaking his head.

Freida shrugged. "No deal then."

"She told us earlier," said the lieutenant colonel. "There's an explosive device in the cabin…" He glanced at his watch. "Set to go off at six."

Whitcomb studied Freida. Her lone eye met his gaze.

"You're telling me this girl has missile technology... memorized?"

She nodded.

"She further stated," said the translator, "that Himmler ordered all records of Germany's ballistic missile program destroyed. The girl might be our only chance of ever retrieving the information."

"What about all of your scientists and engineers?" Whitcomb asked.

"They're being hunted down," she said.

"Hunted down?"

Freida twisted her bumpy lips. "Himmler ordered *all* records destroyed, even human ones."

Whitcomb turned to the translator. "Tell her I have to hear what the girl has to offer first."

She listened to the translator and shook her head. "Not without something in writing guaranteeing my safety—regardless of what she says."

Whitcomb sighed and turned to the lieutenant colonel. "Can we speak outside?"

* * *

"Let's just write something up," said Whitcomb. "We just can't let that girl die...regardless of whether she has information."

"It could be a trap...an ambush."

"Not likely, sir. There are more effective methods, not to mention it would be a suicide mission for her. Besides, it's obvious this woman is trying to save her own neck...literally."

"But this girl... She'd need a remarkable memory."

Removing his helmet, Whitcomb glanced skyward and sighed. "It's what I'm here to find out, sir."

* * *

An hour later, Freida was staring at a typed document in German. It specified that her assistance to the United States and its Allies would be taken into consideration in any post-war litigation.

Freida looked at Whitcomb as she spoke to the translator. "What this girl knows will put you years ahead of any other nation. This is the best you can offer? Consideration in post-war litigation?"

"Perhaps you'd prefer we hand you over to the Russians," said Whitcomb sternly.

Freida glared at him. "If they weren't the dregs of humanity, I might consider it." She stood up. "But if that's your position, take me out and shoot me now."

The two officers looked at each other.

"Fine," Whitcomb relented. He took a pen from his breast pocket and scribbled on the document. "The United States Army hereby offers Freida Geisler unconditional sanctuary. Now," he faced Freida. "Take us to the girl."

CHAPTER 68

Marga sat with her eyes closed, fighting off the fear of what would happen if Freida failed to return when the sound of a vehicle outside drew her attention. She figured Freida had returned and stood, smoothing her skirt. A car door squealed open and then closed. Window shades prevented her from seeing outside.

The door knob rattled—it was locked. Marga tensed. A jarring force hit the door but it held. Another jolt and the door flew open with a splintering crash. She gasped as a German officer, brandishing a pistol, charged inside. Panicked, she tugged on her chain but she was trapped. She hunkered inside the fireplace—waiting and watching as the officer advanced until he stood over her. Marga looked up at him, anticipating the worst, when a wry smile crossed his lips and he holstered his weapon. He crouched and their eyes met.

"Greetings, Fräulein. I'm SS-Brigadeführer Gerhard Pringer. And, I'm very pleased to meet you."

CHAPTER 69

Whitcomb glanced skyward toward the rumble of a Republic P-47 fighter plane circling overhead in the afternoon sky. Its wings bristling with machine guns, the aircraft flew large, lazy circles over the convoy of Jeeps and armored personnel carriers filled with combat troops escorting him and Freida toward the cottage in the woods where she'd left Marga chained to a fireplace.

Reaching their objective, the vehicles halted, and a platoon of soldiers fanned out to create a security perimeter. Drawing his .45 caliber pistol, Whitcomb followed Freida as she pushed open the door that showed signs of having been kicked in. They entered. The cabin was quiet except for a ticking sound and the girl was gone.

Freida stood in the middle of the room next to the table that held the homemade bomb. Her crooked mouth agape, she spun around and yanked the wires off the explosives, and threw them aside. "*Verdammt!*" she blurted in a fit of rage.

Holstering his pistol and removing his helmet, Whitcomb announced, "Well, Fräulein. It appears your collateral is gone."

Freida ignored the translator's words as she stepped to the fireplace and pulled at the dangling three-foot chain. Smacking it against the stonework, she faced Whitcomb. "I know who did this!"

CHAPTER 70

Hands bound, Marga rode in the front passenger seat of Pringer's *Kubelwagen* convertible staff car. Based on the sun's position in the sky, he was driving them eastward following a narrow road winding through the forest. Feigning a yawn, she asked, "Where are we going?"

He ignored her question.

"I know you think I have scientific secrets. Well, I don't. I made the whole thing up!"

His eyes barely visible beneath the visor of his peaked cap, he said, "In that case, you have no value to me."

She realized her mistake.

"Did Freida mention what she was using you for?" he asked.

Marga looked away.

He laughed. "She was bartering you to the Americans."

Marga turned. "Bartering?"

"As am I. Only, I'm dealing with the Russians."

"Russians!"

He nodded. "The war will soon be over, and I have many sins to atone for."

"I'll deny knowing anything!"

"In that case, if you have nothing to offer…We're both dead."

A wind gust made her dress flutter in such manner as to reveal her legs. She saw how he glanced at them, and she quickly covered up.

"However…" He drew a smug grin. "You might be kept alive for…other reasons."

Revulsed, Marga turned away. "I'd rather die."

He smiled. "Don't worry, Fräulein. If you know what I think you do, it'll be the last thing on anyone's mind."

CHAPTER 71

Dawn broke through a canopy of trees as Marga awoke in the *Kubelwagen's* rear seat. Rubbing her eyes and yawning, she sat up and looked around when radio static drew her attention to the raised hood.

"Red Saber...Red Saber...This is Dagger...How copy, over?" Pringer's voice sounded.

Static burst from a speaker, and a husky, heavily accented voice—like that of a Russian—answered in German. "Dagger...Dagger...This is Red Saber! Read you loud and clear!"

Pringer answered. "Red Saber...This is Dagger...Will rendezvous at your location in three hours...Over."

"Affirmative...My location...Three hours...Red Saber out!"

* * *

Flying at 6,000 feet and 40 kilometers to the west, a radio intercept officer aboard an RAF Bristol Blenheim electronics monitoring aircraft eavesdropped on Red Saber and Dagger's radio traffic. Triangulating Red Saber's coordinates, a coded transmission was relayed to RAF Headquarters Command in Belgium.

Jotting a synopsis of the radio exchange, the electronics officer knew that any communications involving Russians, in western Germany and far ahead of their advancing armies to the east, likely involved a Soviet effort to beat their Western Allies to a significant strategic prize—piece of equipment, technology, or someone with a great skill or knowledge.

* * *

Marga emerged from a thicket where she'd relieved herself to find Pringer had just finished lowering and securing the *Kubelwagen's* roof. "We'll have to do without breakfast," he said slipping behind the steering wheel. Marga climbed into the passenger seat and offered her wrists, which bore the red outlines of the binding ropes. He looked at her. "If you promise to behave…It won't be necessary."

Marga sat unmoved.

"Try and run…"

Marga sensed a sinister tone in his voice.

"I promise you," he patted the holstered Luger at his hip. "You won't make it."

Looking away, Marga rested her arm on the passenger door as Pringer started the *Kubelwagen*, shifted gears, and drove off, headed east.

* * *

The intercepted radio traffic between Dagger and Red Saber reached RAF field headquarters in Liege. The British knew of the SS woman who'd surrendered herself to the Americans, offering an asset with information on Germany's rocket program in exchange for asylum. The failed extraction of a German scientist offering the same information in Holland was immediately flagged and a communique was flashed to a forward operations airfield on the Dutch-German border. It was read by Devon Farrington who was there for debriefing following his failed mission.

Like most intelligence operatives, Farrington didn't believe in happenstance. He recalled a German woman's voice at the ambush site. "Come, dear," she'd said to Marga as he feigned death beneath Yorick and Anna's crumpled bodies. "We have things to do and little time to do them in." Farrington surmised the woman had taken Marga to exchange with the Americans for some form of war crime clemency. Now, the male voice identifying as Dagger, had somehow gotten hold of Marga, and was making his own play—only to the Russians. Farrington strapped a leather helmet and goggles to his head and sank into the open forward cockpit of a two-seat de Havilland Tiger Moth biplane. He fastened his shoulder harness while the pilot, seated behind him, started its engine and within minutes they were flying eastward. Their objective: Red Saber and Dagger's rendezvous location. Chambering a round in his semi-automatic weapon, Farrington was determined to get back the German, violin-playing girl—come what may.

* * *

Whitcomb balanced himself against a bank of radios in the back of the Jeep that was following a convoy of half-tracks and armored cars in the search for Marga. He had considered Freida's theory that a superior had snatched the girl from the cabin. It was apparent that Freida had gone rogue and was calling her own shots—making her own deals. And that was why Whitcomb sent her back to field headquarters to be looked after in case her allegiances changed once more. Rubbing his chin stubble, he contemplated another theory:

The British, French, and Russians had similar interests and perhaps one of them had gotten to the girl first. But, he reasoned, if the British or French had taken her, he would have known by now. There were too many leaks between the Allies' intelligence units. However, if the Russians were in the picture and working with Freida's superior officer, then all bets were off and an escape with the girl would lead to the east.

After studying maps late into the night, he and a team of officers had drawn up likely eastward escape routes from the cottage. A military police sergeant in Whitcomb's convoy who was a former Detroit police detective assessed the tire tracks around the cabin and hinted that a large-wheeled vehicle, perhaps a scout car, had been there.

Fighting the morning chill, Whitcomb raised his jacket collar and warily surveyed the surrounding terrain of towering trees and thick vegetation. For an instant, it occurred to him that perhaps it was all a wild-goose chase designed to divert resources. *Hell, the girl may not even exist!* He turned and adjusted the volume on his radios. If any sign of the girl appeared, he would be notified immediately. Digging out a pack of Lucky Strikes from his jacket, he spit over the side of the Jeep and shook his head. *It's going to be a long day.*

* * *

Pringer was relieved to finally reach the edge of the forest with Marga sleeping beside him in the passenger seat. They'd been in the car for two hours, but now had only 40 more kilometers to drive. Glancing at his gas gauge and watch, he warily scanned the open sky. *Another hour, and my new life begins.* He thought once more of living on a small farm in Russia or Poland or perhaps, through Petroshenko's influence, finding a suitable role in Russian occupied Germany. He could work as an administrator or even in a reconstituted version of Sicherheitsdienst. He mused, whom better than someone with his experience to help the Russians with state security over their new citizenry?

* * *

Cruising 8,000 feet over Westphalia, nineteen-year-old First Lieutenant Jib Stokely flew a sleek silver P-51 Mustang on an early-morning patrol. Gazing in the distance, where ribbons of smoke rose from the city of Münster's crooked and artillery-battered skyline, he monitored radio traffic from other aircraft and ground units. He gave his watch a glance and wondered if the mess hall would still be open when he landed within the hour. The thought of scrambled eggs and sizzling bacon tantalized his senses.

He canted his head earthward, taking a soothing breath through his oxygen mask, when something far below, on the ground, caught his eye.

* * *

Marga saw a shadow cross the dashboard. Curious, she looked up, shielded her eyes, and squinted. Something glimmered in the sky. *A plane.*

* * *

Jib Stokely barrel-rolled his Mustang and executed a spiraling descent when the object of his curiosity came into focus: A *Kubelwagen* staff car.

* * *

Marga ducked as the plane roared overhead. Craning their necks skyward, she and Pringer saw the markings on the gleaming fuselage. *Americans!*

Pringer cursed, revved the engine, and shifted gears. Flooring the gas pedal, he caused the *Kubelwagen* to fishtail and accelerate, but it was too late. The P-51's wing-mounted cannons directed bursts of shrapnel into the *Kubelwagen's* path sending the car veering off the road.

Screaming, Marga clutched the dashboard. Crunching metal and breaking glass enveloped her as the *Kubelwagen* rolled over. Riddled with pain, she lay crumpled in a small pocket between soft earth and the floorboard. Smoke swirled around her. Coughing, she clutched her throat. Her head was swimming. She began to lose consciousness…

* * *

"Over there!" Farrington hollered, turning to the pilot and pointing in the distance at the unmistakable silhouette of an American P-51 climbing from a strafing run, a thin veil of smoke rising in its wake. With a nod, the pilot banked the Tiger Moth toward the action.

* * *

Marga fought panic as she repeatedly kicked at the passenger door until it gave way. Grunting and grimacing from the pain, she crawled on hands and knees to get free of the car. Once she was finally beyond the metal cage, she glimpsed Pringer through a veil of smoke. He'd been thrown from the vehicle and lay on his back motionless. She didn't know if he was alive or dead. And, despite blood oozing from his nose and a gash on his forehead, Marga's eyes were drawn to his torn britches revealing a grotesquely twisted leg.

* * *

"Sir!" came a garbled transmission over one of Whitcomb's radios. "Reported contact…Ten miles east of your position…Vehicle engaged by one of our aircraft…Apparent casualties."

Whitcomb scowled and snatched the transmitter. "What kind of vehicle?"

Static flooded the speaker. "Scout car…*Kubelwagen*."

"Grid coordinates?"

"Affirmative, sir."

"Go with them!"

Whitcomb scribbled the eight-digit coordinates and keyed his microphone. "Keep an eye on our German lady friend…As a matter of fact, turn her over to the brigade provost marshal!"

"Sir…" Static rushed through the speaker. "She's gone!"

"Gone?!"

"Affirmative, sir!"

Whitcomb mashed the transmitter and barked into the mouthpiece. "Well, you damn well better find her!"

* * *

As she staggered around the smoking *Kubelwagen*, Marga noticed a puddle of fuel beneath the overturned engine. She had to get away—and fast.

The sound of a droning engine sounded from above. Cupping a hand to her brow, she searched the sky when a canvas biplane buzzed overhead. Recognizing the circular RAF emblems on its wings, she reversed course and darted for cover behind the car.

* * *

Looking down from the Tiger Moth flying over the wrecked *Kubelwagen*, Farrington observed Marga running through smoke and taking cover. Turning in his seat, he pointed to the ground and shouted, "*Put it down! Put it down now!*"

* * *

Pringer's eyes opened as the strange craft buzzed overhead. Turning, he saw Marga hunkered behind the *Kubelwagen*. He tried to speak, but unforgiving pain stabbed his innards.

* * *

The Tiger Moth swooped to a landing on the road. Her heart pounding and limbs shaking, Marga sprang to her feet when suddenly, flames burst from the *Kubelwagen's* engine and a rush of suffocating heat enveloped her. Shrieking and covering her head, she ran through a screen of smoke when a hand snatched her ankle.

* * *

The Tiger Moth halted 100 feet from the burning vehicle.

"Wait here!" Farrington shouted to the pilot over the droning engine as he undid his shoulder harness. Hitting the ground, he sprinted through swirling smoke toward the burning wreck and Marga who, kicking and screaming, fought to free herself from Pringer's grasp.

* * *

Marga looked up. "Abe?!"

He yanked her from Pringer's grip. "You're a hard girl to track down!"

Marga appeared dumbfounded.

"We'll discuss it over tea!" He grabbed her hand, and they ran for the Tiger Moth.

* * *

Flames engulfed the *Kubelwagen* as Pringer observed Marga being escorted to the waiting biplane. As the fire intensified, he had to choose whether to try and stop her or save himself.

He made his choice.

Drawing his Luger, he took aim.

* * *

"In you go!" Abe shouted over the staccato buzz of the engine.

"What about you?" Marga shouted.

He pointed to the front seat when a jarring force propelled his body smack into hers, pinning her against the side of the biplane.

"*Abe!*" she hollered, holding him up.

With blood leaking over his lips, he grunted, "In...you go... love."

Marga looked over his shoulder at Pringer, who was now sitting up and aiming the Luger at them. He squeezed the trigger again, but nothing happened. Fidgeting with the slide, Pringer ejected a round, racked another into the firing chamber, and took aim once more as Marga watched helplessly.

Suddenly, a violent blast shook the air. Collapsing with Abe to the ground, Marga faced the *Kubelwagen*. It had exploded and large chunks of it landed on Pringer, crushing him under its fiery weight.

Powerful hands suddenly lifted Marga and deposited her into the front seat. "Hang on!" said the pilot, belting her in.

Marga looked over the side at Abe, who lay face down on the ground, a dark patch of blood spreading over his back. *"No!"* she shouted, fumbling to unsnap her belt. But the pilot jumped into the rear seat and began revving the engine. The Tiger Moth lurched forward.

"Stop!" she shouted, spinning around, but the pilot ignored her, and the spindly craft took flight. Pushed into her seat, the control stick slapping her knees, she fought for breath while desperately looking back at the grisly scene they were leaving behind—the burning *Kubelwagen* and her savior, Abe, splayed out on the ground, his shirt soaked in blood. She thought she saw him move, but the Tiger Moth banked sharply, whipping her hair into her face, and within minutes, Abe had vanished from sight.

* * *

Like a possessed demon, the Fa 223 twin-rotor helicopter burst from behind a ridgeline firing its nose-mounted cannon. Tracers streaked past the Tiger Moth's open cockpits and tore through its canvas frame. Banking evasively, it dodged the attack, but the helicopter kept pace, firing a torrent of shells until smoke burst from the biplane's engine and the Tiger Moth dove for the forest. A frightening childhood memory of riding a rollercoaster flashed through Marga's mind. Screaming, she braced herself when the biplane leveled-off, its tires skimming the treetops.

Popping rotor blades and an engine's roar suddenly came alongside the Tiger Moth. Turning in her seat, Marga froze. *It couldn't be!* Kneeling in the open cargo door was Morten holding a bolt-action rifle, with Freida, her face twisted into a hateful mask, standing over him.

* * *

"Put a round through their engine!" Freida shouted over the rush of wind and howling engines. Morten aimed, but the bobbing of both aircraft caused him to chase his shot.

Freida punched his shoulder. "Shoot, damn you!"

He fired. The Tiger Moth shuddered, and smoke poured from another hole in the engine.

Freida thrust her head inside the cockpit and barked orders. Nodding, the pilot dipped the copter and eased its thrashing blades into the biplane's wing spars and support cables causing its upper wing to buckle. The Tiger Moth began to shake violently.

"Five minutes to the border!" the helicopter pilot shouted to Freida over the rumble of engines. She looked out the door, her gaze settling on Marga.

"Shoot her!" she bellowed in Morten's ear.

Bewildered, he looked up at her.

"*Do it!*"

He raised his rifle and aimed. The bouncing of both aircraft made it impossible to keep his sights centered.

"*Now!*"

He squeezed the trigger.

"*Idiot!*" She punched him for missing.

Angered, he jumped to his feet and pressed his face into hers when he buckled. Freida met his stunned gaze and followed it toward her bloodied hand clutching the dagger thrust into his gut. Dropping his rifle, Morten fell into her, and with a mighty heave, Freida shoved him out the door.

* * *

Shocked, Marga covered her mouth as Morten tumbled from the helicopter and disappeared into the trees below. Her lone eye aflame, Freida snatched Morten's rifle and chambered another round. The Tiger Moth suddenly jerked to the right, slicing its shattered upper wing through the helicopter's open cargo bay knocking the weapon from Freida's hands. Falling onto the tattered wing, she embraced its torn fabric. As the Tiger Moth canted left, separating from the copter, she rode the bouncing wing like a rodeo rider beneath a halo of whipping rotors.

Marga covered her mouth and looked into Freida's demonic eye and the hollow socket now exposed by the loss of her eye patch. A sinister grin warped Freida's deformed lips as her thin, yellow hair flapped wildly in the wind. The Tiger Moth's pilot worked his pedals trying to shake her loose, but she clung tenaciously to the ragged canvas and managed to draw her revolver. She fired. The pilot shrieked. Marga turned. Blood seeped through his fingers as he clutched his shoulder.

Another shot rang out and Marga flinched as the bullet blasted a hole into her seatback. She looked up through whipping hair to see Freida's incredulous look. The German SS agent gritted her teeth and cocked her weapon, advancing another round into the firing chamber. Through the chaos of rushing wind, growling engines, whirling rotor blades, and gun shots, Marga surprisingly found herself calculating the number of bullets remaining in Freida's six-shot revolver. She'd fired twice—how many more shots could she hope to dodge?

Marga crouched and Freida fired again. Another miss! *That's three shots remaining!* Her adrenaline racing, she inched her head upwards when the control stick, acting in tandem with the inputs of the pilot behind her, smacked her cheek. Marga grabbed at her face—*that's it!* She shot up in her seat as Freida cocked the hammer. "Revolvers never jam," she recalled Freida's boast. Marga steeled herself and grabbed the control stick between her knees and yanked it back. The Tiger Moth lurched upwards into the whirl of beating rotors and Freida, her weapon aimed, burst into a red greasy cloud and scattered into the slipstream.

The sudden impact sent flames shooting from the helicopter's engine and it peeled away, spinning and breaking apart, like a fiery pinwheel into the forest below. Marga spun around and faced the pilot. He clutched his wounded shoulder and tried to make their craft climb. But the smoking, battered plane kept sinking. Fighting for control, he had no time to warn her. It didn't matter—she knew—they were about to crash.

Slicing through a canyon of trees, the biplane's monocoque frame dutifully absorbed the impact—its wheels snapping off, wings shattering, propeller disintegrating. Bouncing and skidding, the Tiger Moth bounded headlong until it ground to a jarring halt amid a smoking cloud of dust.

* * *

Embraced by a benevolent welcoming light, Marga emerged into a lush garden of Egyptian-blue hydrangeas, blood-red roses, and amaranth-pink carnations. Snow-white daylilies bloomed from carpets of kelly-green clovers while atop a boulder, nestled against a flourish of flaming-auburn bougainvillea, Oskar, her beloved orange tabby, who'd vanished one night in her youth, sat with his cool emerald eyes regarding her adoringly. Then, from a shimmering golden mist, Ullie appeared, handsome and unburdened. There were no words, but Marga understood. *We'll be here...waiting.*

Waiting...?

A sudden, suffocating rush enveloped her as if she'd been swept over a thundering waterfall. Smoke and dust choked her lungs and pain riddled her body. Beneath a warm crown of blood, her head swam as she was lifted onto a canvas stretcher. A needle pricked her arm, and blissful darkness, like a welcoming blanket, claimed her senses.

CHAPTER 72

Three days later, in an American army field hospital, the patient in Ward 3, bed 14 slept peacefully. But for a row of cranial sutures, bruises, scratches, and twisted ankle, the young woman was in remarkable condition for having survived a plane crash. The same went for the Tiger Moth pilot who'd been evacuated to England.

Under the watchful gaze of a burly African American military police sergeant, standing guard in the empty ward, two doctors and a nurse studied a medical chart at the foot of Marga's bed.

"So, this is the young lady army intel is so keen on," said Dr. Huston Ames who wore a white lab coat over green fatigues.

"No one is to speak to her without one of their people present," replied Dr. Hugh Folsom, holding a cigarette and massaging a scruffy five o'clock shadow.

"She appears to speak only German," said the nurse. "So, it shouldn't be an issue."

Flipping through Marga's chart, Dr. Ames commented, "A lot of good it'll do them. That bump on her head…"

The nurse mused, "When she was awake, that Major Whitcomb…I think that was his name…Regardless, he asked her, her name, you know, basic things."

"And?" queried Ames.

"The major had the translator scribble her words, thinking they might be important." The nurse hid a smile behind her clipboard. "It turns out it was a poem." She reached into a pocket and unfolded a slip of paper. "*O lieb, so lang du lieben kannst...*by Ferdinand Freiligrath."

"What did the major think of that?" asked Dr. Ames.

Pocketing the paper, the nurse shook her head. "He didn't. Despite repeated questions, all she did was recite the poem."

"I've classified it as a case of retrograde amnesia," said Dr. Folsom. "More times than not, the immediate events prior to the amnesia, in her case, whacking her head on impact, are lost."

"You mean, she'll have no memory of the crash," said Ames.

"Or events leading up to it," Folsom replied.

"How about long term?" Ames asked.

Shrugging, Folsom took a quick drag. "It's early, but if I were the intelligence folks, I wouldn't hold my breath. The brain is a complicated organ. Anything they hope to get from her might take a while, if it ever comes."

CHAPTER 73

Under a cloudless sky, a convoy of Jeeps rumbled to a halt outside a quaint Bavarian chalet nestled against Garmisch-Partenkirchen's green forests and snow-capped mountains. Clutching a holstered .45 pistol, Major Dan Whitcomb trotted up the granite steps into the lobby followed by a cigar-chomping staff sergeant toting a Thompson submachine. A corporal followed close behind them.

Whitcomb hoped this wasn't another frivolous exercise, but he had to corroborate the remarkable claim made hours earlier by a surrendering German scientist claiming to be Magnus von Braun—brother of Wernher—who, with a group of other engineers, wished to surrender to the Americans.

"Greetings, gentlemen," announced a tall, handsome man stepping out from behind a wingback chair facing a crackling fireplace. Despite his accent, he spoke good English. "I'm Doctor Wernher von Braun, and I have a proposition for you."

Stunned, Whitcomb tilted his helmet back and smiled at the sight of the most wanted German scientist in Europe. He laced his thumbs under his canvas pistol belt and asked, "What exactly are you prepared to offer, Doctor?"

"The entirety of the Third Reich's missile program...To include myself and most of my top engineers."

"And in return?"

"Why, I want to come work for you Americans—along with my team of engineers, of course."

"That's a generous offer, Doctor. But we'll have to see what you have before making any guarantees."

"Major, what I have to offer will accelerate America's ballistic missile program by a decade. Not to mention, there's more to our research than simply the V2."

"We'll be happy to look at it," said Whitcomb deadpan like a poker player in a high-stakes game. He met von Braun's gaze. It appeared unmoved and confident. He knew the German held all the cards in any negotiations and would only act once his terms were met. Regardless, Whitcomb took a shot and asked, "Is your cache of documents close-by?"

"Major..." von Braun squinted to read Whitcomb's embroidered name tag.

"Whitcomb...Major Dan Whitcomb."

Von Braun stepped forward and offered his hand.

They shook and von Braun turned to another man, who'd stepped forward from beside the fireplace, and spoke to him in German. The corporal at Whitcomb's side translated von Braun and the other man word-for-word. "Harold, did I not tell you once that I was going into the insurance business?"

"And now it's time to cash in your policy," said Harold.

"That's right," von Braun replied in English looking at Whitcomb. "The records are safe, Major. However, located in a most inaccessible place. I mean, even if I wanted to, I couldn't get to them."

Whitcomb folded his arms and sighed. "You're saying that they're buried at the bottom of a mine somewhere."

Von Braun betrayed a smug grin. "Something like that."

"Okay, Herr Doctor. Give me a list of your demands and I'll speak with my superiors. We'll see where things go from there."

"It so happens, Major…" von Braun turned to Harold who produced a thick, letter-sized envelope from his suit jacket. "You'll find my demands neatly outlined within." Whitcomb took the envelope. "In the meantime, unless you plan to take us into custody, I'd like to remain here until you've reached a decision."

Whitcomb tucked the envelope into his breast pocket and nodded. "I'm posting a security detail around the chalet and armed guards in the lobby. Tell your people to stay on the grounds until further notice."

Von Braun shook Whitcomb's hand again. "Splendid, Major. We'll be here awaiting your response."

CHAPTER 74

Six Months Later – November 1945

Marga stamped her feet, fighting off the clammy chill as a fog-horn sounded across the dark Hamburg pier where she and her parents waited with hundreds of others to board the *S.S. Orion*. The three-funneled passenger liner speckled with glowing portholes and running lights was due to sail with the morning tide.

Marga sunk her hands into her wool overcoat, feeling blessed to have clean, warm clothes. For years, she had been a witness to the devastation of German cities and towns where people in threadbare clothes camped in parks or in gutted ruins.

"Must you stamp your feet like a goat?" her mother asked.

"It's cold, Mama," Marga replied. "When do you think we'll board the ship?"

Erna's frosty breath floated as she spoke. "When they tell us to."

Marga turned to her father, who stood pensively smoking a stubby cigarette. He'd lost weight in the previous months. Though only forty-two, he now had much gray in his thinning hair. But he still looked elegant in his navy-blue suit with matching fedora.

"Are you okay, Papa?" Marga asked.

He drew on his cigarette nodding. "I'm fine, *Liebchen*."

"What do you think America will be like?"

He met her curious gaze and said, "Better than here."

"Are we ever coming back?"

"Marga, don't distract your father with silly questions." Erna straightened her daughter's beret. "He has enough on his mind."

Marga understood her mother. She'd heard it mentioned once in the den of their temporary quarters at a former cavalry barracks in Oldenburg. The so-called Operation Paperclip provided for many of Germany's best minds—chemists, physicians, engineers, and scientists—to relocate to America. Wernher had seen to it that Harold and hundreds of other Peenemünde researchers were included. They would settle in Texas, near the New Mexico border, and work for the U.S. Army developing its missile technology. Perusing an encyclopedia at a Hamburg sidewalk bookshop, Marga had studied images of cactuses, armadillos, and stretches of limitless desert. She thought of Peenemünde's remote beauty and hoped her new surroundings would be as nice.

Thoughts of the future also reminded her of the past and of Ullie and the technical secrets entrusted to her at the Adlon Hotel. If only he'd known of the mine sealed with von Braun's crated V2 documents. It troubled her knowing that it had all been for nothing.

After recuperating from the Tiger Moth crash, she'd found her recollection of the flight remained hidden behind a subconscious wall—perhaps as a defense mechanism. On occasion, she dreamt of a tranquil garden with radiant flowers, a beloved cat, and Ullie. It always made her smile.

The foghorn again sounded and Marga folded her arms against the dank chill when a man's voice suddenly called, "Doctor Toth! Doctor Harold Toth!"

Harold tossed his cigarette and replied, "Here!"

People stepped back as a man in civilian attire strode with authority through the crowd followed by two helmeted military police officers.

"Doctor Toth, I'm Simon Wilson, Army C-I-C." He spoke fluent German and flashed a set of credentials. "We'd like a word with your daughter."

"Our daughter?" Erna stepped forward, shielding Marga. "Why?"

"Not to worry, Frau Toth. She's in no trouble." Simon peered through the darkness at Marga. "Fräulein, would you be so kind as to follow me?"

Marga glanced at her parents then at Simon. She knew CIC meant, Counter Intelligence Corps. She had already sat through countless interviews with them and other intelligence agencies concerning her knowledge of technical data in which she'd told them whatever she knew.

Erna declared, "I demand to know what this is about!"

"Frau Toth," Simon said calmly, "you're welcome to accompany us."

"Maybe I should come too," said Harold.

Simon turned to him. "We won't be long, Herr Doctor. Besides, you'll be boarding soon. It's best you remain here for when they begin calling out the passenger manifest."

Flanked by the two MPs, Marga and her mother followed Simon to a nearby warehouse. They went inside the dark and cavernous building filled with wooden crates and rows of stacked plywood, cement bags, and construction equipment.

They stepped to a doorway of what appeared to be an office.

"Frau Toth," Simon said to her. "Please wait here. We'll be but a few minutes."

Erna took her daughter's hand.

"It's okay, Mama. I'll be fine."

Marga followed Simon through the door into a small, well-lit office. She immediately froze, unable to believe her own eyes. Standing beside a desk, arms folded, was someone she had not expected to see ever again.

"*Abe?* You're...you're..."

"Alive?"

Marga threw out her arms and embraced him.

"I thought..." She stepped back. "How did you...?"

"I was happened upon by an American patrol," he said in his accented German. "Good fellows...Had a top-notch corpsman."

"How did you know I was here?"

He tweaked her chin. "I floated a balloon and made some calls."

Covering her mouth, she blushed and snorted a laugh.

"After all you went through," he said, "I wanted to see with my own eyes that you were safe and back with your family."

"I can't thank you enough."

"And..." He reached behind him and grasped a violin case.

Marga clasped her hands. "A violin?"

He held it out to her.

She hesitated before gingerly taking and examining it. "What's this for?"

"I figured it would help as you start a new life."

"May I look inside?"

He folded his arms and chuckled. "It would be a shame if you didn't."

She placed her gift on a credenza, unsnapped the latches, and opened the case. "Oh! It's beautiful!" She removed the instrument and placed it on her shoulder. "It feels nice. Oh, Abe, how can I ever thank you?"

He smiled. "Play me Brahms."

"'*Wiegenlied*'?"

He nodded. "Lullaby...I'd like that."

She checked the strings' tension, tweaked the pegs, and then placed the violin on her shoulder. Raising the bow, she gently brushed it over the strings, met his gaze, and began playing.

He sat on the edge of a desk with arms folded. His expression melted Marga's heart as she played. After a minute or so, an MP opened the office door and her mother entered the room quietly.

Marga remembered every note of the three-minute piece, and despite her nervousness and excitement, misplayed only a few. With a long, finishing stroke, the final note hung pleasantly in the air. Grinning, Marga lowered the instrument and turned to her mother, who appeared befuddled. "Mama, I'd like you to meet a friend of mine. He saved my life."

Abe stepped forward and planted a soft kiss on the back of Erna's hand. "I now see where your daughter's charm and beauty originate."

Marga thought she saw her mother blush.

Erna cleared her throat. "It's a pleasure to make your acquaintance, Herr...?"

"Farrington," he said. "Major Devon Farrington of His Majesty's Royal Marines, at your service."

Marga looked at him and chuckled. *Devon Farrington?* It was the first time she'd heard his real name.

A phone rang and Simon stepped from a corner and answered. Thanking the caller, he hung up. "I'm afraid it's time to say our good-byes," he said. "They're boarding the ship."

"It's been a pleasure, Frau Toth," Farrington said. He pecked her mother's hand once more, and then turned to Marga. They embraced. "Do great things with your life, young lady."

Marga felt a lump in her throat, and tears blurred her eyes as she buried her face in his shoulder. "I will...I promise."

She replaced the violin into its case and secured its latches. Clutching it, Marga started to follow her mother to the office door when she stopped and turned to Farrington one final time. "Good-bye...Abe." She raised the violin case. "I'll think of you whenever I play it."

EPILOGUE

July 1969

Marga led her husband by the hand into Tony's Satellite Bar and Grille, a Cocoa Beach venue popular with the Peenemünde crowd since the Mercury program days. It featured a glowing neon sign of a spaceman hoisting a mug and hopping back and forth over the moon. By the time of the Apollo program, most of its patrons had their favorite seats and knew the presets on the Wurlitzer jukebox, cranking out The Platters, Steppenwolf, Johnny Cash, Tammy Wynette—and, of course, Elvis.

The place had a breezy feel and reminded her of the drive-in restaurant he'd taken her to on their first date, 21 years earlier and 6 months before they married. The bar was standing-room only, filled with NASA personnel, their wives, girlfriends and patrons celebrating Man's first moon landing. Working their way through the crowd, she offered her cheek for damp kisses and hugged and congratulated many of the engineers who greeted her in their native tongue. She knew most of them remembered her as a bicycle-riding schoolgirl with a violin case slung over her shoulder and books in a handlebar basket. Their elation and relief, after decades of work, of landing a man on the moon was palpable. A smiling, rosy-cheeked Wernher von Braun appeared out of the crowd and pecked her cheek. "Ah, so lovely to see Peenemünde's own Shirley Temple," he said.

Alongside him, clutching an overflowing mug, her father beamed a rubbery smile. "*Liebchen*." He placed an arm around her.

"Papa, Philip and I are so proud of you! All of you!" She kissed his cheek.

"Did you speak with your mother?" Harold asked in his accented English.

"I called her before leaving the house. She told me to tell you not to overdo it."

Harold laughed. "If ever there was an occasion to overdo it!" He raised his mug. "Besides, Wernher and I are sharing a cab home."

"Thank heavens." She caressed his shoulder. "We can't stay long." She turned to her husband. "Philip's electrical engineering team from Grumman is having a cook-out on Merritt Island. I made potato salad…It's in a cooler in our trunk."

"Ah, your famous potato salad!" Harold turned to his son-in-law. "You married a good woman, Philip."

"I did, Harold. And you raised her to be one." They shook hands.

"Bye, Papa." She kissed his cheek and turned to follow Philip for the door when, from an upright piano tucked in a corner beneath a Carling Black Label banner, someone played, "Stars and Stripes Forever." Several patrons cheered; some raised small American flags and began waving them.

"Marga!" a woman called to her.

Marga and Philip turned to see Janet Dobbs, the wife of a NASA engineer, and a regular visitor to their Titusville home. "Tell your mother I loved her apple strudel recipe!" Janet's accent was pure Alabama.

"Oh, she'll be thrilled to hear it," Marga said, clutching Janet's hand. "Is Gene here?"

"Oh, mercy!" Janet looked around. "He's lost somewhere in this crowd! I'd best find him. It's nice seeing you, sugar. Let's get together soon!"

"Let's," said Marga.

Finally, she and Philip got to the door when a few notes of *"Horst Wessel Lied"* plinked from the upright piano. Marga turned. But as quickly as the tune resonated, it ceased, overtaken by gregarious chatter and laughter. She thought she must have imagined it, an echo from long ago...*Perhaps.*

* * *

The following day, Marga drove her station wagon to a secluded beach not found on Florida Space Coast tourist maps and jealously guarded by locals. Parking in a shady lot encompassed by swaying palms, she stepped onto the sun-kissed sand, slipped off her sandals, and hooked them on a finger. She walked to the water's edge where waves swirled around her ankles and her feet sank into the wet sand. A gentle wind fluttered her pink cotton sundress, caressed her warm flesh, and ruffled her wheat-colored hair. Cupping a hand to her brow, she looked out to sea where a fishing charter scrawled a wake and a red-hulled tanker scraped the horizon. Searching the sky's blue canvas, she sought the moon and thought of the effort it had taken to land men on its surface. She thought it mankind's crowning scientific achievement and swelled with pride that her father had figured in its accomplishment.

Pacing the shoreline, water splashed her shins and sunlight warmed her tanned, freckled arms. Relaxed and oddly nostalgic, she thought of days spent on the beach—along the Baltic—with Portia, now an electrician's wife in Cologne, and like her, the mother of three. They wrote each other weekly and telephoned on their birthdays.

Her thoughts soon grew somber. A stubborn ache reminded her of Felix's fate. He had disappeared beneath a barrage of Katusha rockets on the banks of the Oder River. And then there was Walter Mitz, trapped in Berlin in the war's final days—forsaken by a morally bankrupt ideology— who had simply ceased to exist. As always, she saved her final thoughts for Ullie, a sweet memory from a time of naïve yet palpable ardor. She cherished his memory and always saved her last nightly prayer for him.

A seagull's screech drew her eye skyward. Large and white, it hung in the air with its wings extended and she stared at its feathers bristling in the wind. She closed her eyes, entranced by the sound of waves and birds and the salty fragrance of the sea. She imagined laughter—that of Portia and Felix and herself…so long ago. She sighed and opened her eyes. It was time to go, her visitation with ghosts concluded.

Retracing her footsteps through swirling eddies of water, she again looked out toward the horizon. The charter boat had traveled far down the coast, its wake reclaimed by the ocean while the red-hulled freighter had slipped from view like a distant memory…Still there but gone.

* * *

A champagne moon glowed in the Baltic night sky, caressing white beaches and sloping dunes entrusted to nature's silent care. Under the vigil of oxidized ferrous gantries, like sentinels from a forgotten war, a soft wind created a grieving moan from Peenemünde's dilapidated former launch towers, like lost spirits calling to former lovers.

Nestled in the skeletal remains of a deserted tower, an osprey huddled in its nest. Cloaked in darkness, the moon perfectly centered in its golden iris, it suddenly reared its head toward the star-dusted heavens and in a primordial cry, called out on behalf of Peenemünde's ancient soul reaffirming – we remember, and we remain.

The End

AUTHOR'S NOTE

Certain historical events and timelines in *The Rocketeer's Daughter* have been modified to fit the story's narrative. Marga Toth and her family are fictional characters, although countless real-life 'Margas' endured the war. Many belonged to the League of German Girls (*Bund Deutscher Mädel / BDM)* in which membership was 'encouraged' between the ages of 14–18. Despite promoting athletics, scouting, home economics, and public service, the league's primary purpose was political indoctrination by the Nazi party. By war's end, many young women worked in factories, farms, hospitals, and commonly served as searchlight operators and ammunition bearers for anti-aircraft batteries defending German cities.

More people died in the production of the V2 than were killed by its use. (Approximately 10,000 forced laborers versus approximately 5,000 mostly civilian casualties.) Following the war, several overseers of the V2 production and assembly center in the Harz Mountains were tried for war crimes.

Despite its advanced technology, the high-flying, sound-barrier-shattering V2 played no significant role as a tactical weapon but rather more effectively as a psychological one.

Dr. Wernher von Braun and many of his engineers relocated to America through *Operation Paperclip*. Many went on to prominent roles at NASA where von Braun led the development of the Saturn V rocket and headed the Marshall Space Flight Center in Huntsville Alabama.

The rockets that have taken Man into space for exploration and commercial purposes are direct descendants of the V2 and it will forever be the origin of Man's path to the stars.

ACKNOWLEDGEMENTS

To everyone who helped make this book a reality, I offer a heartfelt thank you.

ABOUT THE AUTHOR

Clinton Aldrich is a graduate of the The Citadel and served as a U.S. Army aviator and federal narcotics agent before retiring and starting an interview coaching business. He published *A Republic's Rise* in 2020.

Please visit **clintonaldrichauthor.com** for more information and further reading.